"Thank you, Doug.
You're pretty cool to hang out with.
I really had a good time."

"You're welcome." His eyes dropped from her eyes to her lips. He took a step forward.

Jan took a step back.

"Where are you going? I was just going to give you a hug."

"That's not what it looked like."

"What did it look like?"

"Like you were going to . . . never mind."

"What, kiss you?" He took another step. She was back against the car. "Like this?"

He licked his lips as his head bent slowly toward hers. Just before touching hers he stopped. Waited. She leaned in. Their lips touched. Simple. Innocent. He kissed her once. Again. A final time.

"Call me when you get home, okay?"

"Okay," she managed, hoping her noodle legs wouldn't give out before she got into the car. . . .

Also by Zuri Day

The Morgan Men Series

The Blue-Collar Lover Series

Published by Kensington Publishing Corp.

Packing
HEAT
A BLUE-COLLAR LOVER NOVEL

ZURI DAY

Kensington Publishing Corp.
http://www.kensingtonbooks.com

DAFINA BOOKS are published by

Kensington Publishing Corp.
119 West 40th Street
New York, NY 10018

All Kensington Titles, Imprints, and Distributed Lines are
available at special quantity discounts for bulk purchases for
sales promotions, premiums, fund-raising, and educational
or institutional use. Special book excerpts or customized
printings can also be created to fit specific needs. For details,
write or phone the office of the Kensington special sales
Nmanager: Kensington Publishing Corp., 119 West 40th
Street, New York, NY 10018, attn: Special Sales Department,
Phone: 1-800-221-2647.

Dafina and the Dafina logo Reg. U.S. Pat. & TM Off.

ISBN-13: 978-1-61773-427-4
ISBN-10: 1-61773-427-6
First Kensington Mass Market Edition: March 2016

eISBN-13: 978-1-61773-428-1
eISBN-10: 1-61773-428-4
Kensington Electronic Edition: March 2016

10 9 8 7 6 5 4 3 2 1

Printed in the United States of America

Acknowledgments

What a great time researching and writing this story! Who knew those quiet, often nondescript-looking post office buildings could hold such romantic juiciness! The postal workers who were consulted for this story chose to remain anonymous, but thank you "L" and "J" for helping me "keep it real"! Also, a very special shout out to my motorcycle-riding cousin, Steve Moss, Jr., who offered a peek into his bike world and who makes the antics of my hero seem tame by comparison. Love you, cuzzo. Slow down! ☺ To all motorcycle riders, and all of the men and women responsible for getting our letters and packages where they need to go . . . this one is for you!

1

"Why didn't you tell me about the new girl?"

Doug Carter barely looked up from the stack of mail he prepared for the sorter. His friend and coworker, Joey, the branch's official pretty-boy playboy, was always yapping about something or other, as if he'd die if he didn't talk.

"It doesn't matter. I met her anyway."

"Good for you."

What Joey needed to worry about were the two women he was juggling between the morning and afternoon tours. At times, Doug was tempted to use his supervisor status and move them both to the second tour, the one they were working right now, just to watch him squirm.

"You're over there being real quiet about it. Must have tried to hit on her already and been turned down." Joey palmed a Priority package like a basketball and "shot" it into a bin.

"Believe that if it makes you feel better." Doug reached for another bin of mail and set it on the sorter.

"What man wouldn't? Thick caramel cutie with that stop-traffic booty? Stop acting like you didn't try and get her phone number."

"I could get her number without trying, if I wanted it. Which I don't. I'll agree that she's attractive. But unlike you, I don't play where I get my pay. Finally learned my lesson about that, and I'm a changed man. Right, Pat?"

The unofficial office matriarch who'd worked at the post office for almost forty years, at this branch for the last fifteen, popped a wad of gum as she passed them. "I'm not even trying to be in you all's business. Joey has a better chance of walking on the moon than going out with that cute new girl, but I'm not listening to a word being said."

Doug, Joey, and other nearby coworkers laughed as Pat placed her purse in one of a row of nearby lockers and left the room. In this wide-open space with sounds easily bouncing off the high ceiling and plasterboard-covered walls, now boasting skeletons and witches for a Halloween theme, there weren't many words spoken that couldn't be heard by everyone in the back room. Pat definitely didn't miss much. She wasn't a busybody. Doug knew this for sure. But if needing advice or someone to listen, Pat was usually the go-to choice. She could hold a confidence and wasn't a backstabber. And she knew where all the post office skeletons were buried. Had buried some herself.

A few minutes later, the new cutie walked into the room and over to where Doug sorted mail.

"Excuse me, Doug?"

He turned. "Hey, Janice. How's it going?"

"Okay, I guess."

"It's going fine, from what I can see." Joey turned off the processing machine and walked around the long steel table over to where Doug and Jan were conversing. His obvious flirtation went unnoticed. At least by the one for whom it was intended.

"Is there a certain time for breaks?" Jan asked. "Or should I coordinate with the others at the counter?"

"There is no specified time. Is Pat back up there?"

"Yes."

"Then just make sure she knows you're leaving."

"Okay. And I prefer being called Jan, remember?"

"Oh, right. Sorry about that."

"No problem." She smiled, revealing half-moon dimples on each cheek. Doug found himself wondering if there were dimples in other places, then mentally chastised himself for the thought.

Joey refused to be ignored. "Jan Baker, right?"

"Yes."

"See, unlike my coworker, I remember the important things."

"If that were true, you'd remember to keep your mouth shut." Doug's retort was immediate, with perfect aim. Only the chuckle that followed made it less deadly.

"You'd better listen to him, Joey." The sugar-coated voice of another coworker standing two tables over was paired with an impish smile as she turned around. "When it comes to anything involving the mouth, Doug knows what he's talking about."

Doug's smile faded. *Never could keep our business private. That's why being with you wasn't a mistake I made twice.*

Except for the quiet tittering of the worker hired right before Jan, the room went quiet. Those who'd witnessed the short but fiery hookup between the Normandie Post Office location's nice guy and the one now called Messy Mel did not find her taunt funny. They knew it had been meant to mark territory that Melissa didn't own.

Even Joey ignored the comment, choosing instead to stay focused on Jan. "I thought the two of you would have nothing in common." He took a couple steps forward. Jan took a step back. A slight smirk was the only outward sign that Doug had seen what she'd done and gotten her message. Back off.

Joey neither got the message nor stopped advancing. "It's probably the only thing y'all have in common."

Jan finally looked at Joey, confused. "I don't understand."

"Ha! Don't worry, Jan. Most of the time none of us do either."

Joey dismissed Doug's comment with a wave of his hand. "Don't pay him any attention. That's what he wants." He turned warm eyes back to Jan. "Doug's first name is Douglas. About the only one who still calls him that, though, is his mom. If she uses his full name she's probably angry. When Miss Liz is upset, you don't want to be anywhere around!"

From the would-be respondent? Blank stare.

"Now you and me," Joey continued, even though by now he shouldn't have needed to phone a friend to get a clue. "We can probably connect on several levels. Even our names go together. Joey and Jan. Jan and Joey. Know what I'm saying?"

"No, I don't." Jan spun on her heel and walked down the hall.

The back room erupted.

"Ouch!" Doug's words were for Joey, but his eyes were on Jan, admiring her strong, sure stride and alluring backside as she left the room. This morning, when he'd given her a quick tour of the office located on the street made famous during the Rodney King riots, and set her up at her cashier position out front, she'd seemed quiet and reserved. Now he knew that hidden behind that calm façade was at least a little fire. He wondered what it took to turn that into a flame. Both his heart and his nether heat tightened at the thought of finding out, as the room reacted.

"Whoop, there it is!"

"I guess she told you!"

"Give it up, pretty boy. She's not interested."

"Calm down, everyone." Joey quieted his "audience" with raised hands. "Y'all are all reading the woman wrong. Jan is acting the way someone does when they're totally smitten, overcome with undeniable attraction."

"You got the denied right," said a coworker, appropriate snicker attached.

Doug laughed, too. "I don't know what body you were reading, but the language I picked up said you are dismissed."

"Just give me a minute," Joey confidently responded. "I think she's going to be my next boo thang."

"It's more likely she'll give you the boot," a coworker said. Those listening laughingly agreed.

Jan returned from her break to an empty lobby. An afternoon with few customers was the last thing she needed. Boredom provided too much time to think about things that shouldn't concern her. Like Joey, whose flirting was as subtle as the smell of popcorn at a movie theater concession stand. If lies were bricks, she could have built a house with the ones men with good looks like Joey had told her. Took her a year to lose the extra twenty-five pounds gained after breaking up with her own good looker. One who'd wormed his way into her heart and promptly put a hole in it. She'd tried to fill it with hot wings and chocolate-chip ice cream, but all of the extra ended up on her stomach and hips. A calorie counter and so many Zumba classes she felt she could speak Spanish had her finally back in her size fourteens. Which is why her handsome supervisor wasn't going to work her nerves or her nana. If something got started and didn't work out, it could cost her a job and some emotional-eating-induced extra junk in the trunk. Though she couldn't help but be curious whether or not he was involved with the coworker who'd butted into their conversation. The way she'd looked at him suggested to Jan that something was going on between them. So what if he was? It didn't matter to her.

Still, her mind's eye conjured up Doug's stocky body, lazy smile, and easygoing demeanor. He seemed like a nice enough guy, good for casual conversation and as a comrade in the workplace. Nothing more. After her last breakup she vowed to only date men who were headed in the same direction she was traveling . . . to the top of the music charts! A man like hip-hop artist and producer Nick Starr, who was making a major comeback after ten years out of the game, had just last week told her she had real talent and was in a position to help Jan reach her goal. She didn't look like the average size two pop star, but successful performers like Adele, Kelly Clarkson, and Jill Scott were living proof that in the cutthroat world of entertainment there was a place for somebody who could sing the paint off the wall and look like her.

Jan looked beyond the quiet, empty customer area in the small branch office to the posters lining the far wall. Limited-edition stamps. Information on passport services. A smiling postal worker thanking the troops. They taunted her, mocked her. Reminded her that she was someplace she'd rather not be doing something she'd rather not do. For years she'd lived the life of a struggling artist trying to break into the big leagues. She'd waited tables, done telemarketing, landed a few temp jobs—anything that would bring in enough money to pay the rent on her Hollywood studio. Those carefree years where she dreamed and planned and believed life would happen just the way she wanted seemed a lifetime ago. Back when life was normal. Before the accident, when everything changed.

She turned and reorganized an already neatly arranged box of stampers, just for something to do. Music played in the background, the radio tuned to an old-school station. An Anita Baker song came on. One of Jan's favorite singers. She bobbed her head and quietly sang along.

"Girl, you sound good."

Jan looked over at Pat's pleased expression. "You could hear me?"

"Just barely. But enough to know that you have skill, and a beautiful voice. Do you sing in church or something?"

Or something, she thought. "No," she said.

"Well, with a voice like that you should be singing somewhere. Lord knows there are enough people on the air now who can't hit a note with a two by four."

Jan laughed. Of all the people she'd met so far, she liked Pat the best. Her straightforward yet warm personality was inviting, and the sincerity with which she spoke made those who heard it feel good. Before she knew it, Jan was opening up and sharing with Pat the part of her life that she'd not planned to mix with the day job.

"I sing around town sometimes."

"You do? Where, in nightclubs?"

"Clubs occasionally, but more often at weddings and other smaller special events."

"Well, if you're ever going to be somewhere public, let me know. I love music and would definitely come and support you."

Jan nodded at the older man now waiting to be called up and noted two customers behind the next woman at the counter busy filling out an Express Mail label. Though she was lucky to have this afternoon shift, or tours as they were called, she couldn't wait until six, when the counter closed, and nine, when her day would be over. If she hurried, there might be time to make it to On That Note's Open Mike Night, where Nicholas Starr was holding a chance-of-a-lifetime contest. For the next ten weeks, reality TV hopefuls would compete for a chance to be on his new show—*Starr Power*—where ten singers would be groomed by Starr for the entertainment world. At the end the winner would get $25,000 and a record deal, either one of which would change Jan's life. What made this opportunity unique is the ten-week talent search for these ten contestants, happening at the club where she'd performed open mike for years. Each week, contestants who'd survived the preliminary tryouts could sign up for one of twenty last round audition spots. Some would be eliminated, some would advance, and one would be selected to be on the show. The contest started last week. She had advanced. Getting the afternoon tour that went until nine had almost eliminated her chance to compete. But a phone call to the club's bartender had kept her in the running. They'd known each other a long time. He had her back, and would personally make sure her name was on the list. All that was left was doing her part and making sure she was one of the ten on the reality show.

Jan thought about the jazzy rendition she'd arranged for the hit by Meghan Trainor and got excited. It didn't matter that she'd been up all day, slept little last night, and was exhausted.

Five minutes on stage was more than worth the forty-five minutes it would take her to get there. After eight hours of doing work she detested, she would have driven twice that to do that which she most loved.

2

Thank God for light traffic.

Jan flicked her blinker, veered her car left, and zoomed past the SUV with stick figures depicting the family of four and giving their names to all who found themselves stuck behind the slow-moving driver. Jan shifted back to the right lane and accelerated her car to eighty miles an hour, smiling that the sticker had even included the family pet. It reminded her of Crystal, her married cousin with a brood of eight: a husband, four kids, two cats, and a dog. Back in the day, her cousin had dreamed of babies, a husband, and the white picket fence. But for as long as she could remember, Jan's fantasy had always been the stage. Crystal's dream had come true. Jan hoped there was still time for hers to materialize. But she knew the entertainment industry highly favored the young. Time was running out.

Her cell phone rang. Thankful for the interruption from her thoughts, she tapped the telephone icon on her steering wheel and answered the call. "Hey, Chris."

"Hey, Jan. How's it going?"

"Okay. How are you doing?"

"The usual Herndon household craziness."

"How's the baby?"

"Fine. It's his mama who's ready to run away from home."

"Uh-huh. I told you to think twice about having another child. But no, you had to have balance— two girls, two boys."

"It looked good on paper."

Jan laughed. "Are y'all done now?"

"Hubby wants more, but I told him if that happened, he would have them." Jan laughed. "How's work at the new location?"

"Like I thought it would be. Slow. Boring. I miss the bustle of being downtown. Plus, that was closer to a lot of my gigs."

"But you're closer to home."

"True."

"And the people you work with?"

"Nice, so far, for the most part. Though one guy who thinks he's God's gift to women is already on my nerves."

"On your nerves or on your radar?"

"Trust me, I'm not interested."

"Why not? Is he married?"

"Don't know. Don't care. After all it took for me to get over the womanizer? I'm there to make a paycheck, not a love connection. Plus, the man for me doesn't work in a post office."

"How do you know that?"

"I just do." Jan honked her horn as a car bogarted its way in front of her from a merging ramp. "Crazy Cali drivers," she mumbled under her breath.

"You're on the highway?"

"Yep."

"Where are you headed?"

"Where I'll be every Monday for the next nine weeks. On That Note's Open Mike Night."

"You're still doing that? I thought when you started working at the post office last year you'd put all of that behind you."

"All of that, as you call it, is my dream. My passion. I'll never stop singing. Ever."

"I didn't mean it like that. Of course you'll always sing. But isn't that where they're holding the auditions for Nick Starr's new reality show?"

"Yes. And?"

"Are you sure this is less about singing and more about the crush you've had on him since you were twelve. You were going to marry either him or Usher. Remember?"

"Yes, I remember, and no, this isn't some little schoolgirl crush. Although since he was only fourteen at the time, marrying him is within the realm of possibilities." Jan waited. Silence. "You were supposed to agree with that."

"I would if I believed it."

"Forget you, heifah." They both laughed. "At any

rate, getting that recording contract, heck, even all the exposure of just getting on the show could change my life."

"Do you really want to make a fool of yourself on one of those shows? Reality TV is my guilty pleasure. They're going to bring the drama to get high ratings. Arguing and fighting with kids and slinging the B word? They don't know any better, but you're thirty years old!"

"And the Apollo was ten years ago. Thanks for the reminder. Yet again."

"Jan, you know I'd never try and make you feel bad. I'm your number one fan. That voice you were blessed with can put all of these young stars to shame. But you know how today's industry works. They want someone who looks good on TV."

"And I wouldn't?"

"Of course you would. You'd look amazing. It's just—"

"I know. I'm an over-the-hill thick chick. And you're my ride-or-die cuzzo not wanting me to set myself up for yet another disappointment."

"Hey, when I was seven you beat up the neighborhood bully for stealing my jacket." Jan laughed. "I've got to hold you down."

"And I love you for it. But singing is all I want to do. I've got to try. Listen, I need to call Mom and check on Lionel. I'll talk with you later."

Jan hurried the good-bye to get off the phone. Crystal meant well, but they'd had similar conversations to this one a thousand times. It always led to

Jan feeling badly. She should have been successful by now. When calling her mom and brother and getting voice mail it was almost a blessing. No need to let her spiraling mood drag them down.

Twenty minutes later she arrived at On That Note, where the Open Mike Night was held. Because so many singers had made it past the preliminary rounds, making the list of twenty singers who were able to perform each week wasn't guaranteed. The bartender making sure her name got on it was huge, which is why once inside she headed straight to the bar. She waved at a few regulars along the way.

"Hey, Rome."

Rome barely looked up from the frothy beer filling the glass from a tap. "Damn, about time you got here."

"I should have texted that I was on my way. Sorry about that."

"It's all good." He handed the mug to the waiting patron with one hand while the other grabbed a glass and scooped up ice. Watching him was like watching poetry, or a fighter, bobbing and weaving between pours and scoops, glass washing and counter wipe downs, all while carrying on several conversations at the same time. "All right, man." He scooped up the money, which included a tip. "Appreciate it." He added a splash of cranberry to the vodka he'd poured, winking at the customer as she reached for the glass.

"Did you add my special?"

"I've got you covered." Whirling around for a

bottle of wine, he poured a glass of chardonnay and set it before Jan. "How's the job?"

"It's okay."

"It's going to make you this late every week?"

"Looks like it. Which is why I so appreciate you looking out for me." She pushed a twenty toward him, unusual because Rome never charged her for the single glass of wine she drank each week.

"What's that?"

"For the wine, and the favor."

"Get out of here with that nonsense. Just remember me when you hit the big time. That way you can add a couple zeros to that payback."

"Ha! You're a fool, Rome. And my favorite bartender. When I have the party celebrating the release of my first single, I'll hollah at 'cha."

Rome nodded with a smile, set a mixed cocktail in front of another customer, and walked to the other end of the bar. Jan sipped her wine, watching Starr hold court at his usual table surrounded by the type of women her cousin mentioned—young, beautiful, made for TV. Sure, some of them would undoubtedly make the cut. But Starr was a Grammy-nominated singer-turned-producer. He knew real talent when he heard it. He'd complimented her last week and had encouraged her to return. She'd straight out asked if he thought she had a shot in the music business. He'd said yes. That from the lips of the man who could make it happen! The type of power he wielded excited her. That he was easy on the eyes and her preteen crush just two years her senior didn't hurt either. When Crystal had brought it up she'd downplayed how much she used to fantasize about Nick Starr. But the truth of the matter was she'd date him in a heartbeat. Not some joker who worked at the post office, whether a pretty boy, like Joey, or comfortably handsome, like her supervisor, Doug. Not that her super had flirted, or acted interested. And not that she would have cared if he had, something she felt the woman who yelled out the mouth comment would be pleased to know. Nobody in that building had to worry about Jan Baker wanting their man. She had big dreams and wanted a man who could help her make them happen. A man like the one she now looked away from, to center herself, prepare for the stage, and show him that whether or not he knew it she was the perfect artist for his label, to help him continue his big comeback.

"About time you got here." Doug dodged a punch from his brother, who took a seat across from him.

"It wasn't because I wanted to work late," Nelson replied. "Another travel alert. Extra precautions. Plus, somebody left a bag unattended, so we had to sweep the whole dang airport." Yawning, he looked around his and Doug's favorite late-night diner, surprised to see it almost empty, even on a weeknight. "Where is everybody?"

"A group was sitting at that table when I got here." He nodded toward the recently vacated corner booth. "They just left a few minutes ago. I thought the same thing, though. This place stays packed."

If anyone would know the restaurant flow, it would be these two single Carter brothers. Of the five male siblings, Doug and Nelson worked afternoon shifts, schedules that made eating after midnight a common occurrence. They ate here at least once a week. The physicality of Doug's job helped him keep the weight off. Nelson wasn't as lucky. His less-than-healthy eating habits, and addiction to his brother Marvin's desserts, were showing up around his waist.

"So, what's going on, bro? Anything exciting?"

Doug reached for one of two menus on the table. "Same stuff, different day." He began to flip through the myriad of choices. "New girl transferred to our branch this week. That's about it."

"Is she fine?"

"She's a pretty girl . . . with a bad attitude."

"Why, she turned down your offer for a date?" Nelson laughed as he, too, began to scan the menu.

"Asking her out hasn't crossed my mind, or anybody else at work for that matter. I'm still dealing with the fallout from getting with Melissa. Got reminded what a mistake that was just today."

"How so?"

"By doing the same thing that shut us down in the first place . . . running her mouth. Tried to make it sound like we still had something going, just because Joey and I were talking to Jan."

"Jan . . . that's the new girl's name?"

Doug nodded. "Pat tried to warn me about Messy Mel, but I didn't listen. Had to learn my lesson the hard way."

"You know what Mama says. A hard head makes a—"

"Soft butt," the brothers finished together, laughing.

Both took a moment to scan the menu. Decision made, Doug laid his down and rested against the comfy leather booth. "I don't know, man. Maybe 'bad attitude' is the wrong way to describe her. She's one of those serious, focused kind of women. No-nonsense. No fun. After getting to know us, who knows?" He shrugged. "Maybe she'll loosen up."

"Don't make up your mind too fast about her. Those quiet, serious women are sometimes the biggest freaks." Nelson wriggled his brow.

Doug slowly shook his head. "Trust me when I tell you that is not the case with this one."

"You never know. Who does she look like?" Nelson picked up one of two glasses of water the server had set down.

"Who does she look like?" Doug stroked his freshly trimmed beard. "She kind of reminds me of that actress who used to be on *Martin*, what's her name?"

"The one who played his wife?"

"Yeah."

"Tisha Campbell?"

"Yeah, Tisha. The one married to Duane Martin. She reminds me of her a little bit, maybe a shade darker, a few pounds heavier. Got those nice, thick lips and hips." Doug made an hourglass shape with his hands.

"Hot lips and hips? Sounds like somebody I need to meet!"

"If you wait for me to make the introduction, you'll be waiting a long time."

"Why?"

"As if you don't know. Chasing every skirt you see. Just like Joey."

"I bet that fool was all over her!"

"I wanted to punch him out. Been using the same lame rap for the last ten years. She shut him down like a vice squad raiding a drug house."

"Ha!"

"Surprised me, to be honest. I saw a little heat beneath that cool façade."

"But you're not interested."

"No."

"Because she's your coworker."

"You got it."

"If you saw her in a club, would you buy her a drink?"

"Hell yeah. I'd buy her two."

"What? She'd get you to come off of twenty dollars? Right out the gate? She must be special."

"I'm not that cheap."

"Oh, right. You and Byron call it frugal."

"Financially conservative."

"Aka cheap!"

The waiter came and took their orders. The conversation shifted after that, from family to air travel to who would make the AFC playoffs. Though her name was not brought up again, Jan stayed on Doug's mind. On the way home, he still thought about her. Hell yeah, he'd buy that girl two drinks. Maybe even three.

3

The next day, Doug whipped his blue Kawasaki into the post office parking lot. Seeing an open space, he barely hit the brakes as he turned, skidded, and screeched to a stop.

The quick action of the driver beside him saved her opened door and swallowed the scream brought on by his unexpected arrival. Doug laughed, dismounting from his bike amid a cloud of dust. The smell of burnt rubber wafted around them.

He took off his helmet, reached for the car door, and opened it. "Sorry about that. Didn't see the door until the last minute. If not for your quick reflexes, I might have gone flying."

"And you think that's funny?" Jan got out of the car and slammed the door. She brushed by Doug on her way to the building, tapping the key fob to lock the doors without looking back.

Her unexpected anger caught Doug off guard, but only for a second. "Jan, wait up." He rushed to catch up with her. "I was only kidding. I've been riding bikes since I was twelve years old."

"Like a maniac?"

"Even if you hadn't closed the door, I wouldn't have hit it."

"You don't know that."

"Actually, I do. Like I said, I've ridden bikes for a long time. I've got skills." He broke into a '70s strut, an act that usually evoked laughter. Not this time. Even the birds kept silent.

"I'm sorry if I scared you."

In answer, Jan increased the length of her stride. The post office anchored a string of businesses on a corner lot. By the time they arrived for their afternoon shift the lot was almost always crowded, so they'd been forced to park some distance from the door. No matter. Her five foot five was no match for Doug's five eleven. He easily kept up with her.

They reached the post office building's employee entrance. He opened the door to let her enter. They continued down the hallway. "I noticed that Sonata yesterday in the lot and wondered who owned it. My sister was thinking about getting one of those. How do you like it?"

She reached her locker.

Doug stopped, too. "You're that upset about what happened? It's not like I actually hit your door. No harm no foul, right?"

She gave him a look, then continued placing her items inside the locker before closing the door and securing it with her newly purchased lock.

"So you're just going to ignore me, and not answer my question."

She turned to face him. "I suggest your sister do as I did: go to a car dealer and try one out. A test drive with a competent salesperson should be able to provide any answers that can't be found online."

Doug rose his hands in mock surrender. "Wow, all right. I thought your opinion, as a consumer, might be more valuable than someone who stands to make a commission on the sale, but no worries. Like you said, there are a lot of other ways to get information. Again, I apologize for scaring you."

A curt nod was her only reaction. Doug turned to leave, then stopped. "I know you got trained downtown, but later on, after the counter closes, there are a couple things I want to show you."

She met his eye, her demeanor professional. "Okay. Thanks."

"You're welcome. If you run into any problems, either Pat or I can help you."

Another nod as she came toward him before turning down the short hall and out to the customer counter to begin her shift.

Doug placed his personal items in a locker, then walked over to the mail sorter. Joey started right in. "I guess she told you," he mumbled, a hand over his mouth, his eyes shifting as if to make sure no one else heard. This in a place where even the floor had ears. "It has to be frustrating to work so hard for that which for me comes so easy."

"Shut up, fool."

As proof that Joey's voice had carried beyond them, Melissa, three tables away, turned around. "Doug, are you trying to hit on the new girl?"

"No, so that little quip you threw out yesterday was totally unnecessary."

"What?" Melissa batted her eyes as though innocent or ignorant, when she hadn't been either since dog was a pup. Doug shook his head and pulled out his phone. "Oh, about that mouth of yours and knowing how to use it?" She turned off the processing machine, swayed over to where Doug stood, and pushed her natural DDs against his arm. "Did I lie?"

Doug's eyes didn't move from his cell phone screen. "Go back to work, Melissa."

"That's right," Joey said. "Before your man comes around the corner and sees you flirting."

"What man?"

"The one I saw you all up on yesterday in the break room. The maintenance man, that's who."

"Boy, please. We were just playing."

"That's your problem. You play too much. And then broadcast your business. Not cool." Doug's side-eye glance confirmed that he wasn't talking about video or board games.

"Don't be jealous, Doug." She reached up and ran a manicured nail down the side of his face.

Doug quickly removed it. "Stop."

"You know you miss this." Melissa ran her hands down her sides, then flipped her hair as she walked away. She reached her table and turned around.

"But if you play nice . . . you just might be able to get it again."

Doug swallowed a sarcastic answer, one that was true but uncomplimentary. One thing his father, Willie, had instilled in all of his sons was to have respect for women. "Even a floozy is somebody's daughter," he told them once, when passing by a woman who looked to be a lady of the night. "Maybe someone's mother, too." Doug was only nine or ten years old when this happened, but it's a message he never forgot. It wasn't until after he and Melissa had added a one-night set of benefits to their friendship that he found out how many other coworkers had this status as well. Still, he wouldn't judge Melissa for being "sexually liberated." He wouldn't take advantage of her benefits again either.

After putting out an administrative fire, he settled into work. A few hours later he was ready for a break. To ensure everything was running smoothly before leaving, he chatted with a few workers in the back room and then headed to the counter. There, Pat was dealing with the lone customer. Jan fiddled with her register.

He walked over to her. "How's it going?"

"Fine, no complaints." She cleared the machine before looking at him, her expression not quite angry but not quite welcoming either. "While it's slow, I was going through a couple different postage scenarios. My last customer used media mail. I'd never done that before."

"Pat get you through it all right?"

"Yes, she's a great instructor."

"Pat is good people, period."

"What'd you say about my mama?" Said with mock attitude as Pat winked at her customer and gave her a receipt.

"No one would dream of talking about your mama," Doug said with a laugh. "Or you either."

"That's because you know better." She placed the customer's Priority Mail package into a bin, walked to Doug, and slung an arm around his waist. "How are you today?"

"Always better after seeing you, Miss Pat."

"I've told you about that 'Miss' crap. Don't matter that I'm old enough to be your mama. I'm not your mama. Okay?"

"Okay, Miss Pat."

He dodged her swatting hands and walked over to straighten the Express and Priority mailers on display in disarray.

"I was going to do that, Doug," Pat said.

"No worries. They're always like this before the day is over."

"How are Willie and Liz doing? I haven't seen them since the block party."

"They're good."

"Seems like that 4th of July celebration was just yesterday and here it is October. Is there a block party for Halloween, too?"

"Anytime someone fires up a grill on the block

there's likely to be a party. But a big one like what you attended only happens once a year."

"The people in that neighborhood sure know how to party. I had so much fun. Jan, you'll have to join us next year."

"Is this a post office event?"

Pat shook her head. "It's over in Inglewood, where Doug's parents live. They close off the streets, bring out the bands, and have every type of food and drink you can imagine."

"I'm not much of a partier, but it sounds fun."

"Not a partier?" Pat looked from Jan to Doug and back. "What person your age doesn't enjoy a good party or two?"

"None that I know personally," Doug answered. "But there are other activities to enjoy: cards, dominoes, board games, or rolling with my crew." Doug simulated being on a motorcycle and gunning the engine. He didn't miss the frown that flitted across Jan's face, or how she turned away and disengaged from the conversation.

Pat seemed not to notice. "I'm still waiting on my ride."

"I rode her in today."

"You did? Well, I'm going home at seven, so that won't work."

"What are you doing this weekend? I'll come over and let you ride with me and the gang. We're going to San Diego."

"I'm not going to have all your girlfriends mad

at me. Just take me around the block tomorrow on my lunch break."

"You got it."

"Don't forget and drive your SUV."

Doug headed toward the back as he answered, "I won't."

Pat watched him leave, then spoke. "Jan."

"Yes, Pat?"

"Are you married?"

"No, ma'am."

"Do you want to be?"

"Sure, eventually, if I find the right man."

"Then look no further than Douglas Carter. Not only is he easy on the eyes, but he's hardworking, respectful, comes from a good family. If I were twenty years younger, I'd give you a run for your money. Because that's a good man right there."

4

Jan unlocked the door to the home she shared with her mom and brother and quietly stepped inside. The house was dark. This was not unusual. Her mother's workday began early and ran late. The two of them often passed like ships in the night. But her brother was usually there and still awake. She crossed the living room to the hallway, stopped, and knocked on his bedroom door.

"Who is it?"

Jan made a face. "Who are you expecting?"

"Beyoncé."

Her frown disappeared and a laugh escaped. "Are you decent?"

"Yeah, but it's a boring way to live."

She opened the door to go inside but came to a halt after just one step. "Wow."

"Yeah, I bought a TV instead of the computer you suggested. But it was my money. So don't start."

"But I thought we'd . . . never mind." She continued into the room and over to a newly mounted flat-screen TV, tamping down her annoyance with the half-brother twelve years her junior. Having left home by the time he was seven, they'd never gotten close. Being two totally different personalities didn't help either. But he was family and she loved him to life. Over the past two years, their relationship had strengthened. Wanting to keep it that way, she kept the irritation she was feeling to herself. Playing video games was one of the few pleasures her brother enjoyed. So what she felt an irresponsible purchase may for him have been a necessity. She wouldn't judge. Much.

"It's big."

"Just forty-two inches. I started to get the fifty but decided that for this room this one would do."

"High-def, too, huh? It does make the picture pop." She continued to look around. "DVD player, Xbox . . . coming in here is probably the only way I'll see you from now on."

Lionel focused on the controller he held, his whole body engaged in defeating the enemy in the video game. "You're probably right."

"Did Mom take you to get it on her lunch break?"

He shook his head. "Naw, Bernard drove me over. Then helped me hook everything up."

Again Jan kept her mouth shut. Bernard was the one peer who'd stayed close to Lionel after what happened. The two had grown up together. He wasn't a bad kid, just lazy, unmotivated, and, like her brother, spent too many hours watching television and playing video games. She'd seen and read about many people who became confined to a wheelchair and still lived active, fulfilling, successful lives. She wanted Lionel to be one of them. That was unlikely to happen with Bernard around.

History had shown that it wouldn't happen with her nagging either. More than once Lionel had reminded her that he already had a mother and her name wasn't Janice but Rochelle. He was right. People had tried to discourage her dream of a singing career. She'd not listened either. The closer they became, the more Jan realized that she and her baby brother were more alike than not.

She sat on his bed. "What are you playing?"

Lionel's whole body bobbed and weaved as he directed shooters to take out the designated enemy. "Why? You wouldn't know anyway." His thumbs pushed red and blue buttons in rapid succession, which led to shots, explosions, and advancement to a new level. "That's what I'm talking about!"

In the few seconds where the score and next level were shown, Lionel offered, "It's called Battlefield Hardline. Has several modes. I'm in Heist, where criminals are trying to blow up this vault. No, sucker!" Lionel screamed at the screen and used his whole upper body to help the police officer catch the thief. "See what just almost happened? The police figure out whose thieving and prevent their escape."

Requiring the use of analytical skills, quick judgment,

and decisions. Maybe there's a career path in video gaming. Jan told her mind to shut up.

"Are you any good?" Lionel gave her a snort and a side eye. Jan's phone rang. She stood and squeezed her brother's shoulder as she passed him. "Good night, Lionel."

"Night, sis."

After a shower and bite to eat, Jan fired up her Kindle. Aside from singing, reading had been her only other passion. When Terry McMillan's *Waiting to Exhale* came out, she entertained the thought of becoming a writer. But after several abysmal short stories and one try at an outline, she decided to stay in her lane and keep music at the forefront of her dreams.

She'd heard *Destiny's Captive* was a good book, as was anything written by historical romance writer Beverly Jenkins. She'd downloaded it months ago, along with several other novels, but work had put a serious crimp in her reading schedule. She settled back against the pillows but try as she might, Jan just couldn't get into the story. The hero was her kind of man—successful, take-charge, good-looking—but her mind kept drifting back to her supervisor from the post office. Doug Carter, the good man, according to Pat.

Why am I thinking of him? Aside from their morning encounter and his visit to the front midafternoon, she hadn't much seen him. That was probably a good thing. After calming down she'd realized that her reaction to his motorcycle antics may have been over the top. What he did was stupid, immature, and irresponsible. He'd frightened her and made her angry. But she hadn't been harmed. Unless one counted the way her stomach and a few lower muscles clenched when he pulled off his helmet and looked at her the way he did, his big brown eyes full of apology save for a glint of mischief that still remained even after "I'm sorry." Hadn't she heard he was thirty years old? Too grown to be playing like that.

After going over the same page three times, she gave up reading and turned out the light. If she got up in time, she could put on something in the slow cooker and save her mom from having to prepare a meal later. From early morning till late at night, Rochelle Baker went nonstop. Jan worried about her. There'd been no insurance money, so to handle Lionel's steep medical bill and ongoing treatment her mother had added an evening part-time data entry job to her full-time work as a secretary. Jan had moved back home and taken a steady job to help lighten the load. To Jan, family was everything, so she did what she had to do without complaint. But the change in lifestyle meant she hadn't been able to pursue her singing career the way she once had—staying up till dawn and sleeping in the next day. Getting by on Ramen noodles and beans if the pennies got low. That's why the contest meant so much. Hers wasn't the only life that needed changing.

On Monday night, she'd seen Starr paying special

attention to a young girl with a nice enough voice, but one that was no match for Jan's four-octave pipes. What she lacked in talent she made up in looks: long weave, pretty face, store-bought boobs, five-inch heels, skintight mini, and maybe weighing a buck-o-five soaking wet. Society's version of beautiful to a T. Jan didn't look like that. She was thick and curvy and au natural. And could sing all of them youngins under the table. At the open mike she'd gotten the bigger applause and a pass through to the next week. But buck-o-five had gotten selected for the TV show. This forced Jan to acknowledge a painful truth. A shot at the reality TV show was the closest she'd been to a breakout career moment in a decade, and maybe a last chance to grab the brass ring. Time, and slots, were running out.

The next afternoon she arrived to work early, checking e-mails as she sat in her car. Her plan was to catch Doug somewhere away from the nosy crew, especially Melissa, and apologize. There was a very good reason for the way she'd reacted. But he didn't know that. Plus, he was her supervisor and she needed this job. He was owed an apology.

Ten minutes until time for them to clock in, Doug arrived. She heard him first, or his motorcycle rather, revving at high throttle before taking the curb off Normandie Avenue at an unsafe speed, his bike becoming airborne and fairly sailing into the lot. As soon as it landed, he turned into an open space, effortlessly guiding the sleek motorcycle between two cars. She shook her head, his fool moves making her angry again and second-guessing whether it was an apology that he needed or a whack of common sense upside his head.

Quickly gathering her things, she got out of her car and locked it. Long, angry strides quickly lessened the distance between them. Particles of dust were still flying as she neared him. She stopped, waving them away from her face and pushing up her sunglasses to further shield her eyes.

He took off his helmet, smiling as he approached her, his expression one she imagined saved him from whoopings as a child. "You don't even have to say it. Going too fast. Am I in trouble again?"

She tried to remain angry, but his look of feigned contrition quickly dissipated that feeling, being quickly replaced by an emotion she'd rather not feel. "I was waiting on you," she said without answering his question. "I needed to have a chance to talk before going inside."

"Oh? About what?"

"Before watching your reckless entry into this parking lot, it was to apologize for yesterday's outburst. But what I just saw underscores everything I said. Driving the way you do is dangerous and irresponsible. To do so is jeopardizing more lives than your own."

"I appreciate your concern for my well-being, but I know how to handle a bike."

"There are probably plenty of graves filled with men who said the same. Or the victims of such foolishness who didn't survive." Jan didn't want to get angry. Too late. She already was. "You know what? Forget I said anything. I'll just search the nearby area and find a safer place to park."

She turned to hurriedly put distance between them. But, once again, her legs were no match for his long, sure strides. He caught up quickly and stayed her with a hand on her arm. "Jan. Wait." She stopped but didn't look at him. "Look, I'm not trying to upset you. But I've done that curb trick a hundred times, maybe a thousand. I know it looks scary, but it's really easy."

"My br—" She caught herself, clenched her jaw against a rising tide of emotions. "There's a reason why I feel as I do. But that's no reason to have overreacted, as I did yesterday, or be disrespectful as I was just now. You're my supervisor, and a grown man. I don't want to create a hostile work environment. So . . ." The sentence hung unfinished as she battled between what else to say or whether to say more at all. "So for those reasons, I apologize." Without waiting for an answer, she turned and walked away.

Doug stood unmoving, absorbing what she'd said, pondering what she hadn't. He watched her walk toward the employee entrance, adjusting her sunglasses and appearing to wipe her eyes against the dust he'd stirred up with his bike. At least he hoped that's what it was. She couldn't be crying. Could she? He'd been known to bring a woman to tears before, but not for being unhappy. His strides were slow as he walked to the door, trying to figure out the woman beneath Jan's cool, calm exterior. And just like that, it became his mission. To unlock the mystery of Jan Baker. For professional reasons, he told himself, and for the Carter name. Not to become involved romantically or anything, her being a coworker and all. But he couldn't have a woman thinking he was a jerk, especially one who looked the way she did—expression sexy even in anger; nice, round booty filling out those slacks. No, he'd have to make sure Jan knew the truth. That he was the perfect gentleman who Willie Carter raised.

5

Turns out the schedule provided the perfect opportunity for Doug's "good man glow" to shine. Since it continued to be a slow week at the counter and Joey was home with a sick kid, he pulled Jan to the back to train on sorting mail. After watching him run through the process a few times, she felt ready to go on her own.

"Are you sure?"

"I think so. I can always come find you if I have a question."

"I'm going to be here working, too, so you won't have far to look."

"Oh, okay. Then I'm definitely ready for my first solo batch."

He placed a container in front of her, took another two for himself, and they both got to work. For the first few minutes both focused on sorting the mail in front of them. Occasionally, Doug would stop what he was doing and check Jan's progress.

"You're a fast learner."

Jan's attention remained focused on work. "This isn't that complicated."

"True, but you'd be surprised how long it takes some people to get the hang of it. But you picked it right up. Your administrative background may be a reason."

"Perhaps."

Doug reached for another large batch of mail. "What made you want to work here, or rather, for the post office?"

She shrugged and continued processing mail. "Different reasons," she finally answered, reaching for a bottle of water she'd brought in earlier and opening it to take a sip. "Money, mainly. And benefits. Although my last job ran indefinitely it was classified as a temp job, which meant no health insurance or holiday pay."

Doug nodded. There were other questions he wanted to ask, but Joey had taken the day off and the room had gotten quiet, which meant the others, especially Melissa, were listening to every word. He got the feeling that Jan was a private person who'd come in and do a job, not make friends. This was her first week here. He thought time might prove otherwise. Of course, he'd also thought Melissa a woman who wouldn't put their personal business in the workplace and ended up being as wrong as O. J. Simpson selling knives at the mall. So he'd wait for time to tell.

They continued working, quietly, side by side.

The subtle floral fragrance that wafted his way when she moved was a constant reminder of Jan's nearness, and of her serious nature that was somehow sexy as hell. He made a few more attempts at small talk. It was awkward, stilted, her answers courteous but painfully brief. With Joey absent, Pat up front, and Melissa trying to eavesdrop, the back room was unusually quiet. Since Doug couldn't remember the last time Joey had taken a day off, his friend's absence made one thing clear. For as much as his talking got on everyone's nerves at one time or another, the constant jibber jabber made the time fly. Finishing the mail from the bin seemed to take four hours. But when he looked at the clock, only two and a half had gone by.

"How are you coming with that stack?"

Jan rubbed her neck as she looked over. "Almost done with what's here. But there's more, right?"

"Oh, yes. There's something else I need to show you first." He turned and motioned for Jan to follow him. Her expression turned questioning, but she followed him in silence. They kept walking, past the lockers, the offices, break room, all the way to the door that led outside. He turned just as Jan's mouth began to open, and quieted what he assumed an oncoming protest or question with a finger to his lips.

Her silence ended the moment they stepped outside. "What's to show me out here?"

Doug kept walking. "The convenience store on

the corner. Come on." After a brief hesitation, she complied. "I saw you massage your neck and thought it might be time for a break. And honestly, I wanted to talk to you without everyone listening."

"By everyone, do you mean Melissa?"

"So you've already figured that out? Fast learner, just like I said."

"Her comment on Monday made it clear that everything spoken could be clearly heard."

"About that comment—"

"No need to explain," she interrupted, with a hand up for emphasis. "Even before getting hired I'd heard that what happens in post offices could be reality TV."

"You heard correctly. But I wouldn't be on the show." They reached the corner. Doug pushed the button for a green light. "I like a life that's drama-free, which is why Melissa's comment needs explanation. She and I hung out once, years ago, when I first got promoted and transferred to this branch. We both agreed it was a casual hookup. When she changed her mind and wanted something different, our going out ended."

"For you, maybe. Sounds to me like she still has feelings."

"No, she's just being messy. Melissa has dated plenty of dudes, and wants every new girl to know that I was one of them."

"Well, she doesn't have anything to worry about

here. The only things I'm coming to work for are benefits and a paycheck."

"Ouch."

The light changed.

"Don't take it personally," Jan said as they walked across the street.

"Hard not to."

"I understand. But it wasn't meant as a put down. It's just . . . I mean . . ."

Doug held the door for her, laughing at her flustered expression as she passed him. "I'm just playing with you. I get what you're saying. As the new member on the team, I just didn't want you having the wrong impression about me, thinking I date every new hire who walks through the door."

They reached the refrigerated section at the back of the store. Doug reached for a cola. Jan chose orange juice. They passed through the chips aisle. Doug picked up a bag of those, too. He joked with the petite Asian lady at the register, causing titters and a big smile.

"This all for you?"

Doug looked at Jan. "You want a snack or something?"

"No, the juice is fine."

"Just this and her juice," he said to the cashier.

"That's okay. I can pay for mine."

"I know you can, but I'm going to take care of it."

"Shoot, I forgot. I don't have my purse. I'll pay you back."

"Don't worry about it, Jan. I know those two dollars didn't buy me a date."

"Doug, I in no way meant to imply that you were trying to buy my affection."

She'd stated this so seriously Doug was sure she was playing. Until he looked over and saw her profile. Jan looked as serious as a 100-car pileup in two feet of snow.

"Relax, Jan. I was teasing."

"Oh."

"I take it you don't joke much."

"Not really."

"Come on, now. Life is too hard to be taken so seriously. Better to laugh at it sometimes."

"Focused might be a better word to describe me. It's not like I don't like to have fun. I just don't have time for games."

"Even more reason to be forewarned that the Normandie crew plays games a lot. Harmless for the most part. Letting you know so you won't get offended."

"I'll keep that in mind, and hope that my not participating won't be misconstrued either. I'm a private person by nature, which might come off as standoffish. But that's not my intent."

"From what I see so far . . . I guess you'll do."

He tried to keep his face straight but couldn't. Her reaction confirmed that his intentionally off-handed comment had caught her off guard. And made her smile. Another intention.

"Gee, thanks."

They reached the employee entrance.

"You'd better lose that smile," Doug said, before opening the door. "You'll have people speculating about what I did to put it there."

He ducked into the men's room before she could respond.

Jan lifted her chin and lost the grin . . . just barely.

6

Doug left the bathroom, his eyes automatically searching for Jan as he entered the back room. She'd obviously already gone up to the customer counter. He walked around to the flat sorting machines for the last batch of the day's processed mail, expecting mess from Melissa. She did not disappoint.

"Where have you been?"

"Minding my business." He transferred large stacks from the table to a cart. "What about you?"

"The same: minding your business. I see you and the newbie took your break together."

"That doesn't surprise me. Nosy never misses much. . ."

"I don't see what has you so attracted. She might be cute if she lost some weight, but I don't know if even that would do it." Doug continued gathering mail and imitating speak no evil. "Must be the thrill of the chase," Melissa said with a sigh. "Men always have to see if they can get in the panties."

"There you go assuming."

"Assuming what? That you're interested?"

"That and about her personality. You don't even know her yet."

Melissa fed mail into the machine as though a machine herself. "Doesn't take me long to size chicks up. She's uppity, thinks she's better than us. Coming in here wearing a smile as tight as her clothes are loose. She wants y'all to think that she's off-limits, but she can't fool me. I know a thirsty girl when I see one. Women who act like that are usually the exact opposite."

"Since you're so quick to speak on what you think you know, I hope that when you're proven wrong, you'll admit that just as quickly."

"See, she's got you twisted already. Wait until the next time she comes back here. We'll see how friendly your girl is with her competition."

Doug felt like asking who that was but didn't want to start an argument. With Melissa so far off the mark, there was no need. Jan was attractive, but he had no designs on her. They were too different. He was laidback, no drama, lived life to have fun. He'd not been looking for a promotion when tapped for the supervisor position, and would be fine to ride the position on out to his retirement. Jan was serious; no, focused she called it. Probably already planning to scale the career ladder to the top rank of postmaster. It wouldn't at all surprise him if she wound up being his boss one day.

* * *

Just after six p.m., with the front customer service door closed and locked, Jan and the bubbly and efficient Latina with whom she'd worked the afternoon tour walked to the back room.

Doug looked up and smiled as Jan walked toward him. "All locked up?" She nodded. "And you took your dinner break, right?"

"Yes, I did."

"Good. You can help me process this latest batch."

"No problem. I'll just use the restroom and be right back."

When she returned, Melissa was talking with Doug . . . and waiting. "Hey there, Jan!" Her smile was warm and wide as she watched Jan approach. Messiness aside, Melissa was a pretty girl who could turn on the charm. "How's it going so far?"

"Fine, thanks." Small talk had never been Jan's strong suit, but she managed to strike a cordial tone before walking over to a cart. "Doug, is this it?"

"All keyed in and waiting for you," Melissa offered before Doug could speak. "You seem to be catching on fast. Are you a transfer or new hire?"

Jan paused, then answered while reaching for a bag stuffed full with mail. "Transfer. From downtown."

"How long had you worked there?"

"Not long, data conversion mostly."

"So you just began processing and sorting here? Were you a secretary before working downtown?"

Doug glanced at Jan before fixing Melissa with a

warning glare. Even before their brief talk during break, he'd picked up that Jan wasn't big on chitchat. Her current body language transmitted this message better than a flashing neon sign, but his normally perceptive coworker pretended not to notice.

"I only ask because of how fast you seem to be catching on to everything. Then again, Doug is a very good teacher. Right, Doug?"

Anyone not knowing better would mistake her bright eyes and wide smile for signs of friendliness. Doug knew better. Melissa was up to no good and he knew it.

"How fast she's learning has nothing to do with me," he said.

"Then I guess it's all about your skills, girl; why, you're rolling through those stacks like a pro."

Jan rolled a cart over to the table where Doug worked and Melissa stood. She made eye contact with Melissa and offered a slight smile. "Thank you." Dumping the bin of mail next to a sorter, she began placing the envelopes in stacks.

"What'd you do before coming here?"

"Worked as an admin, like you thought."

"Oh, really? Where?"

"Melissa," Doug interrupted, looking at his watch. "Aren't you off work?"

She looked at him, her sparkling eyes conveying that she knew exactly what he was trying to do and she wasn't having any of it. "Yes. And?"

"You're off work, and we're not. Jan would

probably rather concentrate on what she's doing than listen to your chatter."

"Mind your business, Doug. Jan looks like a multitasker. Unlike men, whose minds tend to be one-track, women can focus on more than one thing at a time. Right, Jan?"

Jan looked up and smiled. "Absolutely."

"Besides, how do we get to know and befriend our coworkers if we don't talk to them?"

"Easy. Invite her to lunch. Chat on a break. But right now"—Doug locked eyes with Melissa—"leave her alone."

"My, aren't we protective. It is time to get out of this place, though." Melissa ran a hand across Doug's backside as she walked around him to where Jan stood. "Do you ever go to Magic's T.G.I. Friday's? Over on La Tijera?"

"When it first opened I went a couple times, but, no, I don't go there anymore."

"Well, it's my and my girls' hangout. Happy hour every Friday. Not officially. They don't sell discount drinks or appetizers. But the bartender is a friend of mine and he always hooks us up, know what I mean? Guaranteed, you'll leave there feeling happy! On Saturday, we hit the club."

Jan paused from her work and looked up. "I already have plans for this weekend, but thanks for the invite."

"Did you hear that, Doug? Jan's whole weekend is booked. With some tall, strapping, packing brother, probably. I'm not mad at you, sister!"

A quick, forced smile and Jan resumed working. "Melissa . . ."

"All right, Doug. I'm leaving. Dang! See y'all tomorrow, everybody!" she sang while sashaying down the hallway.

Upon hearing the exit door clang closed, Pat quickly quipped, "That Melissa is messier than a newborn's diaper."

One sentence and like a can of air freshener, the comment sprayed a reason to laugh over a funky situation.

"Don't pay her no mind," Pat continued, coming around to where Doug and Jan stood working. "All in all, Melissa's a nice girl. She's just nosy, mouthy, and can't stand somebody else getting Doug's attention."

"She doesn't have to worry about me. I'm not—"

"She ain't either. And that's her problem." Without waiting for an answer, Pat spun on her wedged heel and retrieved her purse and other items from the locker. "Have a good evening, everyone." Various responses followed her down the hall and out of the building.

The remaining employees settled into work. Time went by in a flash and before he knew it, the day was done.

His eyes searched for Jan without his consent. He'd never had a younger sister to protect, and the women he dated could hold their own. Jan could, too, he figured. Still, a part of him felt responsible for her happiness here, and her success.

Guess this is what being a supervisor is all about.

This thought even though he'd been a supervisor for more than a year and hadn't felt this way before. But it sounded like a good story for this lifelong player, so he was sticking to it.

He'd just started down the hall when she came out of the restroom. "I was just coming to find you. Wouldn't want to get locked in here and have to spend the night."

Jan grimaced as she fell in step beside him. "Definitely not."

"That bad, huh?"

"No, actually I'm getting the hang of things faster than I thought I would."

"You're doing very well. As messy as Melissa was being earlier, she was right about that."

They reached the lockers. Doug leaned against one while Jan opened hers to retrieve the purse and plastic lunch container inside. Closing the locker door, she was surprised to find him there. "Is there something else?"

"No, just waiting to walk you out."

"Thanks, but I think I can manage."

"Probably so, but it's an unwritten rule. Nobody on the night shifts walks to their car alone."

"Why?" They began walking toward the exit. "Did something happen?"

"No, and we want to keep it that way. I'd put the key in the lock and was ready to turn it until I realized you weren't in the group that just left. You were seconds away from being on lockdown."

"Then thanks for looking out."

"No problem. I hope Melissa didn't make you too uncomfortable this afternoon."

"I've had a Melissa or two in my life before. The new kid on the block always gets attention. Curiosity is natural. But like I said earlier, I'm a private person."

"Don't want people all up in your business, huh?"

"Basically," Jan replied with a smile.

"So in that case I guess I shouldn't ask you whether it's true or not."

The question caught Jan off guard. They'd reached her car, but she didn't reach for the door handle. "Whether what's true or not?"

"If the man you're meeting on Friday night is strapping and packing, as Melissa suggested."

This question got her extremities working. Legs took two steps away from Doug. One finger tapped the key fob while the other hand found the door handle. "Looks like Melissa isn't the only nosy one," she quipped with a laugh before getting into her car. She quickly shut the door and started her car. Doug blocked her planned escape and then strolled to her window. She rolled it down, still smiling. "I know. I forgot to thank you for getting me to my car safely. And for your patience in training me this afternoon."

"You're welcome, but what you forgot is to answer my question. Are you dating someone?"

"And you're asking because . . ."

"Because I want to know."

Street noise filled the seconds of silence that followed. "I told you I was private, right?"

"You did."

"My personal life fits squarely within that private zone. So I'd rather not answer your question."

"Okay."

Perhaps it was, yet Doug's hand remained firmly on the rim of her car window. Her eyes went from his hand to his face and back. "So if you don't mind . . ."

He slowly removed his hand. "See you tomorrow, Ms. Baker."

"See you tomorrow."

Doug stepped back and then turned to watch her rapidly disappearing taillights, the car barely breaking before turning on to the street.

"Driving pretty fast for somebody who chewed me out for speeding," he mumbled, pulling out his motorcycle keys. "Pretty good at not answering questions, too."

He got on the Kawasaki, strapped on his helmet, fired up the engine, and spewed errant gravel as he fishtailed out of the parking lot. His mind stayed on Jan the whole way home, especially why she wouldn't answer a simple question like the one he'd asked her. He told himself that it didn't matter. He wasn't interested in dating her anyway.

She was private and quiet. He liked wild, crazy, outgoing women.

She was always so serious. He liked to have fun.

She probably didn't like sex much. He liked sex very much.

These reasonable objections to any interest in Jan Baker played on loop inside Doug's head.

But she stayed on his mind.

7

When he downloaded his latest favorite hip-hop beat for a ringtone, Doug hadn't been thinking about phone calls coming in at eight a.m. On a weekend. And an off day. With his head pounding. Reaching blindly for the cell phone that lay on the nightstand, he managed one eye open to check the ID, then fell back against his pillows.

"Man, if somebody isn't headed to emergency, later on today I'll be sending you there."

"Just as I figured. Still lounging around."

"Heck yeah, I'm lounging. It's Saturday, fool!"

"It's eight o'clock, fool. The time we agreed I'd pick you up to go running." Silence. "Uh-huh. Thought I forgot, didn't you?"

"Hoping is more like it. Look, Barry—"

"Don't even try it," Doug's youngest, now irksome brother warned him. "Nelson already told me about y'all going out last night and you trying to hang with those hardheads. You know you can't drink. Ha!"

"Look, it's not cool laughing at someone's pain."

"I'm laughing at the fact that you can't drink two beers without feeling woozy. Nelson told me you took a shot! Douglas . . . what were you thinking?"

It's what he'd been determined to stop thinking that made him take Nelson up on his offer to hang with him and some of their old friends from the block. Now younger brother Barry's question brought the reason swirling from somewhere in his cerebral cortex through the throb above his right ear straight into his consciousness.

"Open up, man. I'm here."

"Barry, look, dude. I'm—"

Heavy, constant knocking on his front door interrupted Doug's planned excuse. No need to waste his breath trying to talk sense to the baby of the family. Barry was the most spoiled, annoying, cocky person by far that Doug had ever met. So why he and the rest of the Carter clan loved that rascal to the moon and back was a mystery that none of them had yet to solve. Couldn't live with him, and sure as heck couldn't live without him.

Doug reached the door and yanked it open. Barry stumbled forward, knocking Doug backward.

"Barry, stop playing!"

"I'm not trying to mess with you, Doug. I was leaning on the door!"

Doug walked into the living room and plopped on the couch. He rested his head against the back, rubbing his forehead.

Shaking his head, Barry continued past him into the kitchen. "You got some aspirin?" He opened the refrigerator and pulled out a bottle of water, walked over to Doug, and set it on the coffee table. Kicking Doug's foot, he repeated the question.

Doug groaned, rubbed his face with both hands, and looked heavenward. "What did I do to deserve him in my life?"

"I'm trying to help you, big bro, because we're going running today. There's no getting out of that. All you need are a few aspirin, that entire bottle of water, and a good, greasy meal." Barry pulled out his phone, tapped a smiling face on his contact list, and then hit the speaker button.

Two rings and then an answer. "Why are you calling here at what-the-hell thirty in the morning?"

"Mama, it's after eight."

"Do I have kids under the age of five?"

Barry frowned. "No, but—"

"That's the only reason to be up at ass crack on a Saturday."

"Tell him, Mama!" Doug called out.

"Is that Doug?"

Doug leaned closer to Barry and the phone. "It's your favorite, smartest, and most handsome son."

"Oh, I thought it was Doug. It must be my cute little rapper son, T. I."

Doug laughed, started to respond, then clutching his stomach, raced down the hallway.

"Sorry to disappoint you, Mama, but that was your son who can't hold liquor."

"You're over at Doug's house? What kind of shenanigans did y'all get into last night?"

"You'll have to ask Nelson. That's who he hung out with. I'm picking him up for us to go running in Exposition Park. He wants to get in shape and asked me not to let him talk me out of it. So even with his lightweight hangover, I'm keeping my promise to do just that. That's why I'm calling. We need a couple of your award-winning breakfast sandwiches that we can grab on the way to the park."

"Boy, my last name is Carter, not McDonald."

"Come on, Mama."

"Where we going? To a restaurant so y'all can get something to eat?"

"You're really not going to cook for us?"

"Yeah, I'll make them. Five dollars apiece."

"You're serious?"

"As a venereal disease during a penicillin shortage."

"Dang, Mama. That's hardcore."

"You want sausage or bacon?"

"Both."

"What time y'all coming by?"

"As soon as Doug stops throwing up."

"Lord have mercy, that poor child. I might give him his for free."

Thirty minutes later the Carter brothers were cruising down Crenshaw. For Doug, Liz Carter's sandwich, his father Willie's spicy tomato juice hangover concoction, and four aspirin had worked their magic. His belly was full and his head had stopped pounding. That and the perfect autumn weather had Doug actually looking forward to spending some time outside.

Barry slowed for a red light, his head bobbing to a hip-hop beat on the car stereo. "So how much did it cost?"

Doug looked over at him. "What?"

"The bribe for you to go out with Nelson. He had to pay you something because the club is definitely not your thing."

"Naw, it was a birthday party for a dude from the block. Otherwise I wouldn't have . . ." Doug's sentence faded, his attention grabbed by a scene in a nearby parking lot. He leaned forward, pulled off his shades."

"What's the matter?"

"Nothing. I just thought I saw somebody I know."

The light changed. As Barry drove by the parking lot Doug's eyes stayed trained on the woman in the parking lot helping a wheelchair-bound man into a van. "That was her."

"Who?"

Doug shook his head. "Nobody you know." And somebody Doug figured he didn't know as much as he wanted to. Come Monday, he decided, that was all going to change.

Doug survived the run and his baby brother Barry. Sunday was brunch with the Carters and a day of football. By Sunday night, he felt as good as new.

But as it turned out, talking to Jan at the workplace was easier said than done. Mondays were always busy, but with Melissa deciding to call in sick, today was off the charts. There was barely time for small talk until after the doors to the public had been locked and Jan came to the back to help with the afternoon processing.

"Today proved me wrong," she said once she'd set up shop across from him and began processing her batch.

"How's that?"

"I didn't think this location ever got busy."

Doug chuckled. "You'd be surprised. Wait until the holidays."

"I like it. Makes the day go by faster."

"Yeah, it also gives us a chance to work overtime. I hope you're up for staying a couple extra hours."

Jan's hands stilled as she looked up. "I'm really not."

Doug stopped working, too. "Sorry, but on days like this, it can't be helped. We talked about this during your orientation, remember? Because the branch is small, personnel is low. Sometimes we all have to chip in extra to get the work done."

"I don't have a problem with doing my part. Just not tonight."

"What's happening tonight? Or is that question off limits because it's"—he made air quotes—"personal."

"I have an obligation that can't be canceled. It's very important." Her discomfort was obvious as she began to chew her lip. "What if I work through my lunch break instead?"

"No can do. Breaks are mandatory. Even if they weren't, you'd still have to stay late. We're looking at about two hours over and your lunch break is only thirty minutes."

"And we have no control over whether or not we work over, even if it conflicts with a previously scheduled, very important engagement?"

"Engagement, or date?" Doug smiled to show he was joking. She didn't look amused. "Don't answer that. I was teasing but need to remember that you don't like to play. I'm assuming it's a date because I can't think of anything else important that would start after nine p.m., your normal time off."

"It's not a date." Jan pulled out her phone and began texting. "Just something that I do on Mondays that's very important to me. Not being there could be . . . there could be dire consequences if I don't show."

"I'm really sorry, Jan. If I'd known earlier I could have asked somebody from the day tour to stay."

"If I'd known earlier, I could have informed you."

Jan's frustration was evident, but Doug wasn't going to take the blame for something he couldn't control. "I didn't know either. Obviously this afternoon's rush was something we didn't plan. I'm sorry about whatever it is you wanted to do, but it's part of working this tour at this location. Or any other, really, if they're short-staffed."

Jan said nothing, but Doug could clearly see that she was angry. It wasn't his fault that she hadn't read her orientation information more carefully. Still, he felt bad and for some strange reason felt it was his responsibility to make her feel better.

"Want to take our break before tackling the next bin?"

"Yes, but I'm going to run an errand real quick and grab something from a drive-through."

"Can I go with you?"

"I don't want to be rude, but—"

"You'd rather I not go?"

"I hope you're not offended."

"Does it have anything to do with the guy I saw you with this weekend, the one in the wheelchair?"

Jan's shocked, concerned expression made him regret the question.

"I'm not trying to be all in your business," he continued, his voice low. "Over the weekend I was out with my brother and saw you with him in a parking lot by the Baldwin Hills Crenshaw mall. It got me wondering whether or not he was why you're so serious. And why my antics on the motorcycle make you so angry."

He watched her shoulders slump as she turned off her machine. "Come with me to lunch and I'll answer your question. Maybe it's best that you know."

8

They settled into Jan's Hyundai. She started the car and eased out of the parking lot, careful to look both ways, twice.

"Seat belt," she said as she pulled out into traffic.

Doug quickly complied. "Yes, ma'am."

In spite of her damp mood, Jan found herself smiling. "You answered me as one would their mom. I'm not that bad." She glanced at him. "Am I?"

"Not really. It's just that your buttons are easy to push."

"That's probably true." They reached a bank. Jan parked the car. "I'll be right back."

"Bring me back a hundred."

Jan stopped and quickly turned around, hand out. "Give me your card." She huffed and came perilously close to an eye roll. "Well, where is it? We only have thirty minutes."

"Calm down, Jan. I was just playing!"

She relaxed her stance. "So was I. Be right back."

His laughter followed her to the ATM. She retrieved money, returned the text she'd received from a friend, and walked back to the car.

"I've got to give it to you," Doug said as she entered the car. "For a second there, you had me going."

"Just wanted to show you my lighter side."

"I like that lighter side."

His comment sent Jan's heartbeat into overdrive and sent squiggles down her insides that made her kundalini tingle. They drove a few blocks in silence while her mind tried to convince her body that she wasn't interested in the man in her car. The tall, casually attractive man with swagger who'd occupied her thoughts way too much.

"The man you saw me with this weekend." She began to shift her focus. "That was Lionel, my brother."

Doug nodded but remained silent.

"He was in an accident almost two years ago. A motorcycle accident"—she glanced at him quickly—"that left him paralyzed from the waist down."

"I'm sorry to hear that."

"We all were, and are still coming to grips with it."

"How old is he?"

"He was sixteen when it happened, eighteen now."

"Man. That's a hard blow right there. Real hard.

Now I understand the other day and why you reacted the way you did. I'm really sorry about that."

"It's okay. You didn't know."

"No, it's not okay. I was acting a fool and making light of something that rocked your brother's world, and your family's as well. Can't tell you how many times I've performed crazy antics on my bike. Been doing so since handling my first one at barely thirteen. I consider myself a good rider doing stunts I've pulled for years. But you never know. One wrong, unexpected move and—" Doug shook his head, looked out the window. When he turned back, he asked her, "What happened?"

They stopped at an intersection with fast-food restaurants on three of the four corners. "Hamburgers okay?"

"I was thinking chicken. With red beans and rice."

"That'll work for me." She drove across the street and turned into the drive-through lane already crowded with cars waiting in line. "One of Lionel's friend's uncles had let him borrow the motorcycle. He was only seventeen and, unlike you, hadn't much experience driving one. He was only supposed to take it around the block but ended up over at our house where he asked Lionel to jump on the back for a spin. My brother is always up for adventure and didn't hesitate or think twice. He jumped on the back, without a helmet, for what he thought would be a simple, short ride. And if not for the car that decided to do fifty miles an hour down a residential street, it would have been."

"Damn."

"Lionel was thrown off the cycle. His back hit a tree, breaking his spine and leaving him a paraplegic. Whoever was driving the car was at fault. But not responsible. They fled the scene and abandoned the car a few miles down the road. It ended up being a huge legal mess, one that we're still trying to untangle. We know the owner of the car, but they say it was stolen. We can't prove who was driving. So Lionel's medical and other bills have mostly been on my mom to handle. And even though he was on her insurance, there was a cap on what they'd pay. Once that ran out my mom took a second job and . . ."

"You came to work for the post office."

Jan nodded. They reached the mike and placed their orders. The break from the conversation came just in time. There was a lot to process. Once they'd received their food, Doug suggested a quiet residential street near the post office for them to park and eat, and be away from looky-loos. She followed his direction, parked the car, and pulled their food from the bags. For a while, they ate in silence.

"Is that what you had to do tonight? Something for your brother?"

"No," Jan said, reaching for a napkin. "It's something for me."

"That you can't tell me because it's private."

"It's not a guy if that's what you think. It's what I was pursuing pretty much full-time before the accident. I used to tell everybody who'd listen what I did but found out that everyone isn't happy when you follow your dreams."

"That's what was happening tonight?"

"Yes."

"Now I really feel bad. Not that I could have changed anything but still."

"You should feel bad. And you should let me leave at nine."

"What's happening then?"

"If this ends up in the Normandie branch gossip mill, I'll know who told."

Doug raised his hand. "Your secret's safe with me."

She placed the bone from her chicken leg in the bag and reached for her fries. "I'm a singer."

"Oh, for real?" She nodded. "What does that mean exactly, like for fun or what?"

"It's more than a hobby. Singing is something I take seriously and do professionally as often as possible."

"Wow, a singer. That's pretty cool." Jan smiled, ate in silence. "So you had a gig or something tonight?"

"It's a showcase for a chance to compete on a reality TV show."

"Like *American Idol*?"

"In a way but not quite."

"Oh, I see."

Jan didn't think so. Unless one was an artist or

a person with a dream, it was hard to grasp how important any opportunity to get a break was. That one situation where the right place met the right time when the right person was there, and after ten years of trying you became an overnight success.

"So where are you singing next? I'd like to come hear you sometime."

"I appreciate that, but I like to keep those two worlds separate."

"So nobody who works on your day job can see you at night? Girl, this is LA. Everybody has a side hustle. I know of a few postal workers who've caught a break in entertainment. One reached the finals for a chance to be on *The Voice*."

Jan became quiet, recalling the excitement of her TV debut, and lone such appearance. She'd been young, filled with hope, sure that her appearance on *Showtime at the Apollo* would lead to a record deal, worldwide success, and more money than she could ever spend. It hadn't quite worked out like that.

With a glance at her watch Jan placed her empty containers into the paper bag. Doug did the same. She started the car and pulled away from the curb. Within minutes, she turned into the back parking lot of the Normandie branch, found an open space, and parked the car.

Doug opened his door. "Thanks for the ride."

"Thanks for dinner," Jan responded, exiting the car behind him. "Although it really wasn't necessary for you to buy it for me."

"I know it wasn't. That made it even better. A chance to show one of you modern women that chivalry isn't dead."

"A modern woman? That's how you see me?"

"No, I see you as a lowly postal worker. But if you let me come and hear you sing, I might see you as a superstar."

"Look at you, trying a psychological strategy to get me to change my mind."

"Did it work?"

"No."

"Damn."

They both cracked up.

The unexpectedly heavy workload and short staff made it impossible for Doug to let Jan off early. Instead, they left forty-five minutes past their normal off time.

She looked at her watch and pulled out her phone.

Doug saw her. "Think you can make it?"

"I don't know, but I have a friend there who looks out for me. He'll let me know if there are any slots left." When the call went to voice mail, she sent him a text. "It's probably too late," she said with a sigh. "The club is in the valley, a good thirty to forty-five minutes away."

"I'm really sorry about that."

"It's not your fault."

"I know. But I still feel bad."

As they neared her vehicle, Jan reached into her purse, pulled out a card, and held it up.

"What's this?" he asked, and took what she offered.

"The address to my next performance," she responded. "This weekend, if you can make it."

"For sure I'll be there. Can I bring some others with me?"

"From here?"

"No, a couple of my brothers maybe, if they want to come."

"I guess that would be all right."

"So my psychological strategy worked after all."

"Yeah, but don't push it."

"Hey, I'm just saying . . ." He looked at the card. "I guess I'll come to see you then . . . and find out if you need a bucket to carry a tune."

She opened the employee entrance door and tried to slam it before Doug could enter.

He laughed and pulled it open. Watching the confident sway of her ample hips made his smile widen.

9

Jan's second week on the job looked nothing like the first one. Turns out Melissa hadn't missed Monday because of too much partying. She'd really been sick, not returning to work with a doctor's excuse until Thursday. Joey returned on Tuesday, but for some unexplained reason the lobby was busy all week. Doug was right. If this was any indication of what the holidays would look like, Jan didn't have to worry about spending her afternoons at the counter with nothing to do.

More of a problem was trying to balance her passion with the means for a paycheck. Because of the extra hours she'd worked this week, there hadn't been as much time to rehearse with the band for this Friday's performance. Good thing this was a regular gig with a band she trusted, that she'd sang with off and on for almost a year. They'd done a quick run-through on Wednesday night and rehearsed last night until almost two a.m. Jan was dragging, but she knew that once she hit the stage the excitement at performing would carry her. Plus the club, Breeze, catered to the grown and sexy thirty and older crowd, a receptive audience of other hard workers who lived for the weekend and were ready to party down. She always had a good time there and expected tonight to not be an exception to the rule.

Besides a busy week and a show tonight, there was another reason for Jan's good mood. Doug Carter. With Melissa and Joey absent, she and Doug worked together almost every night once the counter closed. The more she was around him, the better she liked him. Sure, he was a little too carefree for her taste, content to cruise through life being average. But he was thoughtful, caring, and, like her, seemed to love his family. Most importantly, though he'd tease her in secret, he'd kept his word about not sharing her dreams of a singing career with the other coworkers. She almost hoped that he'd change his mind or forget about tonight's singing engagement. But a small part of her wanted him to show up, so she could show out. The stage was one place where Jan let her hair down, relaxed, and had a little fun.

With no time to return home before hitting the club, she'd talked Doug into letting her work through her dinner break, "just this one time, nobody will know," and left the job a half hour early. Fortunately Breeze was off of Manchester Avenue, about ten minutes away. She arrived at ten past eight, with only a couple early birds at the bar and a couple sitting at one of the back tables.

"Hey there, Mr. G." She greeted the man who looked like he'd run security since Jimmy Carter was president. "You going to keep the peace for me tonight?"

He patted his jacket pocket. "If they don't start none, then there won't be none."

Inside the club she greeted a waitress cleaning off tables and hugged the bartender, who poured her usual single glass of chardonnay. She wasn't a huge drinker, so that one glass sipped nice and slow as she dressed and put on makeup loosened her up enough to become the diva the night required.

"You heard from the band?" she asked Frank, the club's manager, whom she passed in the hallway.

"You didn't see Thump out there?"

"Our fearless band leader? No."

"He's around here somewhere. Sunny called. He's on the way. You know how long it takes him to set up that mega drum set."

She laughed. "Indeed."

Frank gave her the once-over. "You're looking good tonight. Got a little pep in your step I didn't see last time."

"Thank you."

"What's got you so happy? You got a new man in your life or something?"

"Yes, his name is Benjamin and he hangs out in my wallet."

Frank laughed. "Sounds like I need to hang out with you. My friends are usually George and Abe."

Jan's phone vibrated. "I'll see you later, Frank."

"Have a good show."

Jan rushed into the office that doubled as her dressing room and hurriedly placed down her garment bag and carry-on to grab the phone from her purse. It was one of two calls she'd hoped to receive. "Crystal!"

"Hey, girl."

"Wait, you don't sound happy. You didn't get a sitter?"

"Yes, but baby has a fever."

"No!"

"Sorry, Jan. Hubby and I were so looking forward to an evening out, but I can't leave with her sick."

"I understand. I was looking forward to having you in the audience."

"Who knows? Maybe there'll be a special man listening to you tonight."

"Will you ever stop trying to get me hooked up?"

"Sure. Once you get the ring."

Jan eyed the clock on the wall and wrapped up the call. She finished applying her makeup while thinking that if Starr acted on the text she'd sent earlier and came to see her performance tonight, she might not only get that elusive record deal, but be on her way to snagging the ring her cousin so wanted her to have. And in her heart of hearts . . . the one she wanted, too.

* * *

Doug slipped the security guard a tip and motioned his guests to follow him. They were led to a side table close to the stage.

"This woman must really be special," Doug's brother Byron commented as he pulled out the chair for his wife to sit. "Not only got you into a club on a Friday night but paying extra for a good table? The only tip you normally leave is how to find lost mail."

"Keep your day job, boy," Doug replied. "The comedian gig is clearly not for you." Doug looked at his play big sis. "Ava, watch your brother and make sure he doesn't embarrass Cynthia too bad."

Byron put an arm around Cynthia's shoulders. "You handle the stage. I'll take care of my wife."

The four ordered drinks and appetizers, trading barbs and jokes that kept the table laughing. By the time their food arrived the band was on the stage, getting the crowd warmed up with a rousing instrumental.

"Ladies and gentlemen," said the man playing lead guitar after walking to the mike. "Please put your hands together and help me welcome the beautiful, talented, one and only Ms. Jan Baker!"

Doug looked around, noting a few whoops and whistles amid the enthusiastic applause.

The band switched songs seamlessly. The bass guitar player moved out of the shadows as the lead drifted back. As he played sharp key licks, a voice rang out from behind stage, singing a jazzy grown and sexy version of how she was all about that bass.

"Good evening, Breeze!" Jan strutted from behind the curtain in a form-fitting leopard-print dress, suede stilettos, and a big-hair wig. She worked the stage as she continued to sing, subtly turning sideways and winking at the crowd as she showed off her body's bass that she was all about.

"She's pretty," Cynthia said as she swayed in her seat.

"And can sing!" Ava added. She turned to Doug. "You say she's your coworker?"

Right now, Doug couldn't say anything at all. He was transfixed, almost spellbound by the super-sexy singer strutting her stuff, working the room, flirting and dancing, and looking like two million bucks. The conservative, pretty-in-a-plain-way woman who worked the counter and helped him process mail was nowhere in sight. Before him was a sultry Siren, a vivacious vixen who made his mouth water and his soldier wake up. In shock, he missed the amused look that passed between his siblings, and the eyes now fastened on him amid a group just entering the club.

Jan commanded the stage. Her smartly designed first set was a perfect blend of fast and slow, old and new. After trading riffs with the bass player to close the first song, she segued into Mary J. Blige's "Real Love." Couples spilled onto the dance floor. Single ladies sang along with their hands in the air.

"Come on, Doug," Ava said, drinking the last of

her lemon daiquiri. "You can't expect to sit all night with the band jamming like this." She stood, dancing in place and reaching for Doug's arm.

He moved it out of her reach. "Girl, you know I don't dance."

"That don't matter." She took a step toward him. "You know I have no problem acting a fool, so if you don't want to be embarrassed, you'll take me out on the floor."

"Ask Byron to dance with you." Doug crossed his arms and affected a look perilously close to a pout. "I don't want to get out there."

Byron leaned forward. "What's the matter, Dougie? Not feeling so fresh? Scared your girl will see your rather limited moves and send you packing?"

"One, she's not my girl. Two, I don't scare easily."

While distracted, Ava grabbed his arm. "Then prove it. Come dance with me."

Reluctantly, he did. Fortunately for him, while out on the floor Ava bumped into a former classmate, literally. He was relieved of duty and made a beeline to the bathroom both to freshen up and to get his head together about how his heart was feeling. Seeing Jan in her element had him about to catch feelings and ready to break his own rule about dating a peer. Two pairs of eyes followed his moves this time.

He was gone less than five minutes but upon returning to his table it seemed the crowd had doubled. He stopped at the bar for another ginger ale and decided to stand there awhile, where he could watch

Jan in near obscurity. He smiled and bobbed his head to the beat as she demanded that men put a ring on it, felt special when she sang one of his old-school favorites even though there was no way for her to know about his boy crush on Michael Jackson, and allowed himself to simply enjoy her sultry, soulful rendition of Jill Scott's "He Loves Me," not realizing that he was jealous of who she might be talking about until much later that night.

What he did realize was an undeniable attraction for the woman who he'd admitted was fine but written off as not his type. Before the night was over, he decided as he watched her sashay from the stage with a wave and blown kiss at the end of the first set, this was a mistake he was going to correct.

10

Jan sat exhausted but happy in the office-turned-dressing room for tonight's show. The wig had come off, the false eyelashes had been placed back in their case, and the torture device advertised as a body shaper had been tossed into her travel bag along with the dress that had made shaping necessary. Now in a much more comfortable flared-leg jumpsuit, Jan gathered the rest of her wardrobe and toiletries while talking to two of her favorite people in the world.

"I still can't believe you tricked me, Chris! You don't even do stuff like—" Her hand stilled in midair as her eyes slid from her cousin to Crystal's husband, Brent. She stabbed him in the chest with a manicured fingernail. "This was your idea."

Rather than deny it, Brent smiled triumphantly, basking in the success of their deception.

Jan looked at Crystal. "So the baby didn't have a fever?"

"She felt a little warm," Crystal replied with a Cheshire smile.

"Yeah, I just bet she did." She tried but Jan couldn't drum up an ounce of attitude. She was thrilled that the two of them were enjoying a rare night out together. "However it happened, I'm so glad you guys could come. It really meant a lot having you here."

"You had a nice crowd," Brent said. "Is it always like that?"

Jan shrugged. "Depends on what else is going on. I think this was one of the largest so far, though. I saw several regulars who've been to all the shows."

Crystal beamed at her cousin. "Look at you. Being all star-like with fans and stuff."

"I don't know about all that." Her smile dissipated. "But speaking of stars, too bad Nick didn't make it. If he'd seen me tonight, I would have definitely made the cut for the reality show, might even have gotten a deal."

"There are more people producing than that egomaniac. Just keep doing your thing, cousin. You never know who'll show up."

"What about the people on your job?" Brent asked. "Did you invite them to come check you out?"

Jan shook her head. "Not everybody. Only my supervisor."

Brent nodded knowingly. "Trying to get in good with the boss. I see you."

"Not at all. But in order to try and get off a little bit early some nights, I had to tell him why."

Crystal's interest was obviously piqued. "Was he here?"

Another nod. "I saw him early on, sitting with a lady and another couple."

"Oh."

"No need to sound disappointed, Chris. It's fine with me that he brought a date."

"I know. I was just hoping—"

"No, you were just meddling." Brent shook his head. "Always trying to play matchmaker."

"Honey, I just want everybody to be as happy as I am, with a wonderful man like you." She watched as Brent searched for a comeback but finding none, offered a sheepish smile. "Yeah, that shut you down, didn't it?"

"I'm about to shut down, too," Jan said between a yawn. "A hot shower and a soft bed are calling my name."

She looked around the office a final time, making sure she had all her things. "Y'all ready?"

Brent and Crystal stood and followed her out of the office and down the hall, waiting while she collected her pay from Frank, who sat at the bar chatting with the bass player.

"Damn! The clock sure struck midnight, didn't it?" Thump teased Jan as usual and got on her nerves the way he intended. Nicknamed because of the way he played the bass, he'd been one of Jan's biggest supporters ever since the day she'd auditioned for his band. He'd hired her on the spot.

"You not only lost your glass slipper but that sexy dress, too."

Jan laughed and punched his shoulder. "Forget you, boy."

"Just messing with you."

"I know."

Frank counted out several twenties and handed them over. "You did your thing tonight, baby girl. People really enjoyed it."

"Thanks, Frank." She looked at Thump. "Bye, fool."

"You take it easy. Hard driving a pumpkin in the city."

She waved him off and motioned for Crystal and Brent as she walked to the door. They stepped out to a comfortably cool night, typical for mid-October, with a light breeze and a full moon. The crowds had left and few cars were on the street.

Brent looked at Jan. "Where'd you park?"

"In the parking lot."

"We'll walk you to your car," Crystal said.

"Thanks."

They rounded the building. Jan's eyes went straight to a sight she'd hardly expected. A shiny, electric blue Kawasaki motorcycle parked by her car. And sitting on it, the man whose image refused to stay away as she earlier sang about walking in parks after dark.

Brent's steps slowed a bit as he asked Jan, "Do you know him?"

"Yes, it's fine."

"Who is it?" Crystal asked.

"My supervisor."

"Oh. And without his date. Hmm . . ."

Jan cut her a look. "Don't start."

The man stood as they approached. "I thought you'd never come out of there."

"I didn't know you were waiting." The three reached him and stopped. "Why are you waiting?"

"Because I had to see if the sister on that stage tonight was really the woman who worked on Normandie Avenue. You look a little like her except she had big hair and even bigger swagger, nothing like the reserved woman I know."

"In that case, I'm sorry you waited. She disappeared as soon as the show was over."

"Man, that's a shame. I wanted to tell her how good she was tonight. She was the truth! Right up there with anybody on the radio; better than most of them actually."

Jan warmed at his praise, and at his gaze. "I'll tell her you said so."

"Excuse my rude cousin," Crystal said, stepping forward. "I'm Crystal, and this is my husband, Brent."

Doug held out his hand. "Doug Carter. Nice meeting you." The men exchanged greetings.

"Jan said you came with guests," Crystal continued, ignoring her cousin's tug on her jean jacket. "They couldn't wait with you?"

"No, my sister, Ava, has an early appointment in the morning. So her, my brother, and his wife left a little ways into the second set. They enjoyed her, too, though. We all did."

"Ah, your sister." Crystal emphasized the word, chuckling as she subtly shifted away from the fingers now trying to pinch her through layers of clothes. "That was nice of you, Doug. Not only coming to show your support but inviting others to join you."

"I wish I could take the credit, but Ava would have come anyway." He shifted his attention from Crystal to Jan. "Turns out she already knew about that bad sistah who throws it down at Breeze. Had been to see you a couple times."

"Really? What a coincidence. I guess even in a city as large as LA it can be a small world. And though your sister already knew about me I appreciate you coming out, and bringing some of your family."

Doug's voice dropped a notch. "My pleasure."

"My goodness, look at the time." Crystal grabbed her husband's arm. "Doug, could you please make sure my cousin gets home safely?"

Jan cut her eyes at a wide-smiling Crystal. "I'll be fine."

"Don't worry, Crystal. I've got her." He looked at Brent. "It was nice meeting you, man. You too, Crystal."

Crystal waved. "Likewise. Hope to see you again."

"Bye, Crystal." Jan was trying to speed her cousin's departure and then her own. "Bye, Brent."

Crystal laughed, wiggling a "toodaloo" as she and

Brent headed toward their car that was parked on a nearby side street.

Doug and Jan watched them disappear around the corner. "You'll have to forgive my cousin. When we were little, she rode the short bus."

"Whoa! That's cold."

"It was. I love her. We're more like sisters than cousins. But she's always trying to hook me up."

"Is that a bad thing?"

"I can handle that on my own. But right now"—she began walking to her car, pointed her key fob, and unlocked the doors—"the only thing I want to handle is sleep."

"I hear that." Doug fell into step beside her. "But what about tomorrow?"

"What about it?"

"Would you like to grab some lunch or dinner?"

They reached her car. "Thanks, Doug, but no. Breaks together at work is one thing, but I don't want to get into anything beyond that."

"So I can't come to hear you sing anymore?"

"I can't control that. Breeze is a public place."

"But I wouldn't come see you if you didn't want me to."

"I don't mind."

"Good, because those words were about to become a lie. I'm definitely coming back to see you again. Girl, you can blow, for real. That's what you want to do full-time, huh."

"Me and half the other singers in the world."
She reached for the door.

"Let me get that." He opened it and waited until
she was in and buckled. "I think you need to re-
think your position about whether or not we hang
out. I mean as friends. I'm not trying to get with
you or anything."

"Then we're on the same page."

"Because just so you know, I don't date coworkers
either."

"You dated Melissa."

"I hooked up with Melissa. One time. We never
dated. And that was almost five years ago. Can't
do nothing about my past. But if I had it to do over,
I'd make better choices."

She started her car. He closed her door. The
window eased down. "Thanks again for coming to
the show. I'm glad you enjoyed it."

"Drive safe."

"I will."

Chancing quick glances in the rearview mirror,
she watched Doug watch her exit the parking lot.
He stood there, helmet in hand, until she could no
longer see him. Getting him to disappear from
her thoughts didn't happen as quickly. For the
rest of the weekend, snatches of their conversation
replayed in her mind. When she thought of the
look of admiration in his eyes while singing her
praises, and the awe in his voice, it made her feel
proud and all girlie inside. She knew he meant it.

When Starr complimented her, it didn't seem as heartfelt. It was never done as effusively as when he praised the beautiful girls, like the twenty-one-year-old everyone called Mariah, because of her strong resemblance to the famous diva. The one who she heard was picked in last week's open mike that she missed. Too bad the similarities between the two ladies ended with looks. When it came to voices, there was no comparison. A mouse squeaking while caught in a trap might be able to beat wannabe Mariah head-to-head. Frank and the guys knew she could sing, and told her so, as did many of the regulars. But from Doug, it was special, a genuine reaction after hearing her for the first time.

On the other hand, every time she remembered how he "didn't want to get with her" and "didn't date coworkers" she told herself that she was glad that he didn't. And no matter how much she ignored it, the twinge in her heart suggested otherwise.

11

Doug wasn't a fan of Mondays, but on this particular one he'd been up and dressed with time to spare. Spent the morning handling personal business and got to work early, a rarity. Didn't even try and lie about why. He wanted to see Jan. All weekend long, she'd stayed on his mind. He couldn't get her stage image out of his head—that lush booty swaying slowly and bringing the animal print she wore to life. Even more, she'd been sexy and classy at the same time. The dress was to her knees and she'd showed little cleavage. Yet a naked skinny girl could have stepped on the stage and for Doug it wouldn't have mattered. He liked a woman with a little meat on her bones. He'd been raised by a woman who looked like that. Would any part of the woman he saw Friday night show up this afternoon? Doug couldn't wait to find out.

The floral scent preceded her, so he wasn't surprised to hear her voice. He gave a casual look over his shoulder. Ms. Conservative was back: loose pants, oversized top, fresh face, her real hair in a short, no-fuss ponytail. There was none of that fire that made her light up the stage, none of that savoir faire that transferred her into a woman for whom he'd break old rules and make some new ones. Crazy that after only seeing that Jan Baker for a few hours, he missed her immensely.

This Monday wasn't as busy as last week, but it was still her first break before they had a real conversation. He caught her standing in front of the microwave.

"Think that corn is going to pop faster if you stare at it?"

She smiled. "My mind was a million miles away."

He looked around and, seeing no one close, leaned in, and said, "On a stage somewhere?"

She gave him a warning look.

"Don't worry. I checked before I spoke." He went over to the vending machine and after some deliberation decided on a bag of popcorn, too. He rejoined her just as the bell dinged and she pulled hers out. He put his bag inside and turned to lean against the counter. "How's your brother?"

Jan looked up, her face one of surprise. "He's fine. Why?"

"I was just asking; have thought about him a few times since . . . you know . . . we talked about him. It's made me think twice out there."

"Good."

"Well, well, well, isn't this cozy?" Melissa sauntered

into the break room, large coffee cup in hand. "You two are sure looking comfy with each other."

"Whatever, Mel." Doug turned to get his popcorn.

"My, aren't we snippy." She watched Jan walk over to get a soda. "I'm just commenting on how close you two seem to have gotten."

"Why? Because we're both in the break room?" He went to get a soda as well.

"Doug, quit sounding paranoid. How are you doing, Jan?"

"I'm fine, Melissa." She walked over to a table and sat; then pulled out her phone. "What about you?"

"I'm exceptional, as always. How was your weekend?"

"It was pretty good." Jan answered without looking up from her screen.

Doug looked at his watch and, with a couple minutes remaining on his break, decided to stay in the room. Something told him that Jan needed guarding.

Melissa poured coffee, sugar, and creamer in the cup and then joined Jan at the table. "Did you do anything exciting?"

"Not particularly."

"What about you, Doug?"

"What about me?"

"Did you do anything fun?"

"Hung out with my family, same as always." He joined them at the table. Ate a couple handfuls of popcorn. "What about you? After meeting your friends for happy hour, did you and your girls hit the clubs and go trolling? That's what you used to do."

For better or worse, Joey walked in on this line.

She laughed. "As a matter of fact, we did." She took a sip of coffee, looking over the brim at Jan as she did so.

"Sounds like I should have been at that club," Joey said, jumping into the conversation without invitation.

"Yes, you should have. They had live entertainment."

Doug noticed that Jan's thumb stilled on her phone before she slowly began scrolling again. The feeling he had a minute ago grew worse. But he maintained his cool. "Oh yeah? Did you have fun?"

"Yes, and I wasn't the only one. Looks like you had a good time, too."

"Me?"

Melissa reared back her head and laughed.

Joey, sensing a scene unfolding that was worthy of the popcorn on the table, joined them, watched as her eyes moved between Jan and Doug.

"I don't know why y'all are hiding? It's what postal coworkers do." She fixed her eyes on Doug. "We hook up."

"Wow," Jan said, putting away her phone. She folded the bag containing the remaining popcorn. "On that note, my break is over."

Doug stood, grabbing his drink and the bag of popcorn. "Mine too."

Joey looked at Doug. "You and Jan? It's like that?"

"I don't know what she's talking about, man," Doug threw over his shoulder.

He followed Jan, who was already out of the room and halfway down the hall.

Melissa leaned forward and raised her voice. "I was there!"

Jan continued walking. Doug stopped, turned, and walked back into the break room. "Where?"

"Breeze."

Doug looked behind him. The hallway was clear. Jan probably didn't hear her but with the two biggest mouths of this branch in the room, he knew that if they didn't already, everyone would soon know where else Jan worked.

"Was that y'all's little secret?"

Doug tried to play it off, acting nonchalant. If he didn't make a big deal of it, maybe Melissa wouldn't either.

"Not at all. You were there? You should have come over to the table."

"It didn't look like you had time for me. Your eyes were glued to the stage."

"I'm lost," Joey said, getting up from the table and crossing to the fridge.

"Our girl Jan is a singer. She walks around here

all mousy and quiet, but believe me when I tell you that at night she reveals her inner diva."

"Word?" Joey said, looking at Doug.

"It's not like that," Doug said.

Two more people walked into the break room, giving Melissa an audience. That's all she needed. "Girlfriend wore a dress that looked painted on, with a pair of stilettos and this Diana Ross-looking wig." She swung her weave from side to side for emphasis. "Showing off her substantial backside to all the men in the crowd. She was working it!"

Joey raised a brow. "That Jan?" he asked, with a thumb toward the counter.

"Yep."

"She's exaggerating," Doug said.

"No, I'm not. What did I tell you about women who come off acting all guarded?" Melissa reached for her purse. "I've got pictures." She pulled out her phone and clicked on images. Soon her phone was being passed around. Everybody had a comment.

Sensing a catastrophe, Doug walked out of the break room and headed for the counter. Fortunately, Pat was with a customer, but Jan was not. He stood with his back to Pat and spoke softly.

"Sorry to be the one to tell you, but your secret is out."

Jan's eyes narrowed. "You told?"

He shook his head. "Melissa was at Breeze Friday night."

"You're kidding."

"Wish I was. She saw you. And me. Took pictures."

"What?"

"She's showing them now to everyone in the break room."

"Of all the people who work here . . ."

A customer entered, ending the conversation. Jan called him forward. Doug reached over and grabbed a pad of Post-its, wrote down his number and a simple message: *Call me.*

12

Jan didn't call Doug as he'd requested. What would be the point? Melissa had been at Breeze Friday night, so now everyone at work would be trying to snoop into her personal life. Pat couldn't understand why people knowing would upset her. Had she been in the back as Melissa was leaving, the reason would have been clear. Instead of practicing the song she'd be singing tonight, Jan's thoughts kept returning to work, and what happened earlier today.

"Why didn't you tell me about your show Friday night?" Pat returned from lunch all loud and excited even though Jan was with a customer and there were more in line.

"Honestly, Pat, I forgot." Jan finished the transaction with the customer in front of her and motioned up the next person in line. "It's one of my regular gigs, which is probably why telling you slipped my mind."

"According to Melissa, it was a show to see."

Jan said nothing. Coming from Melissa, that statement could mean anything.

For the next several minutes the women concentrated on handling the customers. When the lobby was empty Pat walked closer to where Jan stood. "Melissa said you're a totally different woman when you're onstage."

"I'm a performer," Jan said. "It's what we do when we're before an audience. We perform."

"She said Doug was there, too."

"Sounds like Melissa has a lot to say where I'm concerned."

Pat chuckled. "It's where anybody is concerned, girl. Melissa has a lot of potential that gets overshadowed by the fact that she can't shut up." She walked a package over to the appropriate bin and tossed it in. "Though in this instance I don't see the problem. If I had a talent, I'd be telling everybody."

"I used to."

"Why did you stop?"

Jan turned to face her. "Because I learned that everyone smiling in your face doesn't wish you well."

"I know for a fact that's true."

"That's why I try to keep my day job and my night activities separate."

"But you told Doug."

Jan took a calming breath. She believed that Pat's intentions were good, but for Jan, this type of conversation she'd rather avoid. "He's my supervisor, and I needed to leave a few minutes early. That's the only reason."

"Are you married?"

This elicited a frown. "You asked that before and I told you I wasn't. Why does that question keep coming up?"

"It's none of my business, really. But you seem like a nice girl and Doug's a good man. I was kind of hoping he was being invited for a more personal reason. But like I said, not my business, so forgive me for asking." A customer came up to the counter. "But answer me anyway first chance you get."

Jan smiled, thankful for a reprieve from the uncomfortable conversation. It didn't last long. The counter got busy so Pat never got her answer. But once the post office closed and she went to the back, her patience really got tested. Not surprising, Melissa was still there even though her shift had ended.

"Diana!"

A slight look of annoyance, a forced smile, but no comment as Jan passed Melissa and headed to the locker where her purse was stored. She hadn't planned to break for dinner right now, but escape was necessary.

"What? That comparison upsets you? I love Diana Ross! You did pretty good Friday night."

Jan took a deep breath before she turned around.

"Thanks, Melissa. I don't believe Diana and I have anything in common, but I'm glad you enjoyed yourself."

"Honey, I enjoyed *you*! Me and my girls walked into the club and I couldn't believe my eyes. After five, you turn all the way up!"

Joey was all smiles. "You sure do, Jan. I saw the pictures and . . . my goodness!"

Jan reached beyond the leftovers she'd planned to warm up, grabbed her purse, and headed for the exit. "Doug, I'm taking my dinner break."

"All right."

Melissa snatched her purse from the table. "I'll walk out with you."

"Melissa!"

Melissa ignored Doug and caught up with a fast-walking Jan. "You sure are in a hurry. Another performance tonight?"

"I'm always busy," was Jan's noncommittal reply.

"Not too busy for everybody," Melissa countered.

"And my name is Jan, not Diana."

Melissa's sweet demeanor turned sour. "Girl, trust me. That was clearly a joke. For you to be in Diana Ross's league would take way more than a wig. Way more."

Jan reached her car and turned. "Melissa, I know you and Doug have history. But I'm here to work, not date. You don't have anything to worry about where he's concerned."

"Even if you were interested, I still wouldn't be

worried. Because I know Doug's type of woman. You're not it."

The barb on Jan was like water on a duck, thick skin developed over a lifetime of similar put downs. If Melissa feeling superior was what it took to get out of her face, Jan figured it was a very small price to pay.

Later that night, Jan reached the club determined to put the nine-to-five antics behind her and focus on her performance. Walking in and seeing Starr, alone and checking his phone, made this easy to do. She pulled on some of that stage confidence Doug admired her for and strode straight to his table.

"Good evening, Starr."

He looked up and smiled. "Hey, talented lady."

The day was looking better already. "Mind if I sit?"

"I'm expecting some people in a bit but sure, have a seat." He went back to checking his phone.

She sat in a chair across from him. "I hate I missed the showcase last week. Especially since every singer in California wants to compete on your show. But it couldn't be helped."

"Not just California. There's talent from all over the country vying for a spot." He set down his phone and looked at her. "Rome told me about your work situation, and that even though it's supposed to be first come first serve he'd been putting your name on the list."

"I hope he doesn't get in trouble. He knows how badly I want this, how much I need it. And he believes in me, too."

"If it weren't for the fact that you sing like you do, it would have been a real problem. You would have been cut last week." Jan held her breath. "But I decided to let you slide, this time, and cut another chick."

She exhaled. "Thank you, Starr. I really appreciate it. There are a lot of great singers out there, but I know I've got what it takes to be on that show, and to go all the way."

He nodded, then went back to checking his phone. "No doubt you can sing, Jan. You have a really nice voice. On any given Sunday there are sistahs like you tearing up churches all across the country."

Jan was taken aback. "You think I sound like a gospel singer?"

Starr looked at her. "I'm not saying that. I'm agreeing with you that there are a lot of people who can blow. But I'm looking for more than a good singer. I'm looking for somebody to represent my name, to represent the show's name—*Starr Power*. That someone has to have the total package: looks, personality, drive, swagger, that 'it' factor that you can't define but"—he paused, distracted by someone behind them—"you know it when you see it."

Jan turned in the direction where Starr was looking and forced her shoulders not to sag. Clearly, he wasn't going to hear anything else she was saying right about now. Hopefully he'd hear her on the stage and call her name as the next pick. Rising, she portrayed bravado she didn't feel by saying, "Nick Starr, I've always admired your talent. Like me, you can really sing. You're not just hype. And I know that there's a certain look that the music industry has decided as the perfect pop look. I might not fit that mold exactly, but that total package you say you're looking for? You're talking to her."

Starr's gaze slid back to her, his smile sincere. "All right, then, total package. I like that confidence. Keep on bringing it as you work that stage tonight."

"Thank you."

He winked. She smiled, then turned to leave and realized that wink was not for her. The woman who'd caught his eye was now talking to the show coordinator. She epitomized the music industry's standard of beauty, and probably Starr's personal standard, too. Tall, slender, long legs, smooth tanned skin, bone-straight hair nearing her waist, and perfectly proportioned T and A. She was stunning, no doubt, and more beautiful than Jan. Later when each took the stage, Jan's singing was better hands down. She sang better than anybody else in there tonight. The crowd appreciated it. Rome was all smiles. But when Starr announced the next talent who would be joining his cable show, it wasn't Jan. It was Ms. Perfect T and A, just in from

London, who took slot number three for the reality TV show.

Jan walked to her car, feeling defeated. Why was she out there busting her butt trying to break into an industry that clearly didn't want her? Why couldn't she do as her cousin had suggested and give it up, move on, let the dream go?

"Maybe Crystal's right," Jan murmured to herself. She started the car and headed toward the freeway. *Maybe my time to shine has come and gone.*

Her phone rang. Either Mom or Crystal, Jan assumed. She tapped the phone icon on her steering wheel. "Hello?"

"Hello, Jan. It's Doug."

"Doug?" Her face bore a frown even as the sound of his voice sped up her heartbeat. "How'd you get my number?"

"I hope you don't mind that I looked it up in our personnel files. I didn't think you'd call me and seeing Melissa sweating you earlier had me concerned. I wanted to check on you, and make sure you're okay. As a friend."

"Well, put that way, I guess I can't be mad. *Friend.*"

He laughed, low and sexy. It caused a pulsation in places lower than her heart.

"You could be mad, *friend*," he chuckled again. "But that wouldn't be very nice. So, how are you?"

"Honestly, I've been better."

"What's wrong?"

Jan told him what had just happened. "I probably

sound like a hater, but I'm not. She's an okay singer and will be great for ratings. So I get it. I just think that at the end of the day a talent show should be about talent."

"Have you ever auditioned for any of the other shows, like *American Idol* or *The Voice*?"

"I tried out for *American Idol*. Stood in line for nine hours and made it through preliminaries. But I didn't get a callback for the TV rounds."

"Who was judging? A deaf person?"

Jan laughed. "No, they heard me."

"Then they were fools. A woman with your kind of talent should be on the radio and at the top of the charts."

"Thank you, Doug. I appreciate that."

She really did. Thoughts of her dreams were mostly kept to herself. It felt good to share, and be validated.

"I'm saying it because it's true. You're a triple threat, girl. You're smart. You can sing your butt off. And you clean up pretty good."

"Gee, thanks."

"You don't come to work looking like you did onstage Friday night, okay? So you're welcome."

"What I wear onstage doesn't define me. Neither do the clothes I wear to work. I bought that stuff because of the PO dress code. My style is more that of a bohemian funky, casual kind of chick."

"You've still got it going on. That's why Melissa is acting out. She's jealous."

"As pretty as she is? I doubt that. She did think we had something going on, though."

"Is that why she followed you out?"

"Sounded like it. Maybe now that I've put her mind at ease, she'll leave me alone and back out of my business."

"She most definitely needs to back out of mine. But she was right about one thing."

"What?"

"You were working it on that stage, baby. You owned it. So I don't care who they put on these shows or promote on TV. Ain't nobody as bad as you."

13

They talked until Jan was safely in her house, something upon which Doug insisted before he'd hang up. The forty-five-minute drive seemed to go by in five. She was surprised they'd talked that long. She'd enjoyed learning about his family and believed his questions about Lionel's health and quality of life were from genuine concern. His seeming protectiveness toward her and belief in her talent made Jan aware of how long it had been since she'd felt that from a man. Conversation had flowed easily, with no awkward pauses. No drama and no tired, overt flirting from Doug.

He had flirted a little bit, though. And she'd liked it.

The next afternoon she walked into work not knowing what to expect but ready for anything. Joey's overt flirting. Messy Mel's blatant digs. She'd have to brace herself a little to handle Doug's sexy smile, but she was ready for that, too.

She barely had one foot in the room before Joey spoke. "Good afternoon, superstar."

Smiling, she answered, "Good afternoon, Joey." Pat crossed from the break room to her locker. "Hello, Pat." She greeted a couple nearby coworkers on the way to her locker.

Melissa looked on from two tables down. "Are you out of good mornings?"

Jan turned. "Oh, hi, Melissa. How are you?"

"I'm amazing, thanks for asking. Had my parts overhauled last night by the tune-up man."

"A little too much information," Pat said on her way to the counter. Jan was right behind her.

"I'm up for hearing details," one of the male coworkers responded.

"I'm up for seeing them," Joey chimed in. Those who heard it laughed.

Doug walked out of the supervisor's office. "What'd I miss?"

"Nothing that I can't show you later," Melissa cooed.

"Naw, I'm good," Doug threw over his shoulder on the way to the front.

He walked in as Pat asked Jan, "Do you sing at Breeze every weekend?"

Jan shook her head. "The second Friday of most months, unless an out-of-town band gets booked. Otherwise there are four local bands playing different genres who rotate the calendar. Frank likes the diversity because it enlarges his crowd."

"Who's Frank?" Doug asked.

"The manager at Breeze."

"What music do the other bands play?" Pat asked. "I like all kinds."

"The first Friday is a combination of blues and more old-school soul music. Third Friday is jazz and neo soul, and the fourth is hip-hop and alternative. There's more info on their Web site."

Doug checked his watch and went to unlock the door from the thirty-minute lunch shutdown. Pat continued organizing her drawer and work area. "I haven't been to that place in years, at least ten. Started going there years ago, back in the seventies, before I was legally allowed. It was called The Connection back then, and on the weekends, baby, it was the spot! My girlfriends and I would fix ourselves to look as grown as possible and hold our breath until they handed back our fake IDs." She laughed, her eyes looking beyond the building's walls and into her history. "Then we'd hit the dance floor and party till dawn!"

"Sounds like a good time," Jan said.

"The best. It's where I met my first husband. In the eighties it got bought by some dude who tried to take it disco. That didn't work. It closed for a while. Last time I was there, it was to see a group that one of my coworker's husband managed. They were good, too, a little old school. Don't know what happened to them. That's the last time I was there."

"I've been singing there for about a year and

honestly hadn't heard about it until I got with this band."

"So where are you singing next?"

Jan glanced at Doug, who was all ears. "I'm not booked for another show until next month, back at Breeze."

"Will you remind me? I really want to come and support you."

The day passed. Jan was grateful for Pat. She was a genuinely nice woman who made Jan's day more bearable and balanced out Melissa's toxic vibe. Once six o'clock came and the counter closed, processing the mail and preparing the bags for the next day's routes made the remaining three hours fly by.

"Feeling better?" Doug asked as he and Jan walked to the car after locking up.

"Yes, Pat is very encouraging. I like her."

"I love Pat. She's like a second mom." He passed his bike and kept walking.

"Where are you going?"

"I'm walking you to your cage."

"My what?"

"Cage. It's what we bikers call those enclosed traps that cagers—what we call people who drive the cages—seem to love so much."

"I see. So you're walking me to the cage that's only ten feet away from your bike?" Jan chuckled. "I think I'll be fine."

"Man, you twenty-first-century women kill me. You say you want a gentleman, and to be taken care of, but you're so independent that if we try and fill that role, we get that."

"What?"

"A smart mouth."

They reached her car. "Thank you, friend, for making sure I reached my car safely."

"You're welcome, friend. Although I could get diabetes from all of that sugary sarcasm."

They both laughed. Doug walked to his bike, donned his helmet, and within a minute was out of the parking lot.

Jan turned the key as she watched him speed out of the parking lot. Her car engaged but didn't turn over. She knew the problem immediately. No gas. She'd meant to stop on her way home from open mike night, but once Doug called the errand had totally slipped her mind.

With an exasperated sigh, she reached for her phone and then opened the glove compartment for her roadside assistance contact card. "I can't believe I forgot," she mumbled, angry that this minor slip would cost her a couple hours sleep. She was grateful that help was just a phone call away, but in the few times she'd had to use them the wait had never been less than ninety minutes. Tonight, she believed, would be no different.

And then a sight caught her eye. Doug, hopping the curb and roaring to a stop within a foot of her door. Too relieved to be angry, she lowered the window. "Hello, Doug, my gentleman friend."

"Uh-huh." He turned off the motorcycle and got off. "Something's wrong, just as I figured."

"Why do you say that?"

"Because you're being nice."

"How'd you know there was something wrong?"

"I kept looking in the mirror, waiting to see you pull out. When I went through the light and still didn't see your car I pulled to the side, waited a minute, and then came back."

"That's really sweet of you, thanks. You're right. I'm out of gas."

"How did that happen? You didn't see the indicator light saying you were near empty?"

"Of course I did. But last night I got sidetracked by a telephone call and totally forgot to stop." She looked at him pointedly.

"Are you saying it's my fault?"

She nodded, answered with total conviction. "I am."

He shook his head. "Women." He walked to his bike, pulled a second helmet from the trunk, and motioned to her. "Come on."

"Where are we going?"

"To get you some gas!"

"Oh no. I don't do motorcycles. I'll just call roadside."

"And wait two hours? There's a gas station right down the street. And I don't want to leave you alone with a broken-down car."

"I'm not getting on that thing."

He let out an exasperated breath. "Then get out of the car."

"What? Why?"

"Man, I sure couldn't date you because you ask too many datgum questions!"

"And I wouldn't want to date you because you're so demanding. Come here. Go there. I'm a grown woman."

"Yeah, a grown woman who forgot something as simple as putting gas in her car." He shifted his weight, changed his tone. "Would you please come with me as I unlock the door to the post office so you can wait inside while I go get gas for your car?"

"It's really okay, Doug. I don't want to put you out."

Two steps and he was opening her car door. "On the bike or in the building. Those are your choices."

She looked at him, her expression contemplative. "I'll wait inside."

They walked toward the door. "Now, was that so hard?"

"Truly painful."

"Ha!"

"No, seriously, I appreciate your helping me. I'm so used to doing things on my own that I guess it is hard for me to step back and be assisted. Something that happens automatically, that I didn't realize until now."

After seeing her securely inside, Doug went to

the gas station. Less than ten minutes later, her problem was handled.

He relocked the post office door. They reached her car. "Here," she said, pulling out her wallet. "Let me give you something."

"Not a chance."

"But you helped me out. Just a show of appreciation."

"Tell you what. You can pay me by not being so resistant when I'm trying to help you. And with a hug."

"Fine." She stretched her arms to his shoulders, leaving two feet between them, and squeezed.

"What the hell was that?" Which he didn't really have to say because his look already said it loudly and clearly.

"Ha! You should see your face! You've never heard of a church hug? That's what's taught to the singles so that there is no temptation between single men and women who socialize together."

"Damn. No wonder so many women in church are still single. That's a jacked-up hug. Come here."

Without waiting or warning, he pulled her to him and wrapped his arms around her. Her arms automatically tightened, bringing them closer still. The energy shifted. The atmosphere changed. Though he wasn't holding her tightly, Jan couldn't breathe. It was the feel of her breasts crushed against his chest, the heat from his breath on her ear, the nearness of him. Something deep inside

her that had been sleeping came alive. She stepped
back and took a gulp of fresh air.

"You all right?"

"Yes, just . . ." She stepped around him, got into
her car, and started it almost in the same motion.
"Thanks again, Doug. I really appreciate your help."

"Anytime. Drive safe."

Jan pulled off without looking back. One look,
she knew, and any hope of not falling head over
heels for her "gentleman friend" would be gone.

14

Sleep was a wonderful thing, but last night Doug hadn't gotten much. At work for less than an hour, he was already in a mood. An unruly customer had threatened him with a lawsuit because of what she claimed was a lost package. After going through Pat and the coworker handling the special notice window, she had demanded to speak to a supervisor. Lucky him. Usually the Carter charm was the ultimate anger annihilator. Not today. This woman didn't want anything except her mail. At the same time he was dealing with Ms. Congeniality, one of the processors jammed. He thought this was enough to happen before he'd gone through one can of caffeine, but no. He had to get a call from his supervisor about some rules and regulation/protocol nonsense. He had a mind to channel his mama, Liz Carter, and tell his super that today was not the day to use his back to climb the employment ladder, but he stopped himself, let the venting slide off said back, and hung up the phone with his job still intact.

When his message indicator beeped, he thought it was another fire. It was, but not the kind he had in mind.

Do you have plans for lunch? I'm buying.

Jan. The woman who more and more was igniting his passion. And costing him sleep. With one sentence, his day began to look up.

He picked up his phone and texted back.

Sure. What do you have in mind?

Doesn't matter. Something quick.

That'll work. But I'll buy mine.

No. This is for helping me last night.

Okay, if it will make you feel better.

☺

I'ma let you have this one. We'll talk later.

And they did. Within seconds of getting into Jan's car, Doug made it clear that payment for his chivalry would not be a chicken sandwich.

"What about a burger?"

"I did the job. I set the pay, which was a hug. Last night was only partial payment."

"How do you figure and how is that fair? There were no choices in what you got for me. My car needed gas. You bought gas. There was no choice as to whether it would be that or lemonade."

Doug paused for a minute, gave her a look. "Dang, that's a pretty good argument," he finally conceded. "I think women are born with an argument gene."

"Ha! Why, because you don't have a comeback?"

"If you ever meet my mother, you'll know why."

"That's interesting. My mom's the opposite. She's quiet. Hates drama. I can count on my fingers the times I've heard her really upset."

"Even when you were a teenager, probably going against everything she taught you?"

"Hardly. I was one of those boring good girls."

"Yeah, the worst ones always say that."

Jan laughed again, harder this time. Doug determined that he liked the sound of her laughter and wanted to hear it more often.

"You're probably saying that because of how bad you were."

"I'll admit it. I was a knucklehead. But I've never robbed or killed anybody, so . . ."

"Oh my goodness! Seriously? No murder or theft but lesser crimes . . ."

"Hey, I'm like don't ask don't tell. Or as you would say . . . that's personal."

The banter continued. In between they decided on pizza, went to the family-owned shop, and brought the slices back to the post office.

That their lunches were the same did not go unnoticed. But since Melissa had left, it was just good-natured jabbing about their not getting everybody a slice.

Ten minutes after they'd parted in the parking lot, Doug called Jan.

"What do you want?" is how she answered.

"Dangerous question," was his response.

"Not for me it isn't."

"Because you're one of those boring good girls."

"Exactly right."

"I see why you're not married," he mumbled.

"I heard that."

Obviously the mumble wasn't low enough.

"Plus, you're one to talk. I don't see a ring on your finger. Why are you still single?"

"I've got time to get the wife and family. I'm not even thirty yet."

"How old are you?"

"Twenty-eight."

"Is that all?"

"Why do you say it like that?"

"Dangerous question," she said, a smile in her voice.

"Not for me it isn't." He smiled, too. "What, does my bald head make me look old?"

"No, you don't look old at all. Your being a supervisor made me assume you were at least in your thirties."

"No, but I've been there ten years already. Started just after my eighteenth birthday."

"You never thought about college?"

"I thought about it. But there was this bike I wanted. Parents wouldn't buy it. They told me that if I wanted it to get a job. So that's what I did."

"It's not too late, you know."

"I've already got what you go to college for . . . a good job. Right?"

"It depends on what you want out of life."

"Did you go?"

"Yes, Cal State. I have a liberal arts degree."

"And I'm your supervisor. See, you made my point."

"I guess that argument gene malfunctioned."

Doug sensed her change in mood. "Hey, that was a joke. I didn't meant to—" His phone beeped. "Hold on a second." He checked the ID. "That's just Mom. I'll call her back."

"No, go ahead and take it."

"I'll call her in a minute. I don't want to hang up with you mad at me."

"I'm not angry. Your comment just reminded me that I'm not where I want to be. That's all."

"Your goal is a lot higher than mine. Lots of people want to make money as an artist. Few are successful. I admire you taking the chance."

"Thanks."

"Are you at home yet?"

"Yes, just arrived. Making sure I got here safely?"

"Always. So when did you know you wanted to be a singer?"

"I was always singing around the house, but seeing Aliyah on television was the first time I thought about doing it professionally."

"I like her music."

"Her voice was amazing. Gone too soon."

"So you what, started singing around town or trying to get a deal? How does that work?"

Now inside her home Jan headed to the kitchen for a bottle of sweetened tea. "In high school and college I sang wherever I could find an audience. Talent shows, choirs, contests. Hang on." She knocked on the door to Lionel's room, then opened it. He wasn't home. A sense of worry hit her instantly, until she remembered a text from earlier saying he'd be hanging out with Bernard.

"Jan, you okay?"

"Oh, sorry, Doug. Yes, I'm okay. Just checking on my brother and got a little freaked when he wasn't in his room. But it's okay. I know where he is."

"Does he get out much?"

"Not as often as I'd like, or as much as he needs. After the injury most of his friends stopped hanging around. Everyone but his friend and neighbor, Bernard, who he's out with now. He needs motivation, and the feeling that he can do something with his life. Bernard's a good kid, but not the one who is going to motivate my brother."

"Neither you nor I have any idea what he's going through. Give him time, Jan. He'll figure it out."

"I hope so." She went into her room. The phone was already on speaker. She placed it on the dresser while she undressed and donned pajamas.

"So you sang all over LA. Anywhere else?"

"Yes, in New York, once. I got this crazy idea to be on *Showtime at the Apollo* and talked my cousin, Crystal, into going with me. We were both too naïve to know what a crazy idea it was to just go there as if I could walk right on. But basically, that's what happened. I ended up getting on the show and actually winning that night."

"At the Apollo? That's true street cred, girl."

"I know, right? I was on top of the moon, thought I'd be called by every record company in America. Didn't happen. I came back here, worked odd jobs, have played in several bands, and while not having much money I still felt good, like I was going after my dream."

"You're still going after it."

"Yes, but not like I could before the accident. That's why I want this show so badly. It's not just about me, but my family. I want my mom to not have to work two and a half jobs, and my brother to have a better quality life."

"What about you? What do you want?"

"Right now, all I want is to get a spot on that show and to work with Nick Starr. After that, I'll figure out the rest."

"Nick Starr is cool, but he's not the only producer out there. Keep that in mind."

"You sound like my cousin."

"She must be really smart."

"Naw, just opinionated."

"Come with it, girl. Keep making a brother feel good."

She laughed. "I'm just playing."

"What? Ms. Don't Play Games used the P word? I've got skills!"

"You're so silly. Both you and Crystal are right in that Nick isn't the only producer in town. But he's the only one in LA having a contest for singers to be on a reality show. So right now, I'm wishing on a star."

"That was really bad, Jan."

"Just more of you and your skills rubbing off on me."

They talked for another fifteen minutes before ending the call. Doug took a long shower, thinking about everything Jan had told him. Funny how different they were. Her focused and sure about what she wanted. He content to take each day as it came and see what happened next. Working at the post office happened because it was the first thing that came along. His natural skills and infectious personality made it something he was good at. Just as Doug was drifting off to sleep, the craziest notion came into his head.

Maybe those same skills that worked so well for him could help Jan, too.

15

It was Sunday, which meant dinner with the fam at his mama's house. Doug had skipped breakfast and was ready to chow down. His brother Byron didn't even wait until Doug's foot touched the porch before he delivered the news.

"You're in trouble."

"Hello to you, too, Byron."

Byron grabbed Doug's arm and kept him on the porch. "You'll be thanking me later. Mama's upset because you ignored her call and then didn't return it."

"Damn! She called while I was talking to Jan. I forgot all about it."

"Jan the singer?"

"Yeah."

"The one we saw at Breeze?"

"Why are you sounding surprised? You forgot that we also work together, and that I'm her supervisor at the post office?"

"The fact that she's making you forget your

mama leads me to believe that you've stamped her zip code." Byron cocked his head and raised his brow. "Know what I'm sayin'?"

"I know you're a fool. Get out of here with that." Doug pushed Byron aside and opened his parents' front door. There was a living room full of people, but he ignored all of them and called out to Liz Carter.

"I'm sorry, Mama!"

Expectant faces looked toward the kitchen, Liz Carter's favorite place in the house. There was no response. Unusual. His mother always had a comeback. He shrugged and gave a wave and hello to the room before continuing into the kitchen.

Pow!

It took a second for him to figure out what had come upside his head.

"Really, Mama. A loaf of French bread?"

"Be glad I didn't make rolls," Liz calmly replied while pulling a steaming-hot container of baked ziti from the oven. "Because then it would have been a rolling pin."

"What'd I do?"

"It's what you didn't do."

"Mama, you just called yesterday!"

"My point exactly." She removed her oven mitt and approached Doug, a hand on her ample hip. "Who is she?"

"Huh?"

"Don't play dumb."

"That's right. Don't play dumb, boy." Youngest

brother Barry walked into the kitchen and bopped Doug upside the head, a move that led to a retaliatory shove. From Liz.

"Don't you get me started on you, boy! Your hot dog goes between more buns than a Ball Park frank."

"Whoa!" Doug roared with laughter.

Nelson walked in. Looked at the stove, then at Liz. "Are you fixing hot dogs?"

Liz chuckled.

Barry smiled. "Naw, man. She's asking Doug about his latest buns."

"Oh," Nelson replied knowingly, before proceeding to the refrigerator for a bottle of beer. "Probably Jan," he offered just before leaving the kitchen.

"Who's Jan?" Barry asked.

"Yes, who's Jan?" Liz asked Nelson's retreating back. "Boy! Get back in here!"

"I'll go get him," Doug quickly offered, rushing out of the kitchen.

"Don't know why he's trying to be private," Liz mumbled. She ambled over to the refrigerator and pulled out the container of salad that Ava had brought over. "He knows y'all can't keep nothing from me. Not for long."

Fifteen minutes later a rowdy group of Carters, brothers Byron, Doug, Nelson, Marvin, and Barry, father Willie and sister Ava, along with her date and a gaggle of family friends filled the living room, plates in hand, the dining room having been abandoned for a Raiders versus Chiefs football game. It was halftime before Liz picked up the earlier abandoned conversation about hot dogs and buns.

"Who's Jan?" she asked Nelson.

"Are you still on that?" Doug asked his mother with slight annoyance.

"Yes, are you?" Liz replied with a look that caused various humored reactions in the room. "And if so, how long have you been on it?"

"Liz, stay out of that boy's business." This from patriarch Willie, the slow-talking drawl of his Mississippi upbringing still evident after thirty years in LA.

"Watch it, partner, or later tonight I'll kindly ask you to stay out of mine."

The room erupted with laughter and comebacks.

"Geez, Mom!" Byron exclaimed, having just taken a gulp of soda. "You're about to make me choke!"

Once the room had recovered from this round of guffaws, Nelson said, "Jan is the new hire over at the post office."

"And a badass singer," Byron added.

"Oh, really?" Liz's eyes sparkled with mischief and humor. Mama-the-detective had scored again. She looked at Doug. "Is she cute?"

He shrugged. "She's all right."

Liz looked at Willie. "She's cute. And he's sprung."

"She really is a good singer," Byron's wife, Cynthia, commented.

"You've heard her?"

"I sure have, Mom Liz. A couple weeks ago, Ava, Byron, and I joined Doug at her show. What's the name of that club, Doug?"

"Breeze."

"And she sounds good, Byron?" He nodded, his mouth full of food. "The dope must have been good, too."

At this brows scrunched, hands stopped mid-motion, sentences mid-word.

Doug spoke for all of them. "Huh?"

"When an in-law knows about an outlaw before the sheriff gets the news . . . somebody's high."

Willie moaned. "Lord have mercy."

Barry gave her a playful poke. "That was pretty good, Mama. And you came up with that all by yourself?"

She gave him a look, then addressed the room. "And y'all wonder why I say his Crayola box is missing a few colors?"

This led to a round of animated conversation. After it quieted down, Cynthia said, "You know, Doug. Our office has a holiday party planned. We were looking at getting a DJ, but it might be nice to have a live band. Do you think Jan would be interested?"

"I could ask."

"How much do you think she'd charge?"

"I don't know, but whatever it is, you'd need to add twenty percent for her manager."

"Oh, she has a manager? What's his name?"

He looked at her with a straight face. "Doug Carter."

"Oh, brother."

"Hey, you don't expect me to work for free do you?"

"Whatever. Just remind me to give you a business card before I leave that you can pass on to her. Have her call me ASAP. It would be nice if we could book her for the event."

The Chiefs made a touchdown, taking the conversation away from singing and back to football. Doug was a diehard member of the Raider Nation and cheered for his team. All the while, though, he kept thinking about the look on Jan's face when he offered her something that so far Nick Starr had not . . . a job.

16

Over at Jan's house, where dinner was also being served, the atmosphere was remarkably different from that in the Carter household. Fewer people. Less noisy.

Jan's mom, Rochelle, looked lovingly at her two children. She was fifty-three years old, with kind eyes and the dimples her daughter had inherited, but the toll of the last two years made her appear older. "This is nice, our sharing a leisurely dinner like this. When is the last time we've eaten Sunday dinner together?"

Jan paused from taking a mouthful of smothered steak. "It's been a while."

"Too long," Lionel added between forkfuls.

"I agree, son." And then to Jan. "How's the job going?"

"It's a job."

"A good job," Rochelle said. "With great benefits, and security."

"I don't know about all that," Lionel said. "Post

offices are old school. All my friends pay for stuff online."

Rochelle's fork paused midair. "What friends of yours pay for anything?"

"All of them!"

"Humph. That's interesting, since none of them are working."

"They work."

"Where?" Rochelle looked at Lionel, unconvinced.

"Mostly in pharmaceuticals," Lionel said, winking at Jan.

"That's not funny," Jan replied. "You'd better make sure you don't become an employee."

"Don't worry about me. You just concentrate on getting hooked up with Nick Starr. Get that multi-platinum hit and none of us will have to worry about nothing no more!"

Rochelle grunted. "That's a pie-in-the-sky dream that you can't eat. Hard work in the real world, that's what put this food on the table."

Jan bit back a response. She'd stopped sharing dreams with Rochelle Baker a long time ago. It was wasted breath to argue. Her mother had been a practical, no-nonsense person as far back as she could remember. Partly out of necessity, Jan admitted, because of the hand that life had dealt. Some of that practicality had rubbed off on Jan. But she still dreamed.

From the dining room, she heard her phone sounding off in the bedroom and went to retrieve it. It was a number that she didn't recognize. Then she remembered. *Doug.* She answered it.

"Hello."

"I thought you were going to send me to voice mail."

"I didn't recognize the number and almost did. This is my off day, Supervisor, so what do you want?"

Harsh words. Warm tone.

"I told you about asking me that?" His voice lowered, turned sexy. "Do you really want my answer?"

"Maybe 'why are you calling?' would have been the better question."

"Oh, that's right. The boring good girl. So first off, that it's your off day should tell you I'm not calling about work. At least not the kind involving the U.S. mail. I might have another type job for you."

"Doing what?"

"Singing. What else?"

What else indeed? Doug obviously got what her mother did not. The realization was another chink in the armor over Jan's heart.

"Are you interested?"

"Of course I'm interested. Sorry, but I wasn't expecting that answer."

"That's what you get with a Carter, babe. The unexpected. My sister-in-law is one of the people I invited to see your show. The place where she works is having a holiday party and needs entertainment.

I told her you'd be perfect, and that she'd need to pay you well."

"Oh my gosh, really, Doug?"

"Well, not verbatim but . . . something like that."

"Where does she work?"

"An agency called H.E.L.P. They help young people get their lives together."

"I've never heard of it, but it sounds like a good cause."

"It is. My niece was going through some things and the program helped turn her around."

"Where and when?"

"I don't know all that. Told her I'd tell you about it and if you're interested, give you the number to her office."

"Yes, I will definitely give her a call." He relayed the number. "Thanks, Doug. Wow, I really appreciate this."

"No problem. Later we can negotiate my agent or manager compensation . . . whatever they call the person who books you jobs and makes you money."

"And here I thought you were just being nice."

"I am. And when you pay me, that's what you'll be doing."

"Ha! You're a trip."

"I get it honest."

"Your dad's a jokester?"

"No, my mom." A companionable silence fell as neither seemed in a hurry to hang up the phone. "So what did you do today, go to church?"

"No, I didn't make it to church this morning."

"But you're usually there."

"As often as possible, but not as regularly as when I sang in the choir. What about you?"

"Christmas and Easter when I was a kid. But now I'd look kind of stupid just showing up for the candy basket."

"You. Are. Stupid!"

"Hey, I'm keeping it real. Speaking of, what are you doing later?" The flirt was back.

"I thought you said you weren't trying to date me."

"I'm not. I just asked what you were doing. As a friend."

"Uh-huh. Your friend is going over to her cousin's house to spend time with her newest niece."

"Better be careful. Babies are catching."

"Not unless it's by way of immaculate conception."

"Dang, drought season, huh?"

"You know what?"

"Ha! Girl, I'm playing."

"Let me get off this phone before I say something I later regret."

"Something like me helping you make it rain?"

"Bye, Doug."

"So you're afraid to go out with me?"

"Of course not. Why would I be afraid?"

"Since I've said I don't want to date you either, I have no idea."

"I hesitate because men sometimes say one thing and mean another."

"I tell you what, if I ever want to hit it, I'll make sure the request is very clear. Now, do you want to go out or what?"

"Where?"

"Do you like to bowl?"

"I don't know. I've never tried it."

"Never! What was your fun growing up? Skating?"

"No."

"Parties?"

"Are you kidding? Not with my mom."

"What did you do for fun?"

"Hung out with my cousin mostly. We both love music and could spend hours in our rooms just reading about the lives of our favorite artists in music magazines, playing their hits and trying to match them note for note and dance move for dance move in front of my mirrored closet doors."

"Was Nick Starr one of your favorites?"

"Yep, I had a huge crush."

"Uh-huh. That's why you want to be on his show so bad. You've still got that crush."

"Trust me, I am not his type in any shape, form, or fashion. So there is no delusional fantasy happening, just a sistah with a passion wanting a break."

"Let's take one now." When she remained silent, he pushed his luck. "Where do you live? I'll pick you up."

"Thanks, but Lionel, Mom, and I are spending the day together. Lately, we haven't done that enough."

"I hear you. Then what about next weekend, say Friday night?"

"To go bowling."

"Trust me, you'll have a good time. I'll pick you up."

"No, I'll drive myself."

"Damn. Okay sometime between now and then I'll text you the address."

"Sounds like a plan."

17

The week flew by. Once again Jan wasn't this week's reality show pick. But she was still in the running. Even more, on Friday night she found herself doing something she hadn't done for months. Going on a date-that-wasn't-really-a-date. She'd been so focused on singing and work that it had taken Crystal to remind her how long it had been.

"You? Going out?" She'd marveled when Jan called and shared the news.

"Don't act so surprised," had been her response.

"Don't act like this is routine," Crystal had countered. "When is the last time you called and told me about a date?"

It had been six months ago exactly, a doozy of a disaster that began as an invitation to see Jill Scott and Erykah Badu in concert. Unfortunately the date thought a night of sex was included in the ticket purchase price. Toward the end of the concert he asked her to come over and spend the night. She informed him that after the concert she was going to her house, not his. Five minutes later the jerk went to the restroom and never came back. The subsequently required taxi ride cost Jan a bill with Ben's face on it. So when Doug suggested he pick her up and they ride together, she told him she'd meet him instead.

She entered the bowling alley and was immediately assaulted with a cacophony of sound: balls rolling on wood, balls striking pins, arcades pinging, music playing, and at least fifty people chattering at once. After a quick look around and not seeing Doug, she reached for her phone. At the same time, someone tapped her shoulder.

"Looking for me?"

"Hey! Where were you?"

"In the other room. Playing pool."

"The bowling alley seems to be a happening place. Who knew?"

"And here it took almost a month for you to go out with me. See what you've been missing?"

She looked around her. "A lot of fun, from the looks of things."

"I'm glad you recognize. Come on. Let's get you some shoes and get started."

"Why can't I wear my own?"

He shook his head. "I still can't believe you've never bowled."

"I'm not into sports. That's not illegal."

"It should be. Bowling alleys use a special wood on their floors. Regular street shoes will mess it up. So you have to wear bowling shoes. Did you bring socks?"

"I have to wear their shoes and socks, too?"

"Man, newbies." He shook his head. "What am I going to do with you?" Taking her arm, he told her, "Come with me."

They walked to the other side of the counter. Jan's brow raised. "A vending machine? With socks?"

"Yes, for people like you."

After getting Jan properly outfitted, they went to their assigned lane. Doug lifted several balls from the holder before choosing one for Jan. "I think this one will be good for you," he said.

"Why, because it's lavender?"

"No, because the balls are different weights and this one is lighter."

"So, you think I'm a lightweight?"

"No, I know you are. Put your fingers in the hole, like this." She complied. "Now watch a master at work."

She rolled her eyes. "You really need to work on your self-esteem."

Doug's demeanor switched from playful to serious as he walked over to the lane and crouched slightly while studying the pins. Jan watched, noting his nice arms, long legs, and cute butt. *He's not a bad-looking guy.* Though she wouldn't call him "hot," as her cousin had. Jan preferred her men in suit and tie, well-coiffed, understated fine jewelry. She'd dated a couple men who fit this bill. Had their character been as polished as their wardrobe, she'd be like Crystal right now . . . married with children. Nick Starr fit that bill. But for the chance to be his missus, she'd have to get in the back of a very long line.

After studying the lane, Doug took his arm back and then swung it forward, releasing the ball midway. It swiftly rolled down the middle toward the center pin and hit it, which knocked down all the rest.

"Bam!" He turned to her. "Did you see that?"

"You knocked down all the pins."

"Yes!"

"Isn't that what you're supposed to do?"

He gave her a look. "It's not as easy as I make it look."

"You threw a heavy ball at them. How hard can it be?"

"Get your smart behind over here and I'll show you."

Over the next hour Jan learned that not only was knocking down all the pins difficult, for a newbie like her it was downright impossible. For the first several tries she hit nothing but the gutter, no matter where she aimed. Finally, Doug came and stood by her side.

"Let me show you something. Copy my moves, okay?" She nodded. "After focusing on that first pin, and envisioning your ball hitting it squarely in the middle, you want to bend your legs just slightly, balance your weight equally."

"There's quite a bit of it."

He gave her stretch skinny jeans and fitted top emphasizing the girls a quick once-over. "There's just enough. Okay, bend your arm a little, like this." He took her arm, angled it slightly, then pulled it straight back. "Now, keep your wrist straight." He touched it. "Tighten it up a little more. That's it. Okay, when you're bringing the ball forward, you're going to rotate your hand, wrist, everything this way, to the left, and let the ball go somewhere around here." He placed his ball low, near his ankles. "Then you just—" He released the ball. It slowly rolled down the middle of the lane and even without the added force, knocked over eight pins.

"Now, your turn."

Maybe, but Jan didn't plan on hitting pins. That's because after his "just enough" comment, and his quick body scan, his lip perched just so and his fingers gently touching parts of her anatomy . . . she hadn't heard another word he said. He hadn't meant it to be an intimate gesture, she knew, but it had been so long since she'd been handled with such skill that his hand on her wrist alone had produced a heat wave down south. If he'd hug her right now like he hugged her in the parking lot, Jan was almost sure there'd be an orgasm in lane six.

"How long are you going to study those pins?"

"I'm almost ready." Yes, she was. Ready to stop playing and handle a different set of balls.

She forced these thoughts away, concentrated, and released the ball. Where Doug's ball looked like the electric slide, hers looked more like the wobble. But it didn't go into the gutter. Instead . . . she knocked down a pin! Jan whooped as if she'd hit a strike. For this first-timer, it was close enough. In their third game, she even hit a spare.

They played a few more and then turned in their shoes. "Want to grab a bite?"

"No, thank you. I've got a lot of running to do tomorrow and it's been a long week."

They walked outside. "Where are you parked?"

"Over there." They began walking in the direction she pointed. "That was fun."

"I'm glad you enjoyed yourself. After you got the rhythm of that swing, you did okay."

"I was horrible."

"It was your first time. You were fine."

"That's putting it kindly. You're a pro."

"I've been doing it for a long time, since I was a kid."

"So you like bowling, motorcycles . . . what else?"

"Sports, mainly football. Video games. And just about anything with barbeque sauce on it."

"Oh no, you're one of those."

"What's wrong with barbeque?"

She shook her head. "Not that. The video games?"

"What's wrong with those?"

"They're addictive. My brother can play for hours."

"There's worse things he could be doing."

"Better things, too."

"That's you right there, right?" She nodded. "Do you have gas?"

"Ha! Yes, a half a tank."

They reached her car. She hit her key fob. The doors unlocked. "Thank you, Doug. You're pretty cool to hang out with. I really had a good time."

"You're welcome." His eyes dropped from her eyes to her lips. He took a step forward.

She took a step back.

"Where are you going? I was just going to give you a hug."

"That's not what it looked like."

"What did it look like?"

"Like you were going to . . . never mind."

"What, kiss you?" He took another step. She was back against the car. "Like this?"

He licked his lips as his head bent slowly toward hers. Just before touching hers he stopped. Waited. She leaned in. Their lips touched. Simple. Innocent. He kissed her once. Again. A final time.

"Call me when you get home, okay?"

"Okay," she managed, hoping her noodle legs wouldn't give out before she got into the car. Once

inside she waved him away, squeezing her thighs to
calm her throbbing nub. Was it because she'd been
celibate for eight months? Or was it because Doug
had done the kissing? What was it about that man
that so turned her on?

She didn't know. But in this moment she admitted
the truth to herself. She wanted to find out.

18

For Jan, Saturday morning came early thanks to Crystal's wake-up call.

"What do you want?"

"Is that any way to answer the phone?"

"It is when the caller is your cousin, it's not yet eight a.m., and you work the p.m. shift."

"Actually, it's a minute past eight. Being the considerate person that I am, I made sure of that."

"Gee, thanks."

"You're welcome." Jan yawned, stretched, and waited for conversation.

"So . . ."

"So, what?"

"Your date, that's what! How'd it go?"

"Why do you keep calling it that?"

"Because when two people go out, that's what it's called."

"We went bowling. It was fun."

"Bowling?"

"That's how I felt. You know I'm not sports oriented."

"That's why I'm surprised. Both that you agreed to play and that you thought it was fun."

"It was. I'd never been to a bowling alley and was surprised to find it a popular spot on a Friday night. Have you ever bowled before?"

"No, but Brent does and if you can learn how, then I know I can."

"Whatever."

"It could be a great double date."

"Who said I planned to go out with him again?"

"You don't?"

Jan sighed and adjusted the pillow as she stared at the ceiling. "I don't know. Doug is a good enough guy and after hanging with him last night I admit he's a little cuter than I gave him credit for, but . . ."

"But, what?"

"Girl, you know why. I'm not trying to get involved again with someone in whom I don't see a forever kind of future. I tried that before and we both know what happened."

"You can't judge all men on one experience."

"You asked."

"He's a nice-looking guy, works full-time, appreciates your singing, and is obviously interested in you. What's missing?"

"Drive. Ambition."

"How do you know whether he's ambitious or not?"

"If he was, he wouldn't be working at a post office."

"Seriously, Janice? You work there! So do you know how crazy that sounds?"

"For me it's temporary. For him, it's a career."

"You say that like it's a bad thing. Cuz, we're not twelve anymore. Don't you think if your knight was going to ride out of that fairy tale and down your street it would have happened by now?"

"Who's to say it still can't happen? I'm not going to lower my standards just because it's taking me longer than it took you."

"I'm not saying you should lower your standards. But you may want to redefine them."

"I just know what I want. And I don't see the benefit of dating someone just to say I have a man. Even though he is a good kisser and it has been a while."

"So there is a physical attraction. At least now I know you're alive."

"Yes, after last night I had to admit that to myself. He's funny, too, but life is serious. After a while his carefree attitude would probably get on my nerves."

"His attitude is probably just what you need to loosen up."

"I'm not uptight. I just don't have time for fool-ishness."

"It's not foolish to be happy. Maybe if you let go

hurts and current expectations, and unlock your heart, you'll find that out."

They talked a bit more before Crystal was called to mommy duty. For Jan, the rest of the weekend dragged. Doug didn't call and she refused to call him. Told herself there was no reason. As if there had to be. Told herself that it didn't matter. But it did.

On Monday morning, Jan called Cynthia. Doug had stated that his sister-in-law worked nine to five-thirty, so being considerate, like her cousin, Jan waited until a minute past the hour to do so.

"Good morning, this is the H.E.L.P. Agency. How may I direct your call?"

"Hi. May I speak to Cynthia Carter?"

"May I tell her whose calling?"

"Jan Baker."

"One moment, Ms. Baker."

It was a potentially low-paying gig for an office party, but Jan was still nervous. While waiting for Cynthia to answer, she paced the room.

"Hello, Cynthia Carter."

"Hi, Cynthia, it's Jan Baker, the singer who works with Doug."

"Yes, Jan. He said you'd be calling. How are you?"

"I'm good, and you?"

"I'm fine. Glad you called. I really enjoyed you and the band the other night. Is there any chance you're available for a holiday party on December 26th? That's a Saturday night."

"I'm available, but I don't know about the musicians who play with me. I'd have to check with them once I have more details."

"Okay. Do you know about our organization?"

"Only what Doug told me, which is that you work with troubled youth."

"Yes, H.E.L.P. works with not only those troubled and disenfranchised but also disabled, discarded, dismissed, and/or disengaged. We try and help everyone know that despite whatever circumstances may cause them to think otherwise, their lives matter. We are a small organization that is part of a large network that does similar work. This party will involve many of those entities and as such will be on a grander scale than if it was just us."

"How many people are you expecting, and what is the entertainment budget?"

Cynthia told her and explained what type of entertainment they desired. The two women continued to chat, not only about the party but some of the other services they offered. Jan ended the call and immediately called Doug. She now had a reason.

"Hey, Doug, are you awake?"

"I am now."

"Sorry for calling so early. I just finished talking to Cynthia and I'm really excited."

"Oh, you did? What'd she say?"

"She gave me the details on the holiday party. It sounds really nice. I've got to call Thump, though, and make sure the band is available."

"Who?"

She laughed. "Our bass player and the band

leader. Everybody calls him Thump because of the way he plays his guitar. Matter of fact, I don't even know his real name."

"That's pretty crazy."

"Yeah, most musicians are crazy."

"And singers, too, right?"

"I walked right into that one."

"With eyes wide open. What about their budget? Is it enough, comparable to what you normally get?"

"It's more actually. Thump and the guys will love this news."

"See what a good friend I am?"

"Yes, I do. That's another reason I called. To thank you for thinking of me for this job. I haven't had much support in my goal of becoming a professional recording artist. My mom thinks it's foolishness."

"What does your dad say?"

"Not much."

"So he's not supportive either?"

"No, and that's goes for more than my career goals. I didn't grow up with him in the house. He and my mom were never married, and when I was around four years old he moved back to Texas, where he was from. Mom says he was around me a lot before then, but I don't remember. He came back into my life when I was nine and from then until around the age of sixteen I'd go there in the summer and spend two weeks with him. Not a lot of time to really get to know people, you know? I've tried to keep in touch with him, but there's not much of a connection."

"Does he have other kids?"

"Yes, three with the woman he eventually married. They're still married, and my half siblings are grown."

"But you're not close to them either."

"No, it's funny. You can be related by blood but not related by spirit, you know? Plus, I'd see them so rarely, we never got close. I think a part of me resented the fact that I didn't know him like they did or have the life they had, with a mom and a dad. So when it came to establishing a close relationship, I can't say that I tried too hard."

"Wait until you become a star. Then you'll become their favorite sister."

"Lionel is the only one I'm a sister to. Which reminds me. Cynthia mentioned there were some programs aimed at disabled youth. I wanted to know more about it, but she had a meeting and had to go. I'm hoping it's something Lionel can get involved with, a support group of sorts where he can gain the tools to have a real life, and not spend all day watching TV and playing video games, just existing. He could use a role model and more men around him who are doing things in life."

"I could talk to him if you want."

"It couldn't be as though I'd asked you to mentor him. He's sensitive and wouldn't appreciate feeling like a case or something."

"Really? So you think I'd walk in and announce that I'm the dude his sister asked to help get his

lazy, unmotivated behind out of the room because
he needed male mentors and role models? Come
on, Jan. Give me a little more credit than that."

"I didn't think you'd say it like that."

"I know how to handle brothers. I have four of
them."

"Oh, no. There's four more of you?"

"Ha! No, there's four who are worse than me:
Byron, my older brother. Nelson, the middle. And
Marvin and Barry, who Mom obviously had while
feeling sentimental about the seventies."

Jan cracked up. "No sisters?" she asked, once
she'd stopped laughing.

"One, Ava. She's a sister in spirit, as you say, but
we're as close as if it were by blood. She's been in
my life since I can remember."

"She came with you to Breeze?"

"Yes, along with Byron and Cynthia."

"Maybe I'll meet her one day."

"Maybe I'll meet Lionel."

"I'd like that." Noticing the time, she stood. "Let
me run. It's open mike tonight and I still need to
practice. See you later."

"Don't be late."

"I just hope I don't have to stay late. There aren't
many slots left, so I need to go and do my thing."

"Show Starr what you're working with."

"Exactly."

19

The next morning, it was Doug who called Jan. "Good morning."

"Hi, Doug."

"Ooh, obviously not a good morning. What's the matter?"

"Oh, just a bit bummed, that's all."

"What about? Talk to me."

"Still waiting for my spot on the reality show."

"You didn't get picked again?"

"Nope."

"Did you get eliminated?"

"No, thank God."

"Dang, that's messed up, Jan. I'm sorry you didn't get selected. How many weeks are left in the competition?"

"Five."

"Then keep the faith. There are five slots left. All you need is one."

"You're right. And I will. Thanks."

"Hey, I've got some news for you."

"What's that?"

"I talked to Cynthia about the program you asked about, the one for your brother."

"You did?"

"Yes, she said there are several different programs for kids in the chair. Does he like sports?"

"Loves them, especially basketball. Before the accident, he used to play all the time."

"Turns out I know one of the dudes who coaches over there. He handles the basketball program. So this might be a perfect fit."

"You should talk to him about it."

"Okay."

"Do you have time right now? I can see if he's up."

"Sure."

Cynthia muted the call and walked the short distance down the hall to Lionel's room. Her first knock yielded no answer. She knocked harder. "Lionel."

"What?"

"Are you decent?"

"I sure hope not. Those who are live a boring life."

She opened the door. "What are you doing?"

"Nothing."

"Are you okay?"

"Yeah, just bored."

"Then this phone call is perfect."

"Who is it?"

"A friend of mine who knows about a program you might be interested in."

"What kind of program?"

"He's on the phone now and wants to talk about it. Five minutes. Okay?"

He clucked his tongue. "Whatever."

Jan unmuted the call and put it on speaker. "Doug, you there?"

"I'm here."

"I've got you on speaker and am here with my brother, Lionel."

"What's up, Lionel?" Doug asked.

"Yo, man."

"I hear you used to play basketball."

"Yep, used to."

"Would you like to play again?"

Lionel snorted. "I'd like to do a lot of things again, bro."

"I'm sorry about what happened to you, Lionel. I'm a bike man myself. Been riding since I was a kid. Been lucky, too. So while I can't say I know how you feel, I know how I'd feel if I couldn't do that anymore." Lionel nodded but said nothing. "Anyway, nice chatting with you, man. I need to run right now, but I'd like to meet up with you, maybe talk about b-ball, the program, and some other stuff, if you're interested."

"Yeah, I guess that sounds cool."

"All right, then. Jan, you still there?"

"Yes, I'm here." She blew a kiss to Lionel on her way out. Once back in her room with the door closed, she continued. "Thanks for talking to him, Doug. He sounded a bit distant and uninterested, but please don't hold that against him. He's a good kid."

"He's not a kid anymore, babe. He's a man who needs to be around other men. As for his attitude, it's pretty typical and sounds like all the other hard-heads out there who are his age."

"Thank you for taking an interest in him."

"I'm interested in you, which makes me interested in him."

"As a friend, right?"

"Girl, I can't even continue with that bald-faced lie. Not that I date women I work with," he hurriedly added. "But if that were to change, I'd want to date you. Last night I went to sleep thinking about your pillows."

"My pillows?"

"I was wondering if they'd crush my chest when laying down the way they do when we're standing up."

"You're talking about my . . . Doug!"

"What? You think I hadn't noticed? Especially in that top you wore to the bowling alley and the way those stripes cut across them in just the right way. But it's not just that, though. Or the way those pants fit your hips and squeezed your booty, on full display when you'd bent down that little bit the way I showed you and threw the ball. Or," he continued over what was surely an objection, "that spray of freckles across the bridge of your nose that's barely visible and those dimples. Damn . . . they're hella sexy. Even that tiny scar beneath your right eye. I've been meaning to ask how you got that?"

"When I was seven and got pushed into a swimming pool. You should be a private detective or something. Few people ever notice that scar. You've really been checking me out. Why?"

"I just started noticing what I just said, about the physical and all. That was after I realized that while you seemed a bit stuck up—"

"Excuse me?!"

"I didn't stutter. Let me finish. You told me once you could come off as standoffish, and that's true. You also said you weren't into games and again, you didn't lie. Although I'm glad to see glimpses of your playful side. Then again, if people hang around me long enough they tend to come out of their shell, no matter how thick it is."

"Oh, really?"

Doug ignored her smart-alecky tone. "The fact that you're unselfish, a hard worker, goal-oriented, and put your family first makes you good people in my book. A lot of women I know feel it's all about them. They're either self-centered, approaching you with ulterior motives or trying to get with you sexually before even knowing your last name. Don't get me wrong, because I like to get down as much as the next guy. But that you're more careful about that, and think a little differently . . . it's refreshing."

"Hmm."

"Last time I asked about why you're single you told me you'd tell me later. Is this later?"

"I really don't want to talk about that right now."

"What about talking about it this Saturday? When I take you out."

There was barely a pause before, "I'd like that."

"What? No questions? No quippy comebacks?"

"Doug . . ."

"I hear you. Quit while I'm ahead."

"Yes."

"What's your address? Because this time I'm coming to get you. Maybe I can even come earlier and meet Lionel. Talk to him for a minute."

"You got a pen?"

"Just text me."

"Okay."

"And, Jan . . ."

"Huh?"

"Just so you know . . . I'll have more on my mind than just being your friend."

20

On Saturday, Doug pulled into the Baker driveway around five o'clock. They'd decided on a casual evening, so along with a closely cropped cut and freshly shaved goatee he rocked jeans, a Lakers T-shirt, and a pair of sparkling white Nikes. He knocked on the door. Jan answered. He gave her CJ jeans, baby-doll top, and curly do an appreciative once-over before leaning in for a quick hug.

After a minute of small talk, Jan said, "Come meet my brother." Doug followed Jan across the living room and down a short hall where she stopped and knocked on a door that sported KEEP OUT and BEWARE OF DOG signs.

"Yeah," said a gruff voice behind the door, partly muffled by sounds of a video game.

Jan opened the door. Lionel was in his usual spot—middle of the room, directly in front of his new forty-two-inch TV—passionately involved in Grand Theft Auto V. She stepped into the room. Doug followed behind her.

Lionel glanced up at both of them before looking back at the screen. "What's up?"

"Hey, Lionel. I wanted you to meet Doug, one of my coworkers."

"Hey, Doug." Said while successfully popping off five would-be killers. "Not today, muthafuckas!"

"Lionel, that's rude. Can you pause the game long enough to be civil?"

"It's okay," Doug quickly interjected. "Let him handle his business. As hard as he's working, this is probably his highest score. Best not to break his concentration."

"I thought you said Doug worked at the PO, sis."

"That's right."

"Naw . . . gotta be a garbage collector. All that trash he's talking."

Jan snorted. Doug laughed and took a step closer to Lionel, watching the screen intently. "Nothing I can't back up."

Jan read the words scrolling across the bottom of the screen as she watched the criminal (whom she assumed to be Lionel the way he was smiling) who'd just sprayed bullets in a dark alley, then car-jacked a Camaro and dropped off drugs at a house in the hood.

WTH?

"Oh, yeah?"

Lionel asked the question, but Jan's face trans-mitted the same. "You did not just challenge him to a video game."

"I sure did. Baby, I'm one of the best to ever pick

up a controller." Lionel laughed. Doug looked at him. "Think I'm lying?"

"I think that you *think* you're the best. But that's just because you've never played a real ninja."

"Oh Lord." Jan let out an exasperated breath.

"Well, put your money where your mouth is, son. Let's put your theory to the test." He turned to Jan. "Where's another chair?"

"Are you serious?"

"Do I look like I'm playing?"

"Spending the evening in my brother's funky bedroom isn't quite the date I had in mind."

"This butt-whooping won't take long," Doug said.

"No, it won't," Lionel added. "I'ma send your boy out with his tail between his legs real quick. And my room's not funky either."

Jan directed Doug to a dining room chair, which he brought and set next to Lionel. Soon after, he and Lionel were engaged in racing, killing, selling drugs, and "hitting licks." Jan shook her head, brought them cans of soda, and retrieved her laptop from her bedroom. Back in Lionel's room she plopped on his bed, alternately watching the onscreen drama, checking e-mails, and posting on social media.

The game continued. The tighter the score the more Doug and Lionel bantered and the louder they became. When it was over, Lionel raised his hands in victory with a whoop for emphasis.

"I've got to give it to you," Doug said, reaching

over for a handshake. "You're pretty good. But I couldn't beat you up in your own house, in front of your sister."

"Oh, so you let me win."

"Absolutely."

Lionel leaned over engulfed in laughter. "A comedian and a singer. Good match."

Doug smiled. "Hey, man, do you have a cell phone?"

"Yeah."

Doug pulled out his phone. "Give me your number. I need to get Jan out of here before she beats me up, but maybe tomorrow I can call and talk with you about the basketball league that my partner coaches. Maybe even take you over before the season starts to shake the rust off your fingers."

"What, play you?"

"Why not?"

An unreadable look scampered across Lionel's face before he said, "You going to be in a chair?"

"Of course! You think I'd give you that obvious excuse, that I beat you because of legs? Man, I'll lay down and kick your butt."

All three of them laughed this time. Doug and Lionel exchanged numbers and soon Doug and Jan were heading down the boulevard.

"Where are we going?"

"I don't know. Where do you want to go?"

"You came to pick me up with no destination in mind?"

"Oh, I've got a destination all right." He wriggled his brows.

She tsked and shook her head.

"Don't sit over there with an attitude. Sometimes the best experiences in life are those not planned."

They drove a ways in silence before Jan turned to look at him. "It was so good to see Lionel happy, I mean really happy. He hasn't looked that way in a long time."

"I tend to have that kind of effect on people."

She smiled, settled into her seat, and looked at the scenery they passed. "I hope that basketball program works for him. He could make new friends, maybe find some type of employment. I don't want to get ahead of things, but it's hard not to get excited about him living a fuller, happier life."

"That's very exciting. My guy over there who coaches the program is very good at what he does. If anybody can put your brother on the right path, the coach can."

They ended up at the movies, checking out a flick that the week before had gotten rave reviews. It was a romantic comedy, something Doug had balked at but in the end had totally enjoyed.

"See, that wasn't so bad," Jan said on their way out.

"You were right. I told you I enjoyed it." Once outside, he asked her, "How about we grab a meal?"

"After all that junk food we ate in there? Between the popcorn, nachos, candy, and those gallon drinks you brought us . . . I can't eat another bite."

"Do you play pool?"

"No."

"Do you dance? I could take you to my club."

"A club?" Jan's expression was dubious.

"My motorcycle club, the Ace Imperials. They turn it up on the weekends, but they're all good guys."

"I've never been that into clubs. Maybe another time."

"It's too early for me to take you home. What about a drink . . . at my house?"

Jan was silent for so long Doug began to wonder if he'd heard her. But just as he got ready to repeat the question, he got his answer.

"Okay."

He smiled, reached for her hand, and walked to his car.

21

He set his iPod to hip-hop music before heading out of the theater's parking garage. "I don't have any liquor at the house. What do you drink?"

"I'm not much of a drinker. When I do it's chardonnay."

"That's white wine, right?"

"Yes."

"What does it taste like?"

"Kinda sweet, fruity."

"A girlie drink."

"Ask a woman what's she drinking and her answer just might be a girlie drink."

"There goes that argument gene working again." He looked over in time to catch Jan's smile before she forced it away.

They stopped at a store near Doug's house, spent a while in the wine aisle discussing choices and then over to the meat section where Doug informed Jan she was going to cook him a steak.

"How do you figure I'm coming over to your house to fix you dinner? I'm not cooking anything."

Doug went stone-faced. "It's either cook, clean, or make love, woman. Now, which one are you going to do for me tonight?"

It took a whole five seconds for Jan's shock to wear off. Once it did, her answer was simple and very clear. "You need to take me home."

She glared at him.

He stared back.

It was a showdown worthy of the O.K. Corral happening between the chardonnays and the pinot blancs.

Doug clenched his teeth, balled his hands into fists, and began breathing heavy.

"Never mind," Jan said, reaching for her phone. "I'm calling a cab." She spun around and headed toward the front of the store.

"Bwahahaha!" Doug erupted. "Jan, wait!" He was laughing so hard he could barely catch up with her. He finally did, and grabbed her arm. "Girl, wait," he said, almost doubled over. "You should know my talking like that was a joke."

She crossed her arms. "Didn't sound like a joke to me."

"I could tell," he replied, wiping joyful tears from his eyes. "Man, if looks could kill, I'd be a dead man. Remind me to never cross you. The results could be lethal."

"Doug, I don't like to play around like that."

"You sure as hell don't." He adopted her tone

and her stance. "You need to take me home. Now! Never mind, muthafucka," he continued, a hand on his hip and his voice even higher. "I'll call me a muthafuckin' cab."

Jan's mouth began to quiver with the first M.F. By the second over-ghetto-fied profanity, she could no longer contain the laughter. It spilled out of her mouth, down her body, and straight into her heart.

"You are a straight-up fool."

"Whew, girl, you make you laugh." Doug reached for her hand. She didn't pull away. They began walking to the meat section.

"No, you made yourself laugh."

"Don't mess with Jan Baker. She'll cut you with her tongue."

"I did not sound like that."

"Yes, you did."

"I did not. Nor did I curse."

He looked at her. "You wanted to."

She slid her eyes in his direction, suppressing laughter. "I sure did."

The easy banter was back as Doug paid for their purchases and they drove the short distance to his home. "I apologize now if there are any drawers on the floor. I wasn't expecting company."

She just shook her head and as he stepped back walked inside his apartment.

It was clean, almost immaculate.

Another side eye as she looked around. "Nice place, Doug." She took in the tasteful black and tan furniture, large flat-screen on the wall with video game paraphernalia on the console below it, Raider memorabilia scattered about, pictures of who she assumed was his family, and beyond the living/dining combination a kitchen with not one dish out of place. "This looks like you."

"Thank you." He walked into the kitchen and placed the grocery sack on the counter. "I hope these tumblers will do," he said as he pulled two short ones from the cabinet. "I don't have wine-glasses."

"That's fine." She entered the kitchen. "And not too much for me. Just half a glass."

"Do you mind opening it and pouring while I fix my steak?"

"You're really going to cook? It's eleven o'clock!"

"Baby, my stomach don't care what time it is. I'm hungry!"

"Why didn't you just go through a drive-through for a burger?"

"I started to," he said, pulling out a cast-iron skillet, oil, and spices. "But when we stopped at the store I figured to get a steak. It's easy to fix, doesn't take long, and tastes better than any burger I could have gotten."

Jan watched him pour a small amount of oil in the skillet that set over a high flame before shaking a variety of spices on the meat and rubbing them in.

"You act like you know what you're doing."

"I'd better, since you won't cook me dinner."

"That's right. I'm not going to clean your house

either." Said saucily, hands on hips, with a look that dared him to challenge her.

Doug stopped, took in Jan's spread-leg stance and haughty countenance. He was sure she had no idea how sexy that attitude made her look. He allowed his eyes a slow journey from the lips spouting all of that bravado nonsense, down the front of the sweater pulled over her girls, over the hips that put an hourglass to shame, down to the black leather ankle boots that complemented the black and white sweater, stretch jeans, and jewelry she wore to perfection, then slowly made his way back up to her eyes. "That's no problem."

Jan's comment had been delivered with obvious fire. But Doug's reaction—quiet, subtle, barely five seconds long—was a lethal comeback that made Jan hotter than the steak now sizzling in the cast-iron skillet.

Conversation was sparse as she watched him expertly finish cooking, letting the steak rest while he pulled a package of salad out of the fridge and a bag of chips from the counter.

"Would you care to join me for this late-night . . . snack . . . Ms. Baker." His eyes suggested there were many ways to take the question.

So did her answer. "I think I will, Mr. Carter. Watching how you handled that . . . meat . . . has worked up quite an appetite."

Bypassing the dining room table, Doug led them to the living room couch. Using his remote, he turned on the TV to a music channel playing seventies and eighties hits. They sat shoulder to shoulder, bobbing their heads to the likes of Earth, Wind & Fire, the Whispers, After 7, and Johnny Gill, while eating Doug's perfectly medium-well-done steaks. Each bite was tender, juicy, and seasoned just right. And even though the chips were plain and the salad basic, the level of his cooking made them taste better, too.

Jan set her plate on the coffee table and picked up a napkin.

"Wow, Doug, that steak was really good."

He pointedly looked at her cleaned plate. "I can tell." They laughed. "And this from a woman who questioned my even cooking at this time of night."

"I didn't think I was hungry, but . . ."

The way he looked at her made her forget what she was going to say next.

"Coming into my kitchen made you change your mind?"

"Sure did." Her eyes dropped to his lips. Funny, but she didn't remember them looking so yummy. Were they always like that?

He set down his finished plate and wiped his mouth with a napkin as well before picking up and finishing his half glass of wine. "I'm glad you enjoyed it."

"I really did." She finished her wine. "How'd you learn to cook so well?"

"My mama, Liz Carter. She can throw down, and made sure that all of her sons knew enough about cooking to not leave home and starve or exist solely on fast food."

"So at the store you really were kidding when you demanded I come here and cook."

"I told you I was."

Looking around, she continued. "And about cleaning your house."

"Uh-huh."

They looked into each other's eyes as the Isley Brothers suggested that it wasn't yet time to say good night.

"So, Jan." He placed an arm around her shoulder and pulled her close. "Since you enjoyed my steak so much, I'm wondering if I can talk you into dessert."

She wrapped an arm around his waist, rested her head against him. "Probably, and it would be a short conversation."

Doug placed his finger beneath her chin and lifted her lips to his. The air fairly crackled as skin touched skin and tongues quickly darted from their oral caves to become better acquainted.

"Umm," Doug moaned, shifting his body for better access to her thickness. Jan said nothing, only followed his lead.

It was said that the way to a man's heart was through his stomach. It looked like Doug was about to prove that the reverse was also true.

22

The kisses turned from tender to intense. Doug slipped his hand beneath Jan's sweater and stroked her ample breasts. He ran his hand over her stomach and across the waistband of her jeans. Jan's hand moved from Doug's back to his neck, pressing his lips even tighter against hers, dipping her tongue even farther inside his hot, wet mouth. The fruity notes of the chardonnay still played on both their tongues. They were feeling drunk in love, and not from those half glasses of wine now gone.

Doug pulled his lips from Jan's. She followed, not ready for the kisses to end.

"I need to taste more of you," he whispered, his breathing getting more labored. "I need to put my hands all over that lusciousness, girl."

Jan sat up and moaned. "Somebody please stop me from doing what I said I wouldn't."

He reached for the hem of her sweater and effortlessly pulled it over her head. "Baby, you can't stop what hasn't even gotten started." His gaze was fastened on her globes spilling over the cups. He tapped the bra. "Take that off."

She obeyed.

He sucked in a breath. "Damn! You're about to make a brother break his own rule!" He rolled his thumb over her nipple, watching it harden and goose bumps form. "Beautiful." Bending his head, he gently sucked her plumpness into his mouth while his fingers worked magic on her other soft globe.

The combined actions made Jan shiver and unable to think. That must have been it. Why else would she lift her body up, reach for the waistband of her stretch jeans, and begin pulling them down before he'd even asked her?

The move worked for Doug. He stood and reached out a hand. "I think we need to take this party to the bedroom."

"Do you have condoms?" He nodded and turned to lead them into his bedroom. Like the living room it was tastefully decorated, orderly, and neat.

"I can't believe I'm doing this," Jan said.

"Me either," Doug countered.

This exchange as panties joined boxers, jeans, and tops in a pile by the bed, the room lit only by the light cast off from the living room lamp and the glow of the streetlight through the partially opened blinds.

Jan climbed into the bed.

Doug followed. "You move fast, girl. I didn't even get a chance to really check you out."

"That was the plan."

"I know you're not self-conscious about all that juicy you're rocking. Girl, don't believe the hype they're selling on TV and in those magazines. Skinny girls are cool and all, but a sistah with some fatback will make a man like me lose his absolute mind."

Jan giggled.

"You think I'm lying?"

"No, I just never thought my being compared to fatback would make me smile."

"Come here, you." He pulled her to him so they were completely skin-to-skin, ran his hand down her middle, and stroked the top of her paradise. "I've got something else to make that smile grow."

Jan reached for Doug's dick. It was shorter than she'd imagined, but thick and curved. She wrapped her fingers around it and pulled gently, ran her fingers up and down its length, and caressed his sac. "My smile isn't the only thing that's growing," she said.

In answer Doug rolled on top of her and seared her with another kiss. He ground his hips against hers, the evidence of his excitement pressed against her stomach. She ran her hands down his back and squeezed his butt. She liked that he, too, had a little extra cushion for the pushing, which she was ready to get under way. She bent and spread her legs, hoping he'd get the message.

He did.

Breaking the kiss, he slid his tongue down her

neck, nipping and kissing the skin between there and the pillows he loved so much. He lavished each nipple once again before continuing on down her stomach and lower, to her heat. While licking the rectangular patch of hair at the top of her flower, he slid a finger down its seam and slipped it inside.

Jan squirmed, her head tossing this way and that against the pillow. It had been so long. Doug felt so good. She felt a blast of air as he parted her folds and exposed her love button. He taunted and teased it before imparting the most delicious of nether French kisses. Out of control, she swirled her hips beneath the onslaught of lovemaking, grabbed the sheets, and tried not to scream. But as he continued his relentless sucking and licking, she couldn't contain the enthusiasm from the melody Doug's tongue played on her pussy. Her mewling started low and built in volume as an orgasm began at the core of her soul and spread through her body.

"Oh, my goodness! Oh, my goodness! Doug!" she exclaimed before a mind-blowing climax sent her tumbling into an erotic abyss. Just when she thought she'd lose her mind completely, she felt Doug's encore touch the tip of her instrument, felt her walls stretch and invite him in. He quickly set up a rhythm and she just as quickly caught on and matched him note for sensuous note. A one-orgasm woman all her life, she was determined to give him equal pleasure. No one was more surprised than her when the tip of his curved shaft hit her seldom touched G-spot and sent her hurtling over the edge again. It happened once more before Doug directed her to her knees and went in from behind. He placed a hand on each generous hip, rubbed the baby-soft skin beneath his fingers as he stroked the hot, wet flesh around his shaft. Over and over he twisted his hips, tapping her spot and making her already satiated body shiver with each swivel, each thrust, each knead of her cheeks. Until finally he clasped her hips and increased the pace. With a quick intake of breath and a "damn, yeah, damn" chant, he, too, went over the edge.

It was several moments into the silence and their cuddling when he told her, "Girl, that's the best dessert this brother has ever had."

She yawned, already nearly asleep. "Me too."

The next morning, Jan awoke to Doug eyeing her intently. It was kind of freaky and kind of nice at the same time.

"What's the matter?"

"Nothing. Just watching you sleep. You have a cute snore."

Jan sat up. "I do *not* snore."

"Not when you're awake. But when you're sleeping, like a minute ago, you put 'em down, baby. I gave you quite a workout last night, ended that drought. It's understandable you'd sleep deeply. No need to feel shame."

"I can't even respond to that."

"Truth stands on its own."

"Whatever. I know I don't snore."

"I'll record you next time."

"That sure of yourself are you?"

"What? That you snore?"

"No, that there will be a next time."

"That was just a figure of speech, Jan Baker. I enjoyed myself last night." He sat up beside her, waited for a response but got none. "What about you?"

"Earlier I was trying to remember the last time I'd felt the way I did last night." She looked at him. "I don't think it's ever happened. And I know I never had so many orgasms before." She looked at him. "I probably shouldn't have told you that. You already think you're the man."

Instead of a sarcastic comeback he was surprisingly tender. He ran a finger down her arm and gazed at her sincerely. "Nothing wrong with admitting that you had a good time, and that I pleased you. It's good to hear that. I think that sometimes women take it for granted that a man is confident and sure of himself and his skills. I understand that part of that comes from the swagger suit that we wear to protect ourselves against the world. That's why we don't always say it, but we brothers are sometimes just as vulnerable and unsure of ourselves as you women are. So it's good to hear you say . . . that you liked dessert."

Jan gazed at Doug intently before reaching for a pillow and positioning it behind her back. "I liked it a lot." She glanced at him before looking away. "I liked spending time with you. There was something about it that was easy and comfortable . . . like it wasn't our first time. I wasn't nervous or self-conscious. Okay, at first I was. But not after everything started. I just gave in to the moment. That's unusual for me."

Doug relaxed next to her, began intertwining his fingers with hers. "It turns out I was right about you. Your first day on the job, when you checked Joey who was trying to flirt, I saw that fire and figured there was a flame somewhere beneath that cool, conservative façade."

"You've used conservative before to describe me, but I've never seen myself that way."

"Maybe that's not the right word. More like reserved."

"That's my personality."

"I get that now."

"So we've broken our own rules and become a part of the post office player club. What happens now?"

He shrugged. "Go take a shower, maybe grab some food, come back and watch the game—"

She bopped him with a pillow. "I don't mean right this minute. I mean going forward, you and me."

"Oh." He tried to look innocent, but there was no missing the spark of humor in his eye. "Why don't we just . . . let it unfold and see what happens?"

"That's such a Doug answer. Oh my God. How do you live like that? Not knowing what was going to happen or what I was going to do from day to day or week to week would drive me crazy!"

"See, and all that planning and organizing and trying to figure out every detail would raise my blood pressure."

"Well, aren't we compatible."

"In at least one way we are." He ran a hand down her thigh. Goose bumps arose in its wake. "Very much so."

"Let me ask it this way, then. Are you seeing other women, and will you continue to be with them? I realize these are questions I probably should have asked last night."

He furrowed his brow in thought, then began to count on his fingers. "Let's see, there's Debbie, Sue, Wanda, Paula . . ." Jan's brow furrowed, too. "Felicia, Tanisha, LaQuisha . . ."

He glanced at her. "You're lying." She relaxed. A little. Until he laughed. "Why are you always playing? Ooh, you get on my nerves!"

"That's why it's so fun to mess with you. Jan, I'm not running around with a bunch of women. And I don't have anything serious going on. So as long as you let me squeeze that plump rump and rest on your"—he flicked her nipple; she playfully recoiled—"pillows, I would have no problem being exclusive with you."

Jan sat up, covered herself with the sheet. "This was not in my plans."

"That may be a good thing."

"I didn't plan to date anybody at all and definitely not someone who worked with me at the post office." She looked at him. "I don't want anyone there to know about us. I don't want to be part of the postal gossip mill, a character in the Normandie soap opera."

"It's a bit too late for that. Baby, we don't have to say a word and I'm telling you, people are going to know."

"How?"

He chuckled. "I don't know. Maybe it's something in the water over there, but somehow it always comes out. There are eyes everywhere, ears everywhere. I walk by. You look at me and lick your lips and—"

"That's not going to happen! I mean it, Doug. At work we have to act like professionals."

"I'm just saying, when you're feeling somebody and you're with them eight, nine hours a day. It's hard for that not to show."

"I don't want to catch feelings. . . ."

He placed a finger beneath her chin and turned her face to him. "You've already caught feelings. You don't want to get hurt. I don't either. That's why I don't want to try and define or try and lay out what this is, to set up expectations. I'm feeling you. You're feeling me. Let's just keep feeling and see what happens." He held out his palm. "Okay?"

She placed her hand in his and nodded.

"Now"—he reached for the sheet and began pulling it down—"let's lose this. You've got a few more things I want to feel. . . ."

23

The following week, work was different. Life was different. Jan felt different. She wasn't a virgin, so the change wasn't just about having sex with Doug. It was about connecting to a man in a way that she never thought she could. After leaving Doug, she'd thought about the other guys she'd dated and what it was about him and what they'd shared that was different from those other guys. Two words kept coming to her: caring and trust. Doug cared about her feelings and about whether or not she was satisfied. He asked questions and put her feelings first. The result was not only a heightened physical experience but a deeper emotional one as well. Maybe this is why she felt she could trust him. He'd been honest and up front. He'd been a man of his word, even before they were intimate. The space in her heart where the feelings for him were stored was getting larger. She worked hard not to let it show on her face, but from Pat's comment when she showed up to work Monday afternoon, she was only partly successful.

"Looks like somebody had a good weekend."

"Why do you say that?"

"I don't know," Pat said, noticing her from the corner of her eye. "You seem more relaxed this morning. Not that you normally look uptight. But you don't look as wound up as usual."

"Maybe I'm not," Jan replied, careful to keep from making direct eye contact. Instead she rearranged the stamps labeled first class, media mail, fragile, etc. "I didn't have a show this weekend, though, so I did get more rest."

"Remember to let me know about the next one."

"It's this weekend, at Breeze."

"On Friday or Saturday?"

"Friday night. First show starts at nine, second one at eleven."

"Good, because I'm supposed to be babysitting on Saturday. That's something I said I'd never do once my kids got grown. But a grandbaby changes you. Makes it possible to spoil a child like crazy and then send his whiny butt home!"

"Good afternoon, ladies." Doug came from the back to the customer side of the front counter and faced them.

Jan and Pat responded.

"It's obviously good for you," Pat said. "What did the two of you do, breathe the same air on the way to work or something?" Jan kept her face blank as

Doug looked her way. "I told Jan she looked more relaxed today and then you come in here sounding all chipper."

"Pat, stop trying to start something," Doug countered. "I always sound like this. I'm a happy person. When you look the word up in the dictionary you see my picture."

Pat's comeback was interrupted as customers entered. Doug went to the back while Jan and Pat handled several transactions. As soon as the lobby was empty, Pat leaned toward Jan with a knowing look in her eyes.

"Pat, why are you looking at me that way?"

"Because I've been doing this a long time." She kept her voice low. "And I know when I'm looking at two people who are digging each other."

Jan looked around before crossing her arms in a huff. "Doug said we wouldn't be able to keep this a secret."

"Why would you want to? Honey, I'd be putting everybody on notice. There's at least one person who most definitely needs to get the memo, the text message, and a letter delivered by U.S. mail. The one that reads 'hands off.'"

Jan gave Pat a doubtful look. "You think her knowing about anything will matter?"

"Probably not."

Jan no longer looked so relaxed. "Don't say anything, okay?"

"I won't say a word. But you should."

Fortunately for Jan, she got through the rest of
the day without being interrogated. Joey was talka-
tive, as usual, Melissa was her usual sarcastic self,
and everyone else treated her cordial as always.
Thanksgiving was two weeks away, yet the day's customer flow had been light enough for Jan to leave
work on time and head straight to On That Note.
There were only four slots left. Both Doug and
Rome tried to get her not to worry, kept saying
there was no way she wouldn't be selected. But considering who he'd chosen already, Jan wasn't too
sure. Maybe after she performed she'd have a word
with Nick, try to get a feel for how he's feeling
about her. And to maybe lay some of her cards on
the table. Not that it would help, but she wanted
him to know that unlike some of these other performers, for her this wasn't about being famous.
Or getting on TV. It was about using her gift to
change a bunch of lives. She wanted to tell him
about her brother, and how she'd use her good
fortune to try to help the community. One of the
first places she'd donate to was H.E.L.P. In other
words, she wanted Starr to look at her and see a
whole person, not just another singer. Last week,
a guy won. Jan couldn't be mad. She knew about
the man who reminded her of a young Brad Pitt
but surprised everyone by sounding like Smokey
Robinson. She also had no doubt that him in the
reality house, surrounded by at least five females,
would make for good TV. Good move for Starr, but

it made her nervous. There were only four slots left. She really wanted one of them to be hers.

Still, when it was her time to go on, Jan felt good. Doug's compliments about her body had made her think about her style, how to highlight her attributes and disguise the more challenging parts. Yesterday, she'd gone shopping and found a simple black jumpsuit that was perfect. It accented her generous cleavage, cinched her waist, and had pleats that covered her lower abdomen and were slenderizing to her hips. She was singing Beyoncé's "Halo" and knew she'd rock it. And she did.

When Starr took the stage to announce the latest winner, there was an uproar. Audience members were screaming the names of their favorites, Jan's among them. She stood by the bar, next to the bartender, who felt she'd won hands down.

"This is your night, Jan! If he doesn't give you the win, these folks are liable to tear this place down!"

After a few seconds, Starr quieted the crowd. "Wow, these performers did their thing tonight!" Cheering resumed. He put up his hands. "I must say the two standouts were Ms. NeoSoul from New York, Misty Fox!" A loud roar went up for the blond soul singer. "And homegrown California native . . . Jan Baker!" An even louder cheer rocked the rafters. The bartender squeezed Jan's shoulder and gave her a confident wink. Jan began to believe.

"This is going to be tough, one of the toughest decisions yet. In fact, the only reason I am able to make it at all is because there will still be three slots available. Oh, man." Starr teased the crowd by prolonging his decision. She watched his professionalism in working the crowd, building up the anticipation, ensuring high ratings.

"I've got to pick one. They both are amazing! But tonight, the next person with Starr power is . . . Misty Vox!"

A lot of cheers, and a few boos, erupted. "Come back next week, Jan!" Starr shouted. "There's still room for you."

Jan didn't get to talk with Starr. She heard he went from the stage straight to his car. She also heard that Misty went with him. She'd be lying if she said she wasn't disappointed. But he'd told her to come back next week. That there were slots left. Her dream was one week closer to coming true.

24

The sting of getting so close to a spot on *Starr Power* but not getting chosen was made a little easier the next day when she was on her way to work and Thump called.

"Baby girl, I hope that gig is still available."

"Since it's taken you over a week to get back with me, I hope so, too."

"That's how long it took for me to reach all these hardheads and get a firm commitment. I wanted to make sure everybody was onboard before accepting the gig. It sounds like the kind that can lead to more if handled correctly. Believe me when I say I'm just as hungry as you."

"I know. Sorry about snapping at you."

"I ran into Rome last night. He told me about what's been going on over there in the Valley. That punk Starr jerking you around. I told you not to mess with him, or get involved with that Hollywood scene. All that glitters ain't gold, baby. And what looks like diamonds can turn out to be broken glass, the kind that cuts deep."

Jan didn't respond to these comments. Neither one of them was going to change their mind, so what was the use? Though he looked twenty years younger, Thump was almost sixty years old. Had been in the game since he was a teen and had been burned more than twice, including by a record company that stole his music and his money. So around him, Hollywood and music industry were curse words.

"I need to give Cynthia a call and let her know everything's a go and get you two in touch with each other."

"For what?"

"To negotiate the contract."

"Me? Baby girl, you secured this gig. It's your world, I'm just a squirrel trying to get a nut."

"But it's your band."

"Look, you'd better listen to old school and learn how the game is played. Always put yourself first. You get the gig, you handle the deal and the money. Capiche?"

"All right, Thump. How soon can we start rehearsals?"

"Tomorrow."

"That's what I'm talking about. We'll need to learn a lot of new cuts, especially Christmas songs. A lot of influential people can show up to this, so I want us to be on point!"

"You handle your business and I guaran-darn-tee you I'll handle mine."

Jan hung up from Thump and immediately called Cynthia. Two days later she was sitting at a restaurant, going over the details and laying out her terms so the contract could be drawn up. Doug was with her and while she'd told herself it would just make meeting with Cynthia more comfortable, the truth was having him by her side increased her comfort and her confidence. He wasn't familiar with the music industry, but Doug had good common sense and an innate sense for business. She believed her connection to Cynthia's brother-in-law got her and the band members a little more of the budget than would have happened without the family tie. So she was grateful.

She was not only thankful for the gig, but for the rehearsals it required. Throwing herself into them caused her to almost forget about what lay on the line these next few Monday nights. The first rehearsals went smoothly; everyone's song ideas spot-on. Between the rehearsals, the post office, and nights at Doug's place, Jan's head was spinning. But her heart felt good. By the time the following Monday rolled around, she'd forgotten about how badly she'd felt at losing to Misty and again walked into On That Note believing that when all was said and done she'd be the one to beat.

* * *

Maybe he should have told her he was coming instead of planning a surprise. This was Doug's thought as he maneuvered through the packed hallway and main floor of the club, looking for Jan. She'd told him the venue was normally crowded, but he wasn't expecting wall-to-wall humanity. In less than ten minutes he'd had his foot stepped on, a drink splashed on his sleeve, and his butt pinched by a stranger. Now he was almost back to the front of the club, where he'd began, and he still hadn't seen her. When the MC/comedian took the stage and began quieting the lively crowd he temporarily gave up the search, ordered a ginger ale, and claimed a piece of wall near the back by the bar, where he could see most of the room, the stage, and hopefully Jan at some point. If she was here and everything happened the way she thought it would happen, to experience it with her would make it all worth it.

Taking in his surroundings, Doug realized how long it had been since he'd been to a club like this. Outside of Breeze and the Ace Imperials Motorcycle Club, it had been years. He'd never been much of a clubgoer. It had always felt too much like a meat market or fashion show. In that sense, not much had changed. He observed the pretty girls—many with high heels, short dresses, and long weaves—chatting and laughing together while surreptitiously checking to see if anybody noticed. Men trying to look like ballers. Everyone trying to look important. Except for Jan. He saw her now. Naturally pretty, dressed in black leggings, an oversized sweater, and knee-high boots, she walked over to where a group surrounded someone sitting at a table. He started to walk over there, thought about it, and decided to not bother her until after she performed.

That would be a while. Doug stood through several mediocre singers before someone finally got up from a stool at the bar. Once seated, he heard a dark-skinned beauty who wasn't bad, a Latina girl who sounded like Macy Gray on a good day, and a guy who held his own singing The Weeknd's "Earned It." Doug sat back and tried to look at each artist objectively, as a producer or scout looking for talent might. He noticed how a girl might not have the best voice but had the look. Or another had the voice but no personality. Some contained their nerves while others let theirs get away. He took mental notes. Maybe something he noticed could be helpful to Jan.

When she took the stage, Doug immediately recognized two things. One, she didn't have the same swagger as when she performed at Breeze. She appeared more tentative. Less relaxed. Two, she was easily the best singer in the room. Her rendition of Alicia Keys's "Girl on Fire" was flawless, but he preferred the attitude she showed when she sang about her "bass."

Once her performance was over, the crowd was appreciative. But they'd given equal cheers for some of the less-talented, more beautiful singers.

The MC came up and announced a fifteen-minute break. Doug headed toward Jan, followed her eyes as she walked off the stage, and looked over to Starr's table. She waved. Starr gave her a thumbs-up. By then Doug was two feet away. He reached for her arm just as she was about to go down a hall.

She started, ready to jerk her arm away before seeing his face. "Doug? What are you doing here?"

"Checking out the talent, same as everybody else."

"Well, of course, but, I mean, where'd you come from? How long have you been here?"

"Long enough to see you do your thing just now! I got here just before the comedian came on. I looked around for you but didn't see you until the show had already started."

"You didn't tell me you were coming."

"I know. I wanted to make it a surprise."

"You did that."

"Are you mad?"

"Why would I be mad?"

"Don't ask me to try and explain your moods."

She gave him a look. "No, I'm not mad." Then she surprised him with a public kiss on the lips. "In fact, I'm glad you're here."

Doug nodded but was distracted by a stunning brunette walking over to the far table, where Nick Starr sat. "Are they around him like that every week?"

Jan turned in the direction Doug looked. "No, every week the group gets bigger. And so do the boobs. Grab us two seats at the bar if you can. I need to use the restroom. Be right back."

When she returned, there was a ginger ale in front of Doug and a glass of chardonnay in front of the empty stool Jan took. "Thank you."

"Your guy hooked us up."

"You've already met Rome?" She met the friendly bartender's eye. He smiled, nodded a hello, and kept on working.

"Yeah, cool dude. He had all kinds of praise for you. A little too much in my opinion. Might have to check him."

"I thought we were just going to let it flow and see what happened?"

"And that's exactly what I'll be doing when he looks at you the wrong way and I punch him in the face. Showing you what's happening."

"Ha!"

He held up his ginger ale. They toasted.

"This is crazy!"

Jan nodded as she waved at one of the other contestants still in the hunt. "Yes, it's pretty wild."

"If this is show business, I want no part of it. I'm glad you're who you are and can win on your talent. Not that you aren't holding your own in that casual chic kind of way you told me you rolled, but you bring way more than physical attributes to the table." She smiled but said nothing. "What, you don't believe me?"

"I believe that the compliment is sincere, but I'm not totally convinced that it's true."

"What, you don't think you look good?"

"Doug, I was probably in high school before

anybody other than my mother called me pretty. I
was teased, mostly about my weight, and put down
by boys and girls. Boys didn't ask if I wanted to be
their girlfriend and later, in high school, didn't ask
me out. I was the sideline chick, which is almost
worse than the side chick because at least the side
chick gets positive attention sometimes even though
she's sharing. The sideline chick is invisible, watching other girls be admired and desired. So while
I've worked hard to feel good about myself and see
myself pretty, there is a part of me that will probably always be the little fat girl picked last at recess."

"I can't say that I know how you feel. . . ."

"What? You've never been a little fat girl?"

"Not a day in my life. But you know what I've
observed?"

"What?"

"That the little girls who get picked on the most
usually go the farthest."

The MC walked back on the stage to announce
the next contestant. Jan looked at Doug. "After this
set is over, we'll hopefully see this little fat girl go
further in this competition."

"I hope you do, but it doesn't matter. You already
have star power."

When Starr took the stage and announced the
night's winner, Doug was even happier he'd come.
Instead of Jan, the winner was the handsome,
charismatic, and talented guy who'd performed,
and only the second male so far who'd made the
cut. His friend needed his support. At first he

didn't say anything, and neither did she. Didn't have to. Everyone around her voiced their disapproval of Starr's choice and their strong feelings that she deserved a spot.

In between people walking up to say she was their favorite, he leaned in, and whispered, "Don't let it depress you, babe. Stay positive, okay?"

"I'm trying."

From the bartender's expression he was shocked, angry, and hurt for his friend. Suddenly, his expression changed. He walked over. "Jan, I think I know what's going on."

"You're the only one. You and Starr."

"That's what I'm talking about. Starr knows he's going to choose you and is just building up the hype. Look how people are reacting because they think he's not going to choose you. Imagine how they'll be when he does, and how many more will tune in to make sure that you win. I know it's hard for you right now, but from a business perspective . . . that's genius!"

Doug listened as attentively as Jan. Maybe not for the same reasons. He looked at her. "Babe, that does make sense."

"If that's true, why doesn't he tell me?"

"Because he needs your authentic reaction. The people need to see your face drop like it did just now so they can come build you up. The world loves an underdog. You'll be the last one he chooses. Watch."

What her friend and supporter said made a lot

of sense, making Jan's steps a little lighter when she and Doug left a few minutes later. He could tell by the way she interacted with fans as they walked out, and even more so by how she openly flirted with him, which for Ms. Private was an uncommon move that Rome's words had helped change her attitude. He walked her to her car, she drove him a block to his SUV, and as soon as they neared the highway onramp, he called her.

"You're feeling better?"

"I've decided to look at this in a positive way. I haven't been selected. But I haven't been one of those cut either. I'm going to try and focus on that."

"Good idea, baby. Attitude is everything. Instead of seeing each week as a fail, it can be viewed as a performance that's brought you one week closer to your being on TV and getting that contract."

"So you really think I can do it, huh? Get on *Starr Power*? And win it all?"

"Baby, stick with me and the sky is the limit."

Normally Jan would have had a snappy comeback, or a put down. But it had felt good to talk with Doug, to feel his support and even hear his possessiveness. So instead of a comment, she suggested they meet at his house.

Because when it came to Doug and the sky being the limit . . . he just might be right.

25

The next day, Doug approached Jan at her locker. "Hey, you're early."

"Yeah, the errand I ran before work didn't take as long as I thought it would."

"Then can you walk with me to the store? I need to holler at you for a minute."

Jan looked over and noticed Melissa staring at Doug's mouth like she was counting teeth. Turning her back to her, Jan lowered her voice. "Don't look, but Ms. Messy is reading your lips. Maybe you should just call."

"Maybe you should stop being so concerned with what others think about you. We're going to the store. I want a Coke and you want orange juice. Or maybe just exercise. What's the big deal?"

"You're right." She reached for the purse she'd just placed in the locker. "Let's go."

She felt all eyes on them as they exited the building. "I can just about imagine what Melissa is saying right now."

"She's telling lies and spreading rumors. Why do you care?"

He reached for her hand. She jerked it back. "Stop."

"Why? You weren't acting like this last night."

"I wasn't at work last night."

"As far as everyone's concerned, we're screwing anyway."

"Well, now that makes me feel all better."

He laughed and reached for her hand again. She swatted his hand away and sped up. He easily caught up with her. "I can think of worse things to be said about us than that we're dating."

"We're not dating."

"Okay. Effing, then."

She gasped and punched him. "What? I can't say making love because you obviously don't love me. If you did, you wouldn't feel the need to hide that we're friends."

"Is this what you wanted to talk to me about?"

"No, I talked to Cynthia this morning. She said she hadn't heard from you about Lionel."

"I thought you talked to him?"

"I did."

"And?"

"He hadn't decided whether or not he wanted to participate. Said he was going to talk to you about it and then honestly I forgot to ask you about his final decision."

"I'll talk to him tonight."

"Cool, and then have him call me. The winter

league starts in January and I believe they play Saturday afternoons."

"Every Saturday?"

"I'm not sure."

"I don't know if I can commit to transporting him every week, especially on the days I have a show."

"Don't worry about it. Coach and I will work something out."

They reached the corner where a group of rowdy teens were teasing each other, using foul language.

"Hey! Don't y'all see that there's a lady present?" He spoke firmly, but his voice held no malice.

The tall, skinny one nearest him answered, "So what?"

"So you should watch your language. It's called respect, youngblood."

"Man, I don't have to listen to you. You ain't my daddy!"

"No, I'm not. But I'm a man who cares about how you appear to the world. I want you to come off as smart and cool as you think you are. But not everybody is capable of pulling that off so"—he shrugged as the light changed and they started crossing the street—"forgive my thinking you were one of the strong ones. You look like one, though."

"Are you crazy?" Jan muttered under her voice. "You don't speak to teenagers these days. He could have had a gun and shot both of us!"

He looked at her, and solemnly replied, "The day I become afraid of the kids in my community is the day I move out." He looked at her from the corner of his eye. "You need to stop being afraid of your coworkers."

"I'm not afraid of anybody."

"Good. So the next time you walk by me and I'm tempted to pinch that juicy booty it won't be a problem."

"You can try it. But I might pinch back."

They returned to work. Melissa smirked at them but said nothing, partly because of the warning look in Doug's eyes.

That night after work, Jan had barely left Doug in the parking lot before he was ringing her cell.

"Are you out of gas?" she joked.

"I don't want to hide us."

"Huh?"

"I don't want to hide the fact that we're seeing each other, or feel like I have to watch myself around you."

"Doug, you knew when this started that I wanted it kept private."

"We don't always get what we want, and in those moments we have to figure out how to make that work to our advantage."

"What brought on this change of position? I remember a guy who wasn't going to date anybody he worked with."

"Yeah, but you don't remember a brother who was gonna hide it if that happened."

She sighed and hit the brakes as she neared a stoplight.

"What are you afraid of?"

"I'm not. I just don't like people—"

"In your business. Girl, people are going to think they're in your business whether they actually are or not. So trying to keep them out of it is basically a waste of time."

"In your opinion."

"Yes, in my always right opinion." The comment didn't get the response he expected. It got none at all. "I know the problem. You feel some kind of way because of Melissa. If I hadn't slept with anybody at the office, would you still feel so opposed to people knowing we're together?"

"I don't know. Probably."

"Let me ask you something. How would you feel if I was going hard to keep you quiet, telling you I didn't want anyone to know about us? I'll tell you how you'd feel. Hurt. Angry and suspicious, thinking that since I was trying to hide you there must be other things I was trying to hide."

"You think I'm trying to hide something?"

"Or someone."

"You can't be serious. You think I'm seeing someone else?"

"It's not impossible."

"Doug, that's ridiculous and I'm going to act like you didn't say it."

"So if six months from now you decide we'll go

public and then I say no, let's not, you'll be okay."
Silence. "Hello?"

"I'm thinking."

Several seconds went by. And then several more.

"Um, you want to call me back when you have an answer?"

Even with time to think about it, Jan wasn't sure she'd have one. And remembering Pat's earlier comment didn't help. It made her position sound totally crazy.

Doug Carter? That's a good man right there. If it were me, I'd be shouting it from the rooftops.

In that moment Jan decided that Pat was right. "No, you don't need to call me back. I've thought about it and I guess I don't care that everyone knows I turned you out."

"Ha! I don't care either. Because then they'll also know it was some Carter love that put that big-ass smile on your face."

"That's what this is really about. You want bragging rights."

"No, Jan Baker. I just want you."

26

It had been a busy and fast week and by the end of it, Jan felt good about the progress she'd made. Band rehearsals for the holiday party were going well. The contract, one of the more lucrative they'd received, had already been faxed over and signed. Cynthia had also given her the Web site for the basketball program for disabled athletics, along with the director's telephone number, information she'd passed on to Lionel. The end of the year was looking good, and only one thing would make it look better. Securing one of two spots left for *Starr Power*, Nick's reality show. One part of her said there was no way she wouldn't be one of those chosen. But the other part wasn't so sure.

"Good afternoon, Jan." Pat had been at lunch when Jan had arrived, and now joined her at the steadily busy counter. The holiday season had indeed arrived and with it all the residents within a five-mile radius, it seemed, mailing cards and packages to family and friends.

Jan handed a receipt and change to a customer. "Hello, Pat. How are you today?" She motioned for the next customer to come forward.

"Glad I'm on the downside of Friday."

"Do you have plans for the weekend?"

"Just shopping for the Thanksgiving dinner. I like to go before the stores get totally crazy and the shelves become bare. What about you?"

"I'm performing at Breeze again and wanted to invite you."

"On Friday, right?" Jan nodded. "I'd love to go, especially since I wasn't able to make it last month. What are the times again?"

"First set starts at nine, the second one around eleven."

"Ooh, eleven is almost past my bedtime. I'd definitely have to make the first show." The conversation paused as both women waited on customers. "Thanks for inviting me," she said when she'd finished the transaction. "I'm going to tell my daughter about it and see if she wants to come."

"Are you married, Pat?"

"Yes, but Lee doesn't do clubs, honey. He's not just a couch potato, he's a whole casserole."

The afternoon passed quickly. Soon, it was time to lock the front doors and head to the back to help process the next day's mail and set it up for the postmen's delivery routes.

"There's the superstar," is how Melissa greeted her. "I saw where your band is at Breeze this weekend."

"You're on the mailing list?"

"Yep." Melissa cleared her table and walked to her locker. She retrieved her purse and other personal items and stopped by Jan's table. "Can I ask you a question?"

"You can ask," Jan replied.

"Why are you here?"

"What do you mean?"

"Why are you working at a post office? If I could sing the way you do, there's no way I'd be caught at this boring job."

"There are a lot of people who can sing." Jan reached for another bundle of mail and placed it in the sorter.

"Yes, but not like you. I bet if you lost some weight—"

"Dang, Melissa!" said a coworker passing by.

"What? I'm not trying to be rude."

Joey, who was also preparing to go home, chimed in. "It sounded pretty rude."

"Look, superstars are skinny." She turned back to Jan. "If you lost weight and did something to your hair, maybe a weave instead of that wig you wear, you'd look more like what record companies want. Am I right?"

Jan was too stunned for words.

"I didn't mean to offend you. Are you offended?"

"Hell, I'm offended," Joey said.

Logically, she knew Melissa's words shouldn't bother her but emotionally, they hurt. Jan had never understood why women who looked like Melissa felt the need to degrade anyone else. They already had the looks, the men, the popularity. What did she gain by being humiliating? She tried to hide it from Doug, but the comments affected her mood for the rest of the day. When he suggested chicken and waffles after work, she thought the idea perfect. Nothing could make a person feel better than some good old comfort food.

Rather than go in separate cars, Jan followed Doug home. He parked his motorcycle and got in her car. They shared small talk until they'd been seated at the restaurant, placed their orders, and the waitress had brought their drinks.

Doug eyed her intently as he sipped his ginger ale. "When are you going to tell me?"

"Tell you what?"

"About Melissa's messy ass and what she said to you."

"Oh, that. I wasn't going to tell you and it looks like I don't have to. Who opened their big mouth?"

"It don't matter. Fact is, I know."

"Don't make a big deal of it, Doug. That only makes it worse."

"I don't care. She can't talk to you like that and I not say anything."

"I'm a big girl, okay. Let me handle my own battles."

"Okay, but she'd better not be saying anything like that when I'm around."

"What are you going to do, beat her up?"

"No, Willie Carter ensured that that wouldn't happen from a very young age."

"That's your dad?"

"Or drill sergeant, or slave master, depending on the day."

"He couldn't have been that bad."

"He was how he needed to be with all that testosterone in the house who not only taught us how we should treat women, but showed us in the way he treats our mom."

"You were lucky to grow up in a two-parent family."

"I know."

"With such a happy home life, you probably want a family?"

"Some days I do, some days I don't, depending on how my niece, nephew, and cousins behave. What about you?"

"I think so. I used to say no, just wanted to focus on my career. But seeing Crystal and Brent with their brood shows me the good side of having a family. So maybe one day."

"There is something I want for sure," he said once the waiter had brought out their plates and left.

"As soon as we handle this food, I want to go do what it takes to make a baby, how 'bout that?"

Jan took a second to enjoy her bite. "That sounds as good as this chicken tastes."

"Oh, it's going to be finger-lickin' good."

27

The next evening, Doug and Jan arrived early at the club. She went backstage to get dressed. He messed around on his cell phone. Periodically, he watched the door. A little before nine he saw Pat and a younger-looking version of her walk into the club. He stood to get their attention and waved them over.

"How are you, Pat?" He pulled out her chair, then turned to pull out the other woman's chair.

"I'm good," she replied. They sat. "Doug, this is my daughter, Lauren. Lauren, this is Doug Carter, the man I'd marry if I weren't already wed and the one I'd make you marry if you were still single."

They laughed. Lauren held out her hand. "Nice to meet you."

Doug shook her hand. "Likewise." He looked at Pat. "What are you ladies drinking?"

"Heck, this is the first time I've been in this club in over a decade. I'm going to celebrate by having a Long Island Iced Tea."

"Mom, are you sure?"

"I said this is the first time I've been in a while, not my first time ever. Of course I'm sure."

The waiter came over. Doug placed the order.

"What's with the ginger ale?" Pat asked once the waitress left the table. "You don't drink?"

Doug shook his head. "Me and alcohol don't get along."

"Is that code talk for you being a lightweight?"

"Pretty much."

They continued sharing small talk. Their drinks arrived. Pat held hers up. "To Jan, and a great show."

Lauren and Doug joined the toast. He took a sip of his ginger ale, frowned, and set it down.

"What? Too strong for you?" Pat teased.

"Not strong enough. Especially now."

"Why, what's the matter?"

"Trouble just walked in."

Pat turned around to see Melissa and three other women headed their way.

"Well, hello!" Melissa stopped at the table and rested her hand on Doug's shoulder. He shook it off. She laughed. "Why wasn't I invited to join this office party?"

"Obviously because we didn't want you here," Pat replied, not missing a beat.

"Ooh, Pat, animosity doesn't become you."

"It sure doesn't, but truth looks good."

"What about you, Doug? Don't want to share your girlfriend's talent with her coworkers?"

"Looks like you got here without my help."

"I live five minutes away; have been coming to this club for years. Can't say that I ever saw you here, though, until now."

"You're right. I had no reason to come until I heard Jan sing here."

"Uh-huh. I don't know why she tries to act so innocent. I knew from the way she looked at you the first day that the two of you would hook up."

"Why are you so interested in who Jan is and what she does or doesn't do?"

"Please. I'm just making conversation. I could care less what she does with my leftovers."

"Good. Then you and your friends can keep it moving. Have a good night."

"If you wanted to have one, you'd join us. Bye, Pat."

"Bye, Melissa."

Doug laughed. Lauren shook her head. "She still acts like that? What is her problem?"

"Oh, that's right. You've met Messy Mel."

"Unfortunately."

Doug looked at Pat. "Did you hear what she said to Jan the other day?"

"No, and I don't want to. It's Friday night, I'm at the club, and I don't want to bring the workplace in here. Let me head to Long Island and get this party started."

"You know what, Pat? That sounds like a plan."

By the time Jan took the stage Melissa's craziness had been forgotten. It seemed everyone was having a great time, Jan most of all. She laughed and joked with the crowd, comfortable in the place she'd regularly performed for almost a year. After starting the party with fast numbers by Janelle Monáe and P!nk, she turned up her sexy with Toni Braxton. For this number she sat on a stool, showed a little thigh, and popped her fingers as she sang to the beat. The audience did, too, and bobbed their heads. For the instrumental bridge, the band was locked in the pocket, every note perfect. Jan's eyes were closed, she was feeling the groove and thinking about her man when the mood was interrupted by a loud, sustained guffaw, followed by an equally loud comment. "Shut up. She's trying to be sexy!"

This sent all four ladies at the front table howling.

Jan's eyes had popped open with the first sound of laughter. Now they zeroed in on the source, Melissa and her gang. Another day, another time, this type of rudeness would have made her miserable. Tonight, after today, it only made her mad.

As the security guard went over to quiet them, she stood. "That's all right, Mr. G," she said in the same relaxed style she'd been singing the song, her fingers still popping, her mouth still smiling. "I got this. That's right, fellas, keep that groove. While I take something real ugly and handle it real smooth."

An appreciative mumble arose in the crowd. Melissa and her friends continued to smirk. The security guard stayed close.

"So this woman right here." Jan pointed at her. Melissa's smirk eased into a smile as people shifted to see her. "We work together during the day. She thinks I need to change my style, and tried to show me the way."

This brought a strong reaction, especially from the women in the crowd. "She told me I was fat!"

"No!"

"That I needed to lose weight."

"Oh no, she didn't!"

"Told me superstars are skinny. As y'all can see . . . that will never ever be my fate."

The audience laughed.

"She said instead of this wig, I needed to get a weave." She motioned for the band to stop, walked to the very tip of the stage, and looked directly at Melissa. "Whatever your opinion, I don't give a damn. You be you and let me be Jan."

She then turned, switched her ample booty back to the stool, and calmly sat down.

The crowd went crazy! Doug's shrill whistle could be heard over all. Those close to the foursome were jeering and motioning them toward the door. Still playing, Thump began a hip-hop chant. "She. Don't. Give a damn. You be you. She'll be Jan."

Melissa stood, her face indignant. But before she could get a word out, everybody in the club started chanting with Thump.

She. Don't. Give a damn. You be you. She'll be Jan!

Who knew that the "You're Makin' Me HIgh" music would provide the perfect rhythm for a public dis? Jan had made it work! Finally, the four had no choice but to get up and make their exit. Once gone, the crowd cheered Jan for a good two minutes as she effortlessly slid back into the original words and finished the song.

"Melissa really said all that?" Pat asked, wiping tears created from laughing too hard.

"I wasn't back there when this went down," Doug answered, smiling like a proud papa. "But according to Joey, she said even more."

"Wow!" Lauren's eyes were shining. "That had to be planned, right?"

Doug shook his head. "If you knew Jan, you'd know the answer is definitely not."

"So she made up those words now, just like that?"

"I guess so." Doug was still smiling, eyes only for Jan. "She told me she would handle it."

Pat looked at Jan admirably. "Well, handle it she did."

28

"Girl, you are gangster!"

It was thirty minutes after the club had closed. Pat and Lauren had left right after the last set, but not before Pat asked if she could get "Just Jan" for her iPod. Doug and Jan were walking to the parking lot.

"That's not a song." She said this, but her smile showed she wasn't displeased with the title.

"It should be! I still can't believe you called out Melissa like that? You shut her down!"

"I don't know. Just the way she was sitting there, all smug and rude and messing up my show. I just snapped."

Doug wrapped his arm around her waist and pulled her into him. "I hope you never snap on me." He kissed her temple.

"Then don't make me angry."

"My girl is a rapper!" He laughed loudly. "You didn't tell me you had skills, girl!"

"I still can't believe those words came out of me."

"You didn't even think about it, you were free-styling?"

"Is that what they call it?"

"Yes. You've got skills! See you're so talented you can do stuff you don't even know you can do." They reached his SUV. Before opening the door, he gave her a hug.

She hugged him back and didn't want to let go.

No need to worry. Doug moaned and pulled her closer, ran his hand down her back and over her butt.

Jan placed her hands beneath his jacket, began to rub his back, and abruptly stopped. "Doug."

"Yes, baby?"'

"Am I feeling what I think I'm feeling?"

"You're feeling how sexy I think you were on that stage tonight, and how turned on I am right now." He nibbled her ear and made her shiver. "Can you think of anything we can do about it?"

"Yes."

"What's that?"

"Go to your house?"

"What if I can't wait that long?"

She pulled back to look at him. "Then I can't help you because nothing is going to happen in this parking lot!"

"Aw, woman, where is your sense of adventure?"

She reached between his legs and squeezed. "It's right here."

Doug broke the law and made it to his house

in less than ten minutes. They got out of the car laughing, unsnapping, unbuttoning, and unzipping. While Doug unlocked his door, Jan pulled off her shoes. Just inside she shimmied out of her maxi dress and undid her bra. Doug slid off his shoes, ripped off his shirt, and kicked off his pants.

"Come here, girl, and give me some of that sugar. No, give me all of it."

He dropped to his knees and pulled down her panties. She yelped as his strong tongue parted her love-slick lips, grabbed a hold of his shoulders to prevent falling down. He reached behind her and squeezed her cheeks, pushing his tongue deeper into her heat. He sucked her nub with relentless precision, took a finger and played on her anal key.

"Doug, wait. I can't . . . I'm going to fall over."

He sat back on his haunches. "Well, get on down here then and take care of business."

Before Doug, Jan hadn't thought she was too into oral. But she hit the floor and pounced on that curved cock like a rock singer pounced on a microphone. With everything she had.

"Damn, baby, hold up! You want this to be over before it gets started?"

"You told me to handle it."

"Turn around," he hoarsely commanded, lovingly rubbing her butt as she complied. "I'm about to handle you."

The first orgasm came within five minutes. The second one when they moved from the floor to the couch. The last one when they entered the shower, and was so intense Jan probably woke the neighbors.

The next morning, Jan yawned, turned over, and jumped out of bed.

Doug opened an eye. "Babe! What's wrong?"

"I overslept."

"Jan, it's Sunday."

"I know. But Crystal and I are surprising the sisters and taking them to brunch."

"What sisters?"

"Her and my mom are sisters."

"Aw, that's sweet. I wanted us to go to brunch, but Mom trumps that plan. There is an invitation I have for you, though, that you can't turn down. Jan!"

"What? I'm getting in the shower!"

"I want your family to join mine for Thanksgiving." The shower turned on. Doug rolled out of bed and soon his wow was brushing her pow and Jan knew the shower would take a bit longer than anticipated. "Did you hear me?"

"Yes."

"So you're coming?"

"I'll have to ask Mom and Lionel. We usually go over to my aunt Brenda's, Crystal's mom."

"Babe, I want you to meet my family."

"I said I'd ask them."

"I'm asking you."

"Maybe we can do dinner at your house and dessert at my aunt's."

"No way."

"Why not?"

"My brother Marvin, he's a baker. When it comes to desserts, ain't nobody better." He ran a hand over her butt. "There might be something a little sweeter, though."

29

For once Jan was glad for Lionel's best friend, Bernard, being with them. Their arguing about which team would make the Super Bowl and why helped keep her mind off of how nervous she was to be meeting Doug's family. The last true boyfriend she had was three years ago and because his family lived in the South, she'd only met one, his sister, when she came to California for her birthday. Questions crowded her mind and fought for dominance. Would his family accept her? Would his mother be judgmental and overprotective of her son? Was the outfit she'd chosen—burnt orange stretch pants, a brightly colored, baby-doll style sweater brushing her thigh, heeled brown suede ankle boots—too dressy? Not dressy enough? Even though he'd told her she shouldn't bring anything, she'd fixed an appetizer. Would they like it?

They reached the Carter home in Inglewood.

"You can go on up, Jan," Bernard said. "I've got Lionel."

Jan looked at Lionel, who nodded his agreement. "Okay. Thanks, Bernard."

She took a calming breath and walked up the sidewalk. The noise from inside smacked her upside the face. To her right was a doorbell. She pushed it and prayed it was loud enough for someone inside to here.

A young man opened the door. "Hey, there, cutie. You here for me?"

Before she could answer, two big paws snatched him away from the door. "Go sit down, fool, before I have to deck you!" Doug looked at a slightly amused, slightly terrified Jan. "Come on in, Jan. Don't mind Barry. He's the youngest, and was raised by wolves."

"Mama!" Barry yelled. "Doug called you a dog!"

"Stop lying!"

"Yes, he did, Mama, I heard him!"

"Me too, Grandma!"

Jan watched a stout, apron-clad woman with short, curly hair come around the corner. The scene looked like the Red Sea parting as children and adults scampered out of her way. A formidable-looking woman wearing colorful stretch pants, a bright yellow top, and an apron touting Betty Boop came around the corner. She stopped when she saw Jan, looked her up and down. "Are you the one causing this ruckus?" She wore a fierce scowl, but her eyes were dancing.

Jan was too nervous to notice. She looked at Doug and then back at Liz. "Me, ma'am?"

"Aren't you the one I'm looking at or am I cross-eyed?"

Doug put an arm around Jan. "Mama . . ."

"You're about to get put out of my house," Liz said, advancing toward Doug with a pointed finger. "Calling your mama a bitch, and in front of company!"

Jan gasped.

"Mama!" Doug exclaimed, shock on his face.

"I'm a woman. If you called me a dog, then you called me a bitch." She looked at Jan. "Is this the kind of man you want to raise your children?"

The doorbell rang. Jan saw it was Bernard, having gotten Lionel out of the car and into his wheelchair. As relieved as she was to have some family backup, she was just as tempted to run out the door.

"I'm just messing with you, baby," Liz said. "Teasing . . . that's what we Carters do. I'm Doug's mama, Liz. You're Jan, right?"

Jan's relief almost made her swoon. "Yes, Jan Baker. It's nice to meet you."

"You too, honey." Liz looked behind her. "Who's that?"

"That's my brother, Lionel, and his friend, Bernard." Introductions were made all around. While Bernard and Lionel fell right into the football conversation taking place in the living room, Liz pulled Jan aside.

"What do you have there?"

"Just some appetizers. They're called soul rolls filled with smoked turkey, cabbage, carrots and spices, and some dipping sauces."

"Did you make them?"

"Yes, I was going to bake a cake, but I heard there's a professional baker in the family."

"Yes, I am, but I have a son named Marvin who thinks that's his title."

Jan laughed and relaxed a bit more. It was clear that Doug was Liz Carter's son.

"Come on back while I take a look at these. Soul rolls, huh?"

"Yes, made just like spring rolls but with soul food ingredients."

Liz reached the kitchen and set the container on the counter. She removed the lid and took a whiff. "Ooh, these smell good. So you can cook, huh? Never mind, one look at that Carter catcher and I know you can throw down."

"The Carter . . . what, ma'am?"

"That big ass you're working with, child. I got one, so I know. It'll catch them every time. Can I taste one of these? I have to make sure they taste like something before I feed them to my family."

"Sure." Trying to keep up with Liz subject-hopping had Jan flustered, but she liked her. "Oh, those smaller containers are the dipping sauce—barbeque, honey mustard, and ranch."

Jan watched as Liz spooned some of the bar-beque sauce on a roll and took a hearty bite. She watched, waited, and finally asked, "What do you think?"

Liz finished the bite and reached for a dish towel to wipe her hands. "I think you and I are going to get along just fine."

"Mama!" Doug came into the kitchen. "What are you doing, putting my girl to work? She's a guest."

"There's no such thing in the Carter house. You're either family or foe."

"What are these?" Doug spotted the soul rolls, picked one up, and took a bite.

"They are for later," Liz said, placing the lid back on the rolls and taking them to a large table to join other covered dishes.

"Um, those are good. When did you make them?"

"Jan made those."

He looked at her. "You did? Dang, girl, I didn't know you could cook."

"Um-huh," Liz shook her head. "Somebody has been spending more time in the bedroom than in the kitchen."

Before Jan could be embarrassed, more of Doug's family came into the kitchen including Marvin, the brother who worked as a cook and was the family's self-proclaimed baker, Nelson, the middle brother, and two of their cousins along with their dates. Liz shooed out the men and organized the women to help transport the containers of food to the backyard where a rectangular, tablecloth-covered table was set between two round tables. There was also a smaller table for the little ones. By the time everyone arrived and had gathered out back, there were nineteen happy, hungry people ready to give thanks.

After a one-sentence blessing delivered by Doug's father, Willie, with a demeanor Jan felt was more like her, an organized chaos ensued. Plates were filled, drinks were poured, children laughed, and everyone seemed to be talking. Names and faces became a blur as everyone spoke to Jan and made her feel welcome. Doug's happy-go-lucky personality began to make sense. Growing up in this type of household, who wouldn't be?

"Jan, sit here!" Cynthia waved her over to one of the round tables. Jan walked over. "Have you met Ava, Doug's sister?"

"Yes, a little earlier. And . . . I think your daughter?"

"Yes, Leah. That's pretty good after meeting a backyard full of people."

"This is a large family."

"Over here, Dougie Fresh!" Ava yelled for her brother.

"Dougie?" Jan smiled broadly.

"Oh, oh." Ava put a hand to her mouth. "Oops. You're going to have fun with that one!"

"Is it just you and your brother, Jan?" Cynthia asked.

"Yes, and my mom, who's over to her sister's house, my aunt. My aunt only had one child, my cousin Crystal, and I have an uncle who lives on the East Coast."

Doug sat down. After joking with him a moment

Ava returned her attention to Jan. "I really enjoyed you the night I came to Breeze. You have a beautiful voice."

"Thank you."

"Jan will be singing at our holiday party," Cynthia said.

"Oh, really? Very nice."

"Jan's a songwriter, too," Doug said.

Jan gave him a side eye. "Not really."

"Yes, she is! She wrote a song called 'Just Jan' and sang it last weekend." He regaled the table with a spirited recapping of Jan's handling of Melissa at the club.

Ava high-fived her as others who'd joined them congratulated her courage.

"I love that message," Cynthia added. "Is that really a song?"

"No."

"It should be. So many of our kids are bullied and made to feel bad if they don't look or act or talk a certain way. There's so much pressure to conform and not enough encouragement to be uniquely whoever you are. Really, Jan. You should turn that into a real song and sing it at the party. Then I'd incorporate it into our program as one of the behavioral modification tools."

"Are you serious?" Jan asked.

"Absolutely."

Jan shrugged. "I could give it a shot."

"Don't worry, sis," Doug said to Cynthia. "I'll help her out."

"Please don't," Ava deadpanned.

They didn't make it to the aunt's for dessert. Instead the family fun and teasing went well into the night. Regarding his brother Marvin's baking skills, Doug had not exaggerated. Jan ate the most decadent pecan pie ever and the lightest, fluffiest, most flavorful slice of sweet potato pie she'd ever tasted in her life.

Lionel stayed the entire time and had just as much fun. Ava's daughter's boyfriend was around the same age. They and a couple cousins bonded in a den that held a sixty-inch TV screen and multiple video game consoles.

All in all, it had pretty much been the best Thanksgiving Jan ever had. Later, chocolate syrup and whipped cream were some of the props that she used to show Doug her gratitude.

30

As promised, the next Saturday Doug went over to Jan's so he could spend time with Lionel. He looked forward to their outing. Aside from the motorcycle gang, whose hanging out was usually on the road or at their club, Doug only hung out with his brothers.

"Where are you guys going?" Jan asked, after answering the doorbell and greeting Doug with a hug.

"That's for us to know and you not to find out," Doug replied.

Lionel entered the living room. "It's man business."

Rochelle came into the living room. "Hello, Doug."

"Hello, Ms. Baker. How are you doing?"

"I'm fine. Glad to have the weekend off. Please thank your mother again for that Thanksgiving spread she sent over. Everything was delicious and after forgetting to bring leftovers home from my sister's house, right on time."

"I sure will, Ms. Baker. Next time I hope you'll join us."

"Perhaps I will. I also want to thank you for what you're doing for Lionel. It is very thoughtful of you."

"No thanks necessary. It just so happened that my sister-in-law's colleague directs the program I'm taking him to check out today. I'm happy to do it."

"Well, I thank you nonetheless."

"Yeah, yeah, yeah, enough of that yapping." Rochelle frowned. Lionel laughed and rolled over to her for a kiss. "We're out, Ma. Sis. See y'all later."

Since the van was retrofitted for Lionel, it had been decided that Doug would park his motorcycle in the Baker driveway and drive the van.

"Are you sure you can handle it?" Lionel asked once they were in and buckled. "This is a little bigger than that girlie bike you're riding."

"Whoa!" Doug started the car and checked the mirrors before pulling away from the curb. "The trash talking has already started, I see."

"That's no trash talk. Real men ride Harleys. Everybody knows that."

"One trip around the block on my Kawa . . ." The rest of the sentence died on Doug's lips. "Sorry, man. I wasn't thinking."

"No problem. That would normally be the thing to say. This situation I'm dealing with isn't normal."

Doug glanced a look at the now-brooding teen. "Like I've said before, Lionel. I can't imagine transitioning from an independent brother to one who can't live life totally on his own. It's got to be a painful situation to live through. Maybe even to talk about."

"It is what it is."

"Jan said you were riding on the back of someone else's bike. What happened to him?"

"Oh, he fared better than me. He died."

Doug took a longer look at Lionel this time. Was silent until they reached a red light, and then somberly asked, "Are you thinking about suicide?"

"I've thought about it."

Doug let Lionel's words sink in. What could he say to a comment like that? Tell him not to? Give him reasons to live? If Doug were faced with a life such as Lionel's, who was to say he wouldn't think the same thing? And the harder question. Should he tell Jan? The light changed. The silence continued.

"I'm not going to kill myself, man." Lionel sighed as he looked out the window. "But I'd be lying if I said I hadn't thought about it."

"I understand." He did, in a way. But not as comprehensibly as his counselor sister-in-law could. He would never break Lionel's confidence but made a mental note to suggest Cynthia do an evaluation before Lionel began the basketball league.

He had other serious questions but decided to lighten things up. "Do you have a favorite NBA player?"

"LeBron, who else? Plays that position almost as good as me."

"You're a forward."

"Used to be pretty good."

"Life has changed and the situation is different, but you can be good again."

"All right, guys. See you Tuesday at ten." Jan left the studio where the band had rehearsed. She hadn't heard from Lionel or Doug and was tempted to call and see how everything was going. But she decided against it. That neither had been in contact was hopefully a really good sign. With nothing planned for the next couple hours Jan got in her car, pulled off, and called Crystal.

"I'm bored. Please tell me Brent is home and you can sneak out of the house for an hour."

"He's here. An hour to do what?"

"Help me pick out an outfit for the holiday party."

"You've got it. Come on by."

Jan had barely pulled out her phone to tell Crystal she was there before she came bounding down the steps. "Hey, girl."

"Dang, somebody was ready for a break."

"Your timing is perfect. Brent's mom is coming over."

"Chris! And you're leaving?"

"Yes, and hurry up. She called from her car and might be around the corner." Crystal looked around furtively, ready to duck.

"Why are you playing, you love your mom-in-law."

"To pieces. Which is why I wouldn't be able to leave if she was here, but since she's not yet . . . go, go, go!"

"Ha!"

"So how was rehearsal?"

"It was good. We're learning some new material, incorporating some Christmas songs. The guys are excited."

"Since becoming friends with the postal worker, your life keeps getting better."

"You're right."

"What? You're agreeing with me?"

"Completely." Jan told Crystal about Thanksgiving at the Carters. "I never laughed so hard in my life. I fell in love with his mother, and his dad's slow, calm demeanor is the perfect complement to her zaniness. They made me feel totally welcome."

"And the director wants you to write a song?"

"Cynthia, yes."

"Can you do it?"

"I don't know. I'm trying not to force it, but let it happen. Like it did the other night."

"I don't know, girl. You might have to go start something with Melissa, you know, for motivation."

"Listen to you, being as messy as she is."

"I'm just saying." Crystal smiled at her cousin. "I'm happy for you, Jan. You're with a good dude, have a sweet gig coming up and maybe even a reality show. You deserve it all. But I still think you need to beat up Melissa."

31

Monday night and the last open spot for *Starr Power* was going to be chosen. Knowing this, Jan tried to get into it, to bring a little extra. But she knew almost from the beginning that she wouldn't be doing the show. Something about the way Starr looked at her earlier, with a look that was part pity, part guilt. Like he knew that she deserved to be on the show but didn't feel like she belonged in show business. The role of superstar singing female was reserved for skinny girls with pretty faces and the best body that either a personal trainer or money could buy. She'd never been that girl. And as Jan left the venue seconds after hearing the name of the last contestant chosen, she realized something. She didn't want to be that girl. She just wanted to be who she was. She just wanted to be Jan. Was there something so wrong with that?

When her phone rang she didn't even bother to look at the dash. It was either Crystal or Doug and she didn't want to talk to either one of them. The ringing stopped, but moments later began again. When it rang for the fourth time she tapped the icon on the steering wheel and retrieved her voice mails. Only one message had been left.

"Jan, if you don't call me back within the next half hour I'm coming over to your house. So I hope you get this message."

She tapped redial.

"Hey, where are you?"

Jan heard the concern in Doug's voice and felt guilty for ignoring his call.

"On the highway, headed home. And before you ask, the answer is no."

"What?! That's some bull right there. That fool knows good and well you should be on that show."

"Yeah, well, it is what it is."

"I'm sorry, baby."

She sighed. "Me too."

"If you come over I'll try and help you feel better."

"Listen to you trying to sound all sexy."

"Trying? Dang, I didn't succeed?"

Jan laughed in spite of her mood. "I wouldn't be good company. It wouldn't be fair to invite you to my pity party, and I'm definitely having one."

"That's understandable, babe. But don't let some old, washed-up, tone-deaf, blind, wannabe singer producer make you feel bad. You have more talent in your titty than he has in his chump ass body!"

Jan really laughed at that one. "Titty, Doug? Really?"

"Sorry. That's Liz Carter coming out. Sometimes that happens." Jan wanted to respond but couldn't. Reality was replacing shock and tears flowed. "Jan? Are you all right?"

"No."

"Do you need to pull over? Do I need to come get you?"

His caring tone only brought more tears. She spoke through them. "I'm just hurt. And angry! I really believed this was it."

"I'm sorry I couldn't be there, babe."

"Me too. But if you hadn't worked late and Pat hadn't filled in, I wouldn't have been able to compete tonight. Then again, maybe that would have been a good thing."

"Don't say that, Jan. You belonged in that competition and you deserved a slot."

"I don't look like those other women. The ones Starr chose. Doesn't matter that I can sing circles around them. I'm not what that industry promotes. For as much as I hated her for saying it, Melissa was right."

"Just because of the way something is doesn't make it right. There's nothing right about a singing competition that passes over true talent for people who can't sing."

"It doesn't matter anymore. I'm done."

"What do you mean?"

"It's over. I'll still perform here and there, but

it's time I faced reality. I'm never going to be that R & B star topping the charts and playing on the radio."

"You don't know that."

"I do! And there's no use trying to sugarcoat it." Jan cried openly now. "It's over."

"You're headed to my house, right?"

"In this mood I should probably just go home."

"I want to see you." No answer. "Are you coming?"

"I guess."

"Jan."

"Huh?"

"No matter what anybody else says, you're a star. My star."

They talked a bit more before Crystal beeped in and Jan let Doug go to talk to her.

"Hey, Chris."

"Oh, man, Jan." More sisters than cousins, Jan knew her somber greeting would tell Crystal all she needed to know. "I'm so sorry you didn't get it. I know how badly you wanted to be on that show."

"I know. You were right all along. I should have stopped this foolishness a long time ago and come to terms with the fact I'm just not cut out to be in the game."

"That's not true, Jan! You belong in that business as much as anyone. Now, I know I don't always sound like it, but I really want you to succeed in your passion. To be honest, a part of me is a little envious of you."

"Girl, please."

"I'm serious! You've always had a drive to be successful and more importantly, the talent to make that happen. Brent and my family are everything, and I'm right where I want to be. But sometimes I've wondered about who Crystal is aside from wife and mom. What it is that individually defines me. You've never had to ask that question. Girl, that's a blessing. You've always known. And you've been right. You were born to be a singer and I don't care what Starr or moon or sun"—Jan chuckled—"or galaxy or planet or anybody else has to say about it. Don't let them tell you when it's over. You decide when it's over. But don't quit because someone else says you should. Do you hear me?"

"I hear you. Thanks, cousin."

"I love you, girl."

"I love you, too."

Jan decided against going over to Doug's house. It was late, and she was tired. She went inside, fixed herself a large bowl of ice cream, grabbed a sleeve of cookies, and headed to her room. She'd just gotten cozy in her bed and had turned on the TV, when she heard a noise. She stopped, spoon halfway to her mouth, and listened.

There it was again. *Tap, tap, tap.*

She muted the television and listened once more. It happened yet a third time, distinct and unmistakable. Somebody was at her window! Were they trying to break in?

She reached for the phone, her thumb already

on the nine, her mind on the one-one. Easing out of the bed, she turned off the television and threw her room into darkness, hoping she'd see a shadow, a movement or something. She didn't want to call the police and then find out what she heard was a tree branch scraping against the house, or it settling onto the foundation.

Her phone vibrated in her hand. She almost peed right there. Grabbing her chest, she looked at the screen.

"Doug," she whispered so the criminal outside her window wouldn't hear her. "I think somebody's at my window, trying to get in."

"Yeah," he whispered back. "But I'm too big to climb through it. So come open the door."

She'd never wanted to hit, kiss, hug, and hurt somebody all at the same time, but that's how she felt when she opened the front door and let him inside. Soon, however, his kissing and hugging only made her want him to hit it, and love all her hurt away.

That's exactly what Doug did.

32

The next morning, Jan was waddling in the last vestiges of her pity party when her cell phone rang. Doug had definitely made her feel better, but when he left, so did her good mood. She almost didn't answer the vibrating phone, but figuring it might be a time-sensitive issue, she rolled out of bed and engaged the speaker button.

"Good morning."

"Hi, Jan. It's Cynthia. I know you work afternoons and hope this isn't too early to call."

"No, I needed to get up anyway."

"It's about the show, and I hope you don't get offended."

"Let me guess. You showed your party organizers a picture of me and they're opting for a woman who sounds like fingernails on the chalkboard but looks like Beyoncé."

"Goodness, no! Jan, why would you even say that?"

"You haven't talked to Doug today?"

"No, I haven't talked to him since the weekend. Why? Did something happen?"

Jan gave Cynthia a condensed version of what happened at On That Note.

"Jan, I'm so sorry to hear that. You have an amazing voice. Honestly, though, I can't say I'm surprised. We live in a very superficial society that places way too much emphasis on things that shouldn't matter. I'm sad to say that not too long ago I was one of those people. It's how I was raised."

"What happened to change you?"

"A man named Byron Carter. Because of preconceived notions and societal standards I almost let a really good man get away. That's a whole other story. Today I'm following up on the conversation at Thanksgiving. The song I suggested from the incident with your coworker. Have you had a chance to work on it?"

"Not really."

"I hope what happened last night doesn't discourage you from trying. I have a group of girlfriends in Chicago. We've been tight for years and talk almost every week via conference call. On Sunday I shared with them what happened to you at the club and how you handled it. The message resonated with them as it had with me. I told them you were writing a song that encapsulates that message. They asked if it was available for download!"

"I appreciate that, Cynthia, but I don't know if I can do it. Given what just happened last night, the words I said to her sound pretty empty."

"I believe what happened last night makes the message even more pertinent, and important. There's another reason why I'm calling."

"What's that?"

"I'm not a stylist, but I am a professional shopper. Some would say I need a twelve-step program." Jan laughed. "So I thought to offer my services in helping you put together a look for the holiday show. And not because of how you look," she quickly added, "or what you weigh or don't weigh or anything like that. But because there will be a lot of influential people there and I want you to hit that stage looking like you not only belong in the room, but like you own it."

Jan was silent a moment, battling a multitude of feelings. She believed that Cynthia's intent was sincere but at the end of the day it was yet another person commenting on her looks.

"Hello, Jan? Are you there?"

"Yes, I'm here."

"I hope that came across in the way I intended."

"I know you mean well."

"You're upset. I'm sorry. I went back and forth on whether or not to call. But I know some wonderful designers who could whip something up tailored to make you look amazing and—"

"Thanks, Jan, but I already have my outfit for the show."

"Oh, okay."

"My cousin helped me pick it out. It's very rich looking, and I like how I look in it."

"That's great! What color is it?"

"It's a wine-colored velour gown, with a bit of a train at the bottom. I caught it on sale at Nordstrom's."

"It sounds perfect, Jan. Do you have your shoes yet?"

"I have a pair of silver sandals that will work. They're dressy, and will fit into the holiday theme."

"Sounds like the only other thing you need to go with it is an original song."

"No pressure, right?"

"None at all. Just a few thousand young ladies who could greatly benefit from being reminded that they are perfect, just the way they are."

After the phone call Jan stayed in bed remembering that night, what Melissa had said, and her unplanned comeback. Slowly, more words began to congeal. She sat up, grabbed her iPad, and typed the words.

You be you. I'll be me.
I'm the best me there ever will be.
Don't fit your mold? Don't give a damn.
You be who you are and I'll be who I am.

Humming, she got out of bed and continued to think of words and rhymes. Without even realizing it she'd left her pity party and had started writing a song.

33

Jan sat in Frank's office, her dressing room at Breeze. She stared at herself in the mirror and frowned at who looked back at her. A look that reflected society's standard of beauty. In that moment, she felt like a caricature of herself. Without thinking, she'd brought and put on her "show costume." Even as she'd talked Thump into opening the show with a song about authenticity. Even as she was writing a song about being herself, she looked at the reflection of a stranger.

Before she could tell her hands not to, they were reaching for the wig she wore and tossing it across the room. She ran her fingers through the natural twists her hairdresser had given her last week, just to take a break from the press and curl. Looked into the mirror, and smiled. She kept on the damnable body shaper but traded the silk maxi dress for what she'd worn to the club—black stretch pants, a pink, black, and turquoise baby-doll top, and pink high-top sneakers. Eyeing the pile of clothes on the floor and herself in the full-length mirror, she began to giggle. She felt like a little girl about to do something naughty. With the hourglass shaper and playful apparel, she felt girlie too. Girlie and cute. But she wasn't without apprehension. What would the crowd think about this new look? What would Doug think? If Melissa decided to show her heckling face, would the crowd now agree with her? Frank was either going to applaud her or tell her she'd lost her mind. Thump was probably going to have a heart attack.

All Jan could hope for was a doctor in the house. Because she'd decided to be her song's working title, "Who I Am." There was no turning back.

Frank's two-fisted knock signaled it was show-time. With one last look in the mirror and a deep, calming breath, she opened the door, threw on a cloak of confidence, and belted out the first line to India Arie's "I Am Not My Hair."

Frank's brow raised. Thump's jaw dropped. The crowd applauded and shouted their appreciation, especially when she changed the last words of the chorus and sang that she was "just Jan."

"You go, sistah!"

"You look beautiful, girl!"

"Way to love yourself, Jan!"

During the instrumental bridge she freestyled the recent chorus she'd written. As the song ended with the band jamming on a prolonged instrumental loop, it took a second for her to realize that the room was chanting, and what they said.

Don't fit your mold. Don't give a damn. You be you. I'm who I am!

As a single tear rolled down her face, Jan realized something else. Doug's was the loudest voice of them all.

Normally when the show was over, Jan would say, "Thank you and good night!" and walk off the stage. The band would continue playing for a minute or so and end in a grand finale. Tonight was no different except for when she walked toward stage right and her exit, a woman was waiting there.

"Jan!"

Jan turned to see a woman, about her age she guessed, short, cute, and overweight. She was crying.

"Hold on a minute, I'll come down." Jan left the stage and went around to the door that led out to the club where the woman was standing. She stepped out and was met by a big hug.

"Thank you, thank you," the woman said as more tears continued to run down her face. "Thanks for what you said tonight. Those words are powerful and I so needed to hear them. You just don't know!"

"Yes, sister, I do."

"I grew up in a family where I was the only fat one, and have been teased all of my life. Then when I was twenty I had a baby and the extra weight stayed on. I've tried dieting and exercise but have never been able to stay on a program long enough to see real results. I'd hate myself for failing, and what do I do to ease the pain?"

Jan knew all too well. "Eat."

"That's right. But, girl, what you said tonight encouraged me to try again."

"I so know how you feel." Jan hugged her again. "I'm glad what I said encouraged you."

"Is there somewhere I can buy that song?"

Jan smiled. "Not yet, but maybe soon."

"Let me know, okay. I have a niece who's going through the same thing I went through as a child. I'd love for her to be able to hear it."

As they talked, several other women had come over. They all expressed how empowered they felt by what Jan said. After twenty minutes she was finally able to go backstage and change. She did so knowing that she was on to something good.

The last confirmation of the night came as she and Doug walked to the parking lot. "Jan, you looked beautiful up there tonight. I'm so proud of you."

"Thank you, Doug. I don't know what came over me."

"Whatever it was, I hope it stays." They reached her car. His bike was parked nearby. "Did you just make that up, what you were chanting?"

"No. Remember on Thanksgiving, when Cynthia asked about me writing a song?"

"Yes."

"I've been working on it."

"For real?"

Jan nodded. "She thought the message was one that the girls in her program could benefit from and might use it as a counseling tool."

"You say you're working on it. Are you almost done?"

"No, I've written the chorus to a song. Haven't gotten the verses down yet."

"That's pretty cool, Jan. Stick with me, girl, and we're going to be rich!"

"We? How do you figure?"

"You just said it yourself that this happened because of my big mouth. Clearly I was the catalyst to this situation. And your inspiration. Hey, that rhymed. I think I've got skills, girl." He kissed Jan's incredulous face. "Don't worry, girl. I'll help you out. We'll knock out that song, no problem."

He opened her car door. Shaking her head, she got inside. "I have no words."

"That's why I'm here. To help you write this hit and make this money."

34

Doug bounded up the steps to the Baker residence and rang the doorbell. The door opened almost immediately. "Thanks for coming over so quickly," Jan said, breathless.

"Why are you out of breath? Did you go jogging or something?"

"I need to. But I'm just excited. And nervous. Thump sent over the music for the song I'm writing."

"Correction. We're writing."

She gave him a look. "Yeah, okay."

"The music is so good, Doug. I can't wait for you to hear it." She grabbed his hand, pulling him inside. "I hope you like it."

"Your liking it is all that matters."

"I want Lionel to hear it, too." She knocked on his door. "Lionel! I need you. Come out of your cave!"

"Yeah, and don't make me have to come in there after you!" Doug added.

"Sit there. In the dining room." Jan rushed down the hall and came back with her iPad just as Lionel came out of his room.

"Damn, girl. I've already been run over once."

"I'm sorry, Lionel."

"That's all right. Hurt me and I'll sue. What's up, doughboy?"

"Your sister is about to blow up, that's what. And I'm going to be her manager, so if you're planning on suing her, you'll have to come through me."

"Neither of you is getting my money, and both of you need to sit and zip it." She clicked on an icon. "Pay attention, Lionel. I need to write a song that will resonate with your generation."

"Well, for starters, don't use no big-ass words like res-o-nate. For someone my age to like it you need to come hard and bring the fye."

"The who?"

Lionel shook his head. "Fire, Jan."

"Well, why didn't you say so?"

"I did."

"Shh!"

The three listened as a medium-speed, percussion-driven sound—a combination of hip-hop and world beat with a side of pop—filled the room. Instantly, Doug and Lionel began bobbing their heads.

"That's dope," Lionel said.

"I like it," Doug added.

Jan's comment? "Shh!!!"

For the remaining two minutes, the two men dutifully obeyed.

When the music finished, Jan looked from one to the other. "Well?"

Doug feigned sign language. Jan gave him a look. "Hell, I'm just making sure that if I open my mouth I won't get shot!"

"I wasn't that bad," Jan said.

Doug and Lionel spoke in unison. "Yes, you were."

"Who did that music?" Lionel asked.

"The bandleader of the group I'm in, the group you've never heard because"—she used air quotes—"the Breeze is old school."

"It is!" Lionel looked at Doug. "You been to see her?" Doug nodded. "You see anybody in there my age?" Doug shook his head.

"Ha! I rest my case."

"Good, because instead of a case I need some words that will do justice to that bomb beat! Okay, y'all want to hear what I have so far?" She spoke the chorus that had come to her the other morning.

"The best me there ever will be," Lionel sang with a hand in the air and one on his heart. "Sounds like some Oprah feel-good Super Soul Sunday stuff."

"What's wrong with that? I like Oprah, feeling good, and Super Soul Sunday!"

"Sounds corny."

"So come with it then!" Doug challenged. "Over

there jaw-jacking about what it isn't. Bring the flow. Tell us what it is."

"Man, shut up."

"I'm just saying. Create, don't agitate."

"Hey, I like that!" Jan said, chin in hand as she pondered. "Can't use it in the song, though."

Lionel chuckled. "Y'all are both whack." Maybe, but he seemed to be enjoying himself just the same. "Play it again."

They did. Over and over. With every replay more words came. Some rhymes worked. Others didn't. Cynthia felt that she could turn her feelings into a song that inspired. With every line added, Jan, too, started to believe. They worked on the song for hours. Jan's enthusiasm, Doug's encouragement, and Lionel's witty prose had created what they considered was the rough cut of a masterpiece— a first for them all.

As soon as they finished, Jan called Thump. Even though it was after two in the afternoon, she knew she was taking a huge chance by calling him "so early." Thump kept vampire hours.

"What?" is how Thump answered the phone, his voice raspy with sleep.

"It's early. I know, and I'm sorry."

"Jan?"

"Yes."

"Damn, I answered the phone and this isn't even a booty call?"

"No, fool, it's work. Now wake up. I want you to hear the words I put to the music you sent me."

"Okay, come on over."

"Come over? I was going to do it over the phone."

"I don't work like that. Plus, you can't really hear how it sounds until it's recorded. I've got a little mixer in my house."

"Oh, cool. That way I can send a sample over to Cynthia."

"Who's that?" Jan told him. "She married?"

"Very and to the brother of the man I'm dating. So when you meet her, mind your manners and your business."

That night, Jan e-mailed a thirty-second MP3 file to Cynthia with the following note:

Here's a sample of the song I'm writing, the chorus and a little bit of a verse. Let me know if you like the direction we're headed. Thanks, Jan.

In the morning, on her phone, Jan saw Cynthia's four-word response.

Love it! Keep going!

That's exactly what Jan did.

When Doug and Jan arrived at work Monday afternoon, they were still giddy, shining with satisfaction at having created something all felt was bigger than them. Well, except maybe Lionel. Within minutes of finishing the last lyric he was already talking record albums and collaborations with Kanye and Dre. This recollection had Doug and Jan laughing as they entered the back room.

"Ooh, somebody's happy," Melissa said, without turning around.

She'd been angry at Jan ever since the Breeze showdown. Had even threatened to sue. Jan's response? "Go ahead."

"Last night must have been pretty good."

"It was, girl . . ." Jan teased, confidence showing. "Until three a.m."

Joey looked up in surprise and caught the huge grin on Doug's face. "You?" Doug nodded. Joey looked at Jan. "And you?" Jan nodded, too. "You're admitting it?"

"She said that last night was good, and it was. That's what I'm admitting."

Melissa turned around. "Oh my God! Your hair!"

"Yes," Jan calmly replied, patting her curls. "It is."

"I like it," Joey said.

Jan turned and smiled. "Thanks."

Melissa . . . not so much. "What happened? Too busy to get to the beauty shop?"

"Is that your attempt at a dig, Melissa?"

"I think she's trying to expand her fifteen minutes," Doug said. "Get you to sling another verse about her at Breeze."

"I dare you," Melissa warned.

Jan stood her ground. "Unlike you, I'm not messy. Missed you at the show, though." She winked at Doug. Joey cracked up.

"I might be messy, but at least I look good doing it." She gave Jan one last dissatisfied face and flung her weave as she turned her back.

"I'm more interested in the last night comment," Joey said. "What was so good about it?"

"Most likely Doug Carter," Melissa answered, unable to keep out of other folks' business. "I know that from experience."

"You know a lot from experience," a fellow coworker shouted.

"Shut the hell up!" Melissa growled. "You're just mad you haven't experienced it."

"It's not like I couldn't," he confidently replied.

"In your fantasies," Melissa countered.

Various reactions and responses were lost on Jan as she headed to the counter. There were no customers waiting and with Jan wanting to do nothing more than be in a studio with her band and her song, this was going to be a long afternoon.

"What is going on back there?" Pat turned to ask her. "Wow! Look at your hair! I love it!"

"Do you?" Jan asked, having left her shield of feigned confidence in the back room.

"I really do." Pat walked over for a better look. "You have such a pretty face and the short style emphasizes it."

"Thank you."

"Is that what has everybody cackling back there?"

"No, that commotion comes courtesy of Melissa."

"Oh Lord."

"She insinuated that Doug and I were together last night," Jan said, beginning to yawn. "And I cosigned because it's true."

Pat looked over, her expression one of "no you didn't" and "tell me more." But all she said was, "Oh, really now."

Jan laughed. "Yes, but not in the way you're thinking."

"I don't know, girl. You're yawning pretty hard. So much you've got me doing it," she finished, her mouth stretched wide.

Jan chuckled.

"And you're all happy, laughing and everything. Whatever happened last night is looking good on you today."

Jan walked closer to Pat. "If I share, promise to not tell anyone else?"

"Of course."

"We wrote a song together."

Pat's expression went from expectant to perplexed. "Is that all?" Then her eyes lit up. She leaned over, and whispered, "Was this afterwards, you know, in the afterglow? You put it on him so tough that he broke out singing? Is it more like R. Kelly or what's that young man's name . . . The Weeknd?"

"Ha! What do you know about him?"

"Girl, I've got grandkids."

"No." Jan leaned against the counter. "It's more like Pharrell."

Pat's look was priceless. When her first customer stepped to the counter, Jan was still laughing.

As soon as the lobby was empty Pat came over. "Now tell me more about this happy song that's put such a happy smile on your face."

"Okay, I'll tell you because it's not a secret anyway. The smile isn't just because of the song. Doug and I are together."

"You're not telling me anything I didn't already know. I'm just glad you finally stopped lying."

"I didn't lie to you, Pat!"

"No, but you omitted." Pat widened her eyes as she emphasized the word. Jan cracked up. "I'm so happy for both of you. I was hoping like everything the two of you would get together."

"So anyway, about the song—"

"Sorry to interrupt you, but I can hear about the song later. The juicy details of this new love affair is what I want to hear right now."

"We're dating. That's pretty much it."

"Since when?"

"We went out about a month after I got here."

"Where?"

Jan giggled. "Bowling."

Pat nodded. "Good move. I like a man who can think outside of the dinner and a movie box."

"What did you think after that first date?"

"Honestly? That I wanted a second."

"Ha!" Pat held up her hand for a high five. "Now you're talking like a woman with sense. And I already know who, Mr. Doug Carter, so since we've handled the five W's, I'm ready to hear about your song."

"Well, it was inspired by the night I was heckled by Messy Mel . . ."

35

"Awww, look at your tree!" Jan stepped into Doug's apartment, her mouth and eyes wide. It was Christmas Eve. They'd just come from dinner with Crystal and Brent, a raucous restaurant experience that lasted three hours. "When did you do all this? It wasn't up the last time I was here."

"It wouldn't be Christmas without a tree, babe. Plus, I knew you'd be coming over, so if nothing else I needed some mistletoe."

He kissed her.

"Why'd you do that?" she asked afterward, looking up. "I don't see a mistletoe."

Doug reached for her hand and headed toward the bedroom. "You're not going to see one in a few minutes either, when I kiss your other lips."

An hour later, the two satisfied lovers cuddled in bed, surrounded by a comfortable silence. "What are you thinking?" Jan finally asked.

"That I'm not twenty."

She looked up quickly. "That's a strange answer."

"Not when you just got through effing nonstop for forty-five minutes. I'm tired as hell."

"Ha! Nobody told you to give me multiple orgasms."

"Yeah, and nobody told me not to."

She snuggled closer. "Tonight was so good, baby. You had me on fire! When you're handling your business like that, I'll never tell you to stop." She peered over his shoulder at the clock on the nightstand. "It's after midnight. Merry Christmas, Doug Carter."

"Merry Christmas, Jan Baker."

"Did you get me a Christmas present?"

"I just gave them to you . . . multiple, in fact."

She swatted his arm. His look was unchanged. Hers was incredulous. She sat up. "That's why you rode me like an Amtrak going cross-country? Because it's Christmas?"

He shrugged. "Aren't you merry? You were a minute ago. My neighbors probably heard how merry you were." He tried to hold her stare, but she looked so forlorn that he couldn't stop the smile that crept on his face.

"Are you teasing me?" He started laughing. "Doug!" Her swats were now punches he artfully dodged before rolling over on her, pinning her arms and trying to kiss her.

"No!" She twisted her face back and forth.

"What's the matter? You knew I'd get you a Christmas present. You wouldn't have come over if you hadn't thought that."

She stopped squirming. "That's not true."

"Oh, so if I didn't get anything it's okay?"

"It's not like, I mean, it's not just . . . I got you something!"

"Really, baby? You got me a Christmas present?" She nodded. "You have it with you now?"

"Yes."

"You shouldn't have." He sighed.

"Why not?"

"Because . . ." Doug took in the crestfallen expression she tried to hide. "You should have gotten me multiple gifts, like I did you."

"You're lying!"

"Sit down."

"What?"

"Sit!" She did. He walked into his closet and came out with a large holiday bag stuffed with boxes. "I was going to drag out the deception, but you looked so hurt I couldn't. Merry Christmas."

"All of these for me?" She kissed him. "You're a good man, Doug. Thank you. Wait, let me get your gift."

"Open yours first."

"Okay."

She started with the first of four boxes. By the time she'd opened them all she had the perfect accessories for her next show: crystal-covered stilettos, matching dangly earrings, Jan's favorite cologne, and a pair of designer sunglasses.

"I love everything!" Jan exclaimed, removing

her shoes so she could try on the heels. "You picked all this out yourself?"

"I can't take full credit. Cynthia helped me out."

She put on the heels and stood. "They fit perfect. Ooh, they're so pretty! And they'll go perfect with my gown! I never would have bought shoes like these, but I really like them. Thanks, babe!"

She threw her arms around him and gave him a kiss. That kiss became several.

Doug reached for the hem of Jan's top. "Come on. I want my Christmas present now."

"Oh, okay." She tried to turn, but Doug didn't release her.

"No, not that one." He tweaked her nipple. "This one. You. Right here. Wearing nothing but those shoes."

It was quite a while before Doug opened his gift from Jan, head-to-toe Raiders apparel, including hat and slippers. He enjoyed them, but not nearly as much as his first present that day.

36

The week was a whirlwind. Rehearsals every night. Work every day. Stolen moments with Doug in between. Still, Jan felt more alive than she ever had. Just when she thought her dream of singing as a career was over, she got handed a gift. Cynthia's request to Jan had opened an area of music that Jan hadn't before considered. Songwriting. Not only opened it but exposed it as a passion, one that Jan wasn't too bad at . . . if she must say so herself.

She wasn't the only one. When Jan sent the rehearsal tape of the finished "Who I Am" track, Cynthia had called screaming with delight. She'd asked for permission to send it to one of the board members. Jan was hesitant but in the end gave the okay. Even without *Starr Power,* Jan had written a song and people were listening to it!

These thoughts and a million others littered her mind as she packed her bag for tonight's holiday party, one that looked to be bigger than she'd first imagined. She'd gone online and researched the agency that Cynthia directed. H.E.L.P. was an acronym for Healthy Empowerment through Living Productively. In addition to helping troubled youth, it provided a variety of other social services to disempowered, disenfranchised communities, including a gardening program giving urban neighborhoods access to fresh produce. Their board membership was impressive and included celebrities. Jan's gut clenched as her nervousness intensified. *What if celebrities are here tonight?* She repeated her freshly penned words. *Just be who I am.*

Thirty minutes later she was riding in the back of a luxury sedan. She'd balked at the offer but was now thankful that Cynthia insisted that Jan be chauffeured to the event, stating that the service was included in the performance fee. Not having to deal with LA's Friday night traffic gave her time to think, run through the night's repertoire of songs, focus . . . and calm down. It's also why she hadn't accepted Doug's offer to accompany her but rather asked that he meet her there. So that she could center herself and summon the superstar, the diva, the confident woman who walked across the stage like she owned it, when in reality she was shaking in her body shaper. And considering the contraption gripped her like the jaws of life, that was a feat!

From the second she arrived at downtown Los Angeles's Omni Hotel, Jan went from worrying about whether or not she'd perform for a celebrity to feeling like one herself! Cynthia had assigned one of her clients to act as Cynthia's personal assistant so that Cynthia could focus on her performance.

I could get used to this!

The young woman's name was Tamika. She looked to be around eighteen, tall, slender, with cocoa eyes, golden brown skin, and a smile like sunshine.

"Ms. Baker, I'll take your bags."

"Oh, that's okay I'll just—"

"It's my job," Tamika said politely, her voice soft, the grip on Jan's bag unyielding. Jan released the bag. Tamika smiled. "This way, please."

Tamika headed toward the elevator.

Jan walked beside her. "Are we headed to my room?"

"Yes, if you need anything, I can bring it to you there."

"Including the room where we'll be performing?"

"Excuse me?"

Jan laughed. "I'd like to take a peek at the room where the party will be held to get a look at both the layout and the stage."

"Oh, okay. That's on the other side." Tamika led them across the lobby and down a hallway. "How'd you get to be a singer?"

"I was born to sing," Jan answered. "Have been doing it for as long as I can remember."

"I mean, professionally, like with a band and everything."

As they entered and walked around the room

that was still being set up, Jan gave Tamika a brief rundown of her history, including her lone brush with fame on the Apollo stage.

"That's so cool," Tamika said when she'd finished. "I've never been to New York. I've never been out of LA."

"I wasn't there long and haven't been back. I do remember its excitement, though. The crowds, Harlem, Times Square, and riding the subway. Now that was an adventure. My girlfriend and I missed our stop and wound up in Queens!"

"Where's that?"

"Too far to walk back to our hotel! Queens is a borough of New York, part of what makes up New York City. Kind of like how Hawthorne or Gardena or Hollywood are parts of what makes up metropolitan Los Angeles."

"Oh, I get it. I'd like to go there someday."

"You should," Jan said. "How old are you?"

"Eighteen."

"I was nineteen when I went there, almost twenty. It opened my eyes and showed me there was a whole world out there beyond the ten square blocks I'd grown up in. Gave me the desire to do more, and be more, and helped me continue to pursue my dream of doing what I'm doing and being . . . who I am," Jan finished with a smile.

They got on the elevator and reached her floor. Jan saw immediately that Cynthia had continued with the star treatment. The room was actually a massive suite with separate living room, overlooking the water court at downtown's California Plaza.

"This is nice," Tamika exclaimed, walking over to the window's magnificent view.

"One day, I want to be a star like you."

"Girl, I'm no star. During the day I work at the post office."

Tamika looked back at her surprised. "You do?"

"Sure do, the Normandie branch."

Tamika looked out the window. "Yeah, but right now you're in this beautiful room and tonight you'll be onstage singing for a roomful of people. That's like a star to me."

"You know what, Tamika. You are absolutely right. I guess I am a star. And so are you."

"Babe, you look amazing."

It was two hours later, almost showtime. Jan had enjoyed a long soak in the whirlpool tub and the first-time treat of having a stylist and makeup artist help get her ready for the show. She felt glamourous in the wine-colored stretch knit velvet dress, set off perfectly with Doug's Christmas gifts. The shoes added tons of bling. The big, dangly earrings cast beams around the room as they caught the glow of the lighted mirror. She wore no necklace. Instead all attention went instantly to her substantial cleavage perfectly displayed by the cut of softly rounded neckline, cinched waist, and form-fitting skirt that flared from the knee down. Her short curls glistened. Glittery eye shadow and kohl liner made her eyes pop. Wine red lipstick emphasized the whiteness of her teeth. Tamika's word came back to her. *Star.*

Who needed Nick's validation? She had Tamika's.

Doug answered a knock at the door.

Cynthia entered and stopped short. "Jan! You. Look. Stunning! Oh my God, that dress is everything on you." She stepped back, appraising. "The hair, makeup, everything's perfect. And wherever did you get those shoes and earrings?" She winked at Doug. "Whoever picked those out has great taste!"

Doug brushed the lapel of his tailored black suit. "Thank you very much."

"You look amazing, too," Jan said to Cynthia. "Like a model about to walk the runway."

And she did. Cynthia's upswept hairdo emphasized a long neck and a diamond teardrop earrings and necklace set. Her stark white dress with a spattering of rhinestones complemented strappy rhinestone sandals on freshly pedicured feet, the bright red polish on her toes being the only splash of color in her ensemble.

"Thank you."

"And thank you for this room," Jan added, spreading her arms and looking around. "It is incredible. Tamika said it was the room of a star."

"Tamika's right. By the way, did she take care of you all right?"

"Yes, she did. Very professional."

"Where is she?"

"I told her she could go on down, that I was fine."

"Good." Cynthia looked at her watch. "I'm going down now. You're on in about thirty minutes or so but can come down anytime. Are you sure you don't need anything?"

"If you can make sure that there's a bottle or glass of water on the stage that I can access. Oh, and a hand towel?"

Cynthia nodded. "I'll take care of it." She walked over and gave Jan a hug. "The crowd is going to love you," she said. "I cannot wait to see their reaction to 'Who I Am.'"

She was right. The crowd loved Jan. The dance floor stayed packed from the time she stepped on the stage singing Chaka Khan's classic "I'm Every Woman," until she ended the night with "Who I Am."

Their reaction to that was incredible. They cheered and whistled, whooped and hollered until Jan sang it again for an encore.

I'm fed up. Boiling over. I've had enough of society.
Taking shots. Photoshopped. Their perfect plan of what I should be.
Wait a minute. Slow your roll. Who made you, God? Did you make me? No!
So let me win in my own skin. The world is the same different. Represent!

You be you. I'll be me. I'm the best me there ever
could be.
Don't fit your mold. Don't give a damn. You be
who you are and I'll be who I am.

Ostracized. Isolated. Because my ways you don't
understand. Got—
Skinny. Fat. Piercings. Tats. And every other other
that's known to man.
Don't be blue that I'm not like you. Looks like that
was the master plan.
So let me win in my own skin. Everybody's more
alike than different. Represent!

You be you. I'll be me. I'm the best me there could
ever be.
Don't fit your mold. Don't give a damn. You be
who you are and I'll be who I am.
You be you. I'll be me. I'm the perfect plan of what
I should be.
Don't fit your mold. Don't give a damn.
You be who you are and I'll be who I am!

37

After the show Jan and Doug were invited to join Cynthia and Byron in the Presidential Suite, where the H.E.L.P. staff were entertaining board members, VIP supporters, and executives from sister organizations. As she entered, the room broke into applause. Jan was stunned.

"See," Cynthia said as she hugged her. "I told you they loved it! Come on, I have some people for you to meet."

Within minutes Jan's mind was whirling with the flurry of names she'd heard. She laughed and smiled, all the while dreaming of nothing but sitting down and taking off the cute crystal shoes that were now killing her feet!

Just when she was about to beg Cynthia for mercy, a man approached. He was handsome, older, his salt and pepper hair giving him a distinguished air even as his boyishly blue eyes still held their devilish twinkle. Two words in and Jan knew he was English.

"Good evening," he reached for her hand and kissed it. "I enjoyed you immensely. Your show was flawless."

"Thank you so much."

"I don't think I've had the pleasure of meeting you," Cynthia interjected, hand outstretched. "I'm Cynthia Carter, director of H.E.L.P."

"Ah, you're the Cynthia my wife raves about."

"Who's your wife?"

"Betsy Thomas. My name is Chandler."

"Betsy! Love her! Your generous donations have helped hundreds of teens choose differently and better. Thank you so much, Chandler. Programs like these couldn't exist without people like you."

He turned back to Jan. "And you, Ms. Baker, are a star."

Jan bowed her head, truly humbled. "I don't usually, but tonight I'm beginning to think of myself that way."

"As well you should. Such a talent! And that song you wrote? Incredible, it was hands down the best song of the night."

"Thank you."

"You did write it, correct?"

"Yes, myself along with"—Doug gently jabbed her side—"my boyfriend here, Doug Carter."

Doug shook Chandler's hand.

"Who is my brother-in-law," Cynthia added.

"Nice to meet you, sir," Doug said.

"Likewise."

"And my younger brother also contributed."

"Is it copyrighted?"

"Not yet."

"You should get that done immediately, like tomorrow. The process is easy. You can do it online."

"Okay."

"I'm serious. Will you do that?"

"Tomorrow's Sunday but since it can be done online, sure. I'll take care of it."

"Good. Because I really love the song, the message most of all. And if you'll forgive my presumptuousness and forthrightness, I will add that I also believe there is a way the song can have wider appeal, worldwide even."

Jan looked from Chandler to Doug and Cynthia and back again. "How's that?"

"If it is given more of a rock edge, and professionally recorded."

"Rock?" Doug asked.

"Recorded?" Jan followed.

"Yes, my brother a well-known record producer; he handles some of the hottest rock bands in England. I could get help from him for one of them to back you and put this song out for the world to hear."

Jan was floored. "You've got to be kidding."

"I'm totally serious." Chandler reached into his coat pocket and pulled out a cell. "Please call me next week. I'll tell you more of what I have in mind. Will you do that?"

"Absolutely, Mr. Thomas. Wow. I can't believe this is happening."

"Talk to you soon."

"Okay. Bye!"

The three of them watched Chandler Thomas walk away. "I told you if you stuck with me you'd be famous," Doug said. "I think my manager fee just went up."

"Shut up," Jan said with a laugh, looking at the card Chandler had given her. "I wonder if his brother is as big as he says."

"Doesn't matter if you're going to get a professionally recorded song out of the deal. That can be your calling card for more work."

"That's true."

Cynthia was still looking at Chandler, who'd stopped to chat with a group several yards away. "I don't know about his brother, but I know about Betsy Thomas. She's from the East Coast and very connected. Old money. Lots of it." She eyed Jan pointedly. "They get things done, so if I were you, I'd be trying to channel a rock star and make some moves like Jagger."

38

"Oh, Crystal! I wish you'd been there. Everything about the night was amazing: the venue, the people, the sound system, the food. And they loved my song!"

"The song that I still haven't heard even though I'm the cousin who's more like a sister."

"We just finished it!"

"I'm messing with you, girl. And so proud of you."

"Thank you, cuzzo."

"And here you were all down and out over a fallen star."

"Crazy, isn't it? Two months ago Nick Starr and his cable show was like the Holy Grail, the end all, be all. I actually felt like if I didn't get on that show, it was over. And I didn't! And for a minute, I was done."

"But then the man you initially dissed took over, and now look. You're a songwriter about to record! Who knows where this could lead?"

"First of all, I never dissed Doug."

"Yes, you did. You said he wasn't datable because he only worked at the post office. Now, act like you didn't say it."

"I'm not sure it came out quite that way."

"Ha! Well, I'm sure, heifah. It came out exactly like that. Matter-of-fact, as much as you tried to hide it, you had a thing for Nick Starr! Are you going to try and deny that, too? And don't forget who you're talking to. The girl who knew you when you used a permanent magic marker on your face 'cause you were trying to look like Left Eye in TLC."

"Ha! And your brother scared me half to death, telling me the ink was poison and I'd go blind." They howled at this comment. "I'm not going to deny anything you said. And I'm also big enough to admit that my attitude about Doug was totally wrong, and unfair, too. He really is a good man."

"So you'll finally admit that y'all are dating? And the four of us can go out, as couples, officially?"

"Girl, that news has been out."

"To who, because it sure wasn't me."

"The job. Everybody knows my business."

"Well isn't this something. I'm the last one to hear the song and get the news." She looked at Jan, her smile big. "So we can all go out then."

A long pause and then, "I guess so."

Crystal whooped and broke into an off-key rendition of a TLC classic, causing Jan to crack up again.

That Friday, Crystal, Brent, Jan, and Doug enjoyed dinner at Brent's favorite Mexican restaurant.

Minutes after they'd finished their entrées, the waitstaff headed to their table, singing "Happy Birthday." One carried a candle-bearing slice of gooey caramel flan. He was encouraged to make a wish and blow out the candle.

"How old are you, Brent," Jan asked. "Thirty-nine or forty?"

"Forty," Brent deadpanned. "I'm almost as old as you."

Jan didn't miss a beat. "You're confusing me with your wife."

"Hey!" Crystal reached over with her fork for a bite of Brent's cake. "Leave me out of it."

"Do they always act like this?" Doug asked Crystal.

"As long as I've known him. Like two peas in a pod."

"It's actually a good thing. If I tease you, I like you." She reached over for a bite of Brent's cake. He raised his fork. "I just want a bite!"

"Get your own."

"Babe, you need to tease me more." Doug got the attention of the waiter. "Yes, I'd like to order that dessert for these two women who when asked told you they didn't want any. So the man can enjoy his cake in peace."

Brent lifted a fist. "Thank you, my brother."

"No worries." Doug bumped his fist. "I've got your back."

"You're supposed to have my back!" Jan huffed.

"No, I'm supposed to have your backside."

Crystal groaned. "Oh, brother."

Jan leaned into Doug, who'd placed his arm around her shoulders. "So you guys have not one but two babysitters tonight. Must have a wild night planned."

"Oh, there's going to be some chandelier swinging for sure," Brent said as a yawn chased the sentence.

"With four kids seven and under and a perpetual lack of sleep, we'll be lucky to not fall asleep before the eleven o'clock news."

Doug squeezed Jan's shoulder before removing his arm. "In that case I suggest we get those desserts to go, let you two enjoy some alone time."

"What are you two going to do?" Crystal teased.

Doug shrugged, while stroking Jan's thigh under the table. "We'll get into something."

The couples left in their separate cars.

"What do you want to do?" Doug asked.

"Nothing really. We rehearsed every night this week. The only reason we didn't tonight is because Thump had another gig." She gave Doug a sympathetic look. "I'm sorry, Doug. But I'm exhausted. I think I'll just go home."

"Why not come to my house? You can sleep there."

"If I go there, you know we won't sleep. Plus, I want to sleep in my bed tonight. With work and rehearsal, I've got a ton of wash and other household chores that need handling." She looked out the window. "This is the time when being a thirty-year-old still living with your mother is so not cool."

"Why don't you move out?"

"I'm helping out financially. Lionel's medical bills wiped Mom out. She can't handle everything on her own."

The conversation shifted to other things. They reached Jan's house. Doug parked and turned off the engine.

"What are you doing?"

"I'm coming in and hanging out with you."

"You don't have to do that, Doug."

"I know I don't. I want to. What, you have a secret lover or something? Trying to rush me off before he gets here?"

"Yes, that's it." She opened the door and exited without a good-bye.

"Jan!" Doug grabbed his keys and jumped out of the car. He hurried up the walk to catch a fast-moving woman. "I was just teasing, woman!"

"I don't like teasing like that."

"Okay, geez." They entered a quiet house. "Where's Lionel?"

"Probably out with his friend Bernard."

"What about your mom?"

"In her room watching TV most likely." Jan walked into the living room and turned on the flat screen. "Why are you just standing there?"

"I'm a guest who won't assume that I can just sit down like it's my house."

"It's been so long since I've had a guest I forgot how to act. Please, have a seat." She motioned to a comfy, oversized couch across from the television. "Can I get you something to drink?"

"You have soda?"

"Yes, but not ginger ale."

"Anything is cool."

She got the drinks and cozied up next to him on the couch where Doug was channel-surfing.

"Find anything?"

"Not really."

"I'm not surprised. We've got two hundred channels. There should always be something interesting to watch."

"Oh, here we go." Doug set down the remote and settled his head on Jan's shoulder. *"Friday After Next."*

"The sequels weren't as good as the first one."

"Yeah, but it's still funny. Mike Epps is a fool."

They settled in to watch a show both had seen numerous times. Just watching TV and cuddling. About thirty minutes in Jan had a frightening thought. *I could get used to this.* An even more frightening thought followed that one. She wanted to get used to it.

39

Neither Doug nor Jan was ready for the holidays to end. But the second of January saw both of them back at work. With both Pat and Melissa still off, however, it was a light crew.

Joey was there, though, and, as always, was ready for news.

"How was your New Year?" he asked Doug.

"It was good. Yours?"

"Watched the ball drop with my girl, my kids, and dog and thought . . . I'm officially old." Doug chuckled. "What did you do? Hang out with Jan?"

"Went to a dinner party over Byron and Cynthia's new house in Venice."

"Venice?" Joey was shocked. "Day-um! Bus driver salaries have gone up!"

"His wife found the house. It's a pretty cool spot, with the patio on the roof. She's turning Byron bourgie, though, man. Waiters serving us, chef in the kitchen, using seven, eight different plates for one meal. I asked her, why can't you put all my food on one big plate?

"Instead of her answering, Byron had the nerve to speak up. 'They're courses,' he informed me." Doug mockingly imitated his brother, accent clipped, back ramrod straight. "I'm, like, fool the last course you took was high-school gym. Shut the hell up!"

Joey and everyone else in the back burst out laughing.

"What about the food?" an eavesdropper asked. "Was it good?"

"It was delicious, I can't even lie. Steak, salmon, duck . . . and some other stuff I couldn't recognize or pronounce. I tease her a lot, but she's good people, and crazy about my brother. We had a ball."

"And by 'we' you mean you and Jan? You skillfully dodged that question the first time around."

"Not that it's your business, but I wasn't trying to dodge anything. Yes, Jan and I brought in the New Year together. Is that clear enough for you?"

"I heard it!" said a voice from across the hall.

"No doubt," Joey replied with a shake of his head. "Melissa probably heard it and she's off today."

A second later, Jan appeared. "Everybody heard it." She spun around and walked back to the counter.

Doug made a face and followed behind her. "You okay?"

"Yes, you've totally ruined me now. Not only dating a man I work with, but now involved in the soap opera as well."

Pat, who'd heard the comment, too, said, "Looks like you've never been happier."

"Pat, I hated the thought of coming to work here. But it's turned out to be one of the best things that ever happened to me."

"He's that good, huh?"

"Pat!"

"Baby, I'm just—how do you young folk say it— keeping it real!"

"Ha! I didn't mean him. I mean, I did, but not like how you're . . . oh Lord."

"Man got you where you can't think straight."

"No, this is your doing."

Pat laughed.

"Doug makes me happy, but there are some other things happening that have me feeling really good about life right about now."

"Something to do with your singing?" Jan nodded. "Ooh, girl, tell me."

"I want to, but I can't. Not yet. Once it's finished, then I'll share with you. Just be praying for me, okay, that everything will go perfectly."

"I'm happy for you, Jan, and I will surely do that. As for you hooking up with the man who put that big smile on your face, I'm happy about that, too. I told you when you started a couple months ago that he was a good man. When I met you I thought you were a pretty smart girl. Looks like I was right."

With Christmas over, the afternoon dragged. After the counter closed, processing and sorting mail, the time went a bit faster.

Once they were off and walking to their cars in the lot, Doug asked, "Are you coming over?"

"No, I ran around so much during the holidays that I think I'll head home."

"All right, then."

"What about you?"

"I might head over to where Marvin works, grab a bite to eat."

"Where does he work?"

"That new restaurant off of La Brea and Slauson. I'll take you there the next time we go out. The food is pretty good."

They said their good-byes and soon Jan was pulling into her driveway. With both Lionel and her mom's bedroom at the back of the house it was normally dark when she drove up. Tonight there was a light in the living room.

She got out and went inside. Rochelle was sitting in the living room, going through the mail. "Hi, Mom."

"Hello, Jan."

"You didn't have to work tonight?"

"No, they didn't have any more data entry for us tonight so we got off early. I thank the Lord for that."

Jan went and sat beside her mother. "I wish you didn't have to work so hard."

"Me, too, but these bills won't pay themselves. I appreciate what you're doing, Jan. I know you'd rather be in your own place, especially now with that good man you're dating and all. I wish I could see a way out of this debt, but short of a miracle or a lottery win . . ."

Jan struggled with a thought, then made a decision. "I have some news to share. It may not be a million-dollar miracle, but it puts me on the radar of possibilities."

"What's that?"

"I wrote a song and it's going to be professionally recorded."

"Hmm."

A disappointing reaction, but Jan pressed on. "It's an empowering number about being happy in your own skin, with being who you are. Doug's sister-in-law heard about my struggles in the industry, of not being that perfect size 2 like most pop stars. She encouraged me to write my feelings about the experience and then Thump, the bandleader in the group I front one Friday a month, put some music to the words. We performed it at the holiday party last week. The crowd loved it!"

"I'm happy they liked your song, Jan. But let me ask you something. How much money is this recording going to cost you, and what will you do with the song once it's on tape? You have a beautiful voice, Jan, I've always told you that. But there are thousands of women with beautiful voices and millions of records out there. So what do you hope to gain from recording this song?"

Jan told her about the Englishman who approached

her at the party. "He was out of town last week when I called, but his assistant told me to call back tomorrow, which I will, first thing. What do I expect to get out of it? I don't really have any expectations. But this is costing me nothing and will give me a professionally recorded and mastered song to use for auditions. I might even get it made into a video and upload it to YouTube. Who knows what might happen?"

"I understand you taking advantage of an opportunity, but I sure hope you're not thinking about quitting your job to pursue this again full-time."

"No, Mom. I'm not thinking that." Jan watched her mom place aside the letters and envelopes and run a weary hand across her face. Her heart broke for the woman who gave so much to her and Lionel and seemed to get so little in return. "Mom, have you ever had a dream, or wanted something out of life and went for it?"

Rochelle thought for a minute. "I wanted to be a wife, a mother. That didn't turn out quite like I planned it, but I have no regrets. Even with the situation being what it is, you and Lionel are blessings in my life."

"So that was your only dream? To be married with children?"

"Growing up the way I did, we weren't encouraged to dream. Life was looked at from a very practical point of view." Her mother paused, looked off into the distance. "I used to draw, back when I was a kid."

"Really?"

"Uh-huh. Was pretty good at it, too."

"Why'd you stop?"

"I don't know, really. Before your dad I dated this one guy who was a lot like me. Practical. No-nonsense. He was a good man, really hard worker. Never relaxed. Never just sat around and did nothing. If he came over and saw me doing that he'd say I was lazy."

"He saw you drawing and said that?"

"No, I think I'd already stopped by then. But I used to love crossword puzzles, stuff like that. I'd sit and do that after coming home and cooking dinner, waiting for him to come over. He would and if I was sitting there doing puzzles or watching TV he'd shake his head as if I'd committed a crime. After a while I made sure not to be doing that when he came over and then I guess, slowly, I just stopped doing it at all.

"Then I met your dad, had you, and started working. After that it was all about his dream."

"What was that?"

Rochelle looked at Jan, her expression unreadable. "He wanted to own a supper club."

"What? Daddy?"

"Yep, your daddy was one of those suave fellas, classy. He had an idea to operate a club where we'd put on these shows and serve great food. He was a musician, played the saxophone, but a business-man, too. You're a lot like him."

"Wow, Mom. I don't remember ever hearing you guys talk about any of this. I had no idea." They were both silent, lost in thought for a beat or two. "So what happened?"

"His current wife. They met and the next thing I knew we were divorced and he was in Texas. I heard he started a barbeque restaurant down there and then sold it several years later. Made a little profit, too. I guess that's the closest he came to the supper club dream." Rochelle looked at Jan, her smile bittersweet. "I'm glad you've got this chance, Jan, to have your song recorded. Maybe you'll let me hear it when it's done."

"Of course, Mom, I'd love that."

"I know I'm not one of those show moms pushing you toward that life. It's always been one of fantasy for me, something I can't even imagine. I live in a very literal reality. What's important to me are those things I can see, touch, actualize as something I can do. But I love you, Jan, both you and Lionel, and I want you to be happy. It looks like you are."

"I want you to be happy, too, Mom. You do for us, but you need your own life. And maybe even a boyfriend, or companion."

"Now you're talking crazy."

"Why, you're not that old? I can't remember the last time I heard you mention a man. How long has it been since you've dated?"

"Not long enough." Rochelle stood. "I'm going

back in the room to watch a little television. Get to bed early."

Jan stood, too. "Thanks for sharing with me about Dad, Mom. I'm glad you want to hear my song." She put her hands around a mom who rarely showed such affection. "I love you."

"I love you, too."

40

"What are you doing today?"

"A whole lot of nothing." At eleven in the morning on this chilly Saturday she still lay in bed with no guilt at all.

"You should come riding with me."

Jan looked at her phone as if Doug could see her. "Riding what?"

"My bike. What else?"

"You know I don't do that."

"I know, but you should."

"And why is that?"

"Because you're my ride-or-die chick."

"That I could die riding is exactly my point."

"You can die crossing the street, or watching TV. When it's your time, it's your time."

"I'm trying not to go before my time."

"Jan . . . don't you trust me? I'd never do anything to jeopardize your safety."

"This from the guy who on my first day at work almost ran me over."

"You're being dramatic. At no time that you've seen me riding have I not been in control of my bike." Silence. "Come on, Jan. I want to see that bunch of plump you call a booty on my seat, have your arms wrapped around my waist and your titties smushed into my back. Get you some black leather pants and some thigh-high boots with real tall heels."

"Oh, so you want me to fall before getting on the bike."

"Don't worry about any of that, baby. I've got you."

"I'm sorry, Doug. It's not just that I don't like motorcycles. I really don't feel like getting out."

"Okay, but know that before it's all over I'm going to have you on my bike."

"We'll see."

"At the very least you can come hang with me at the club. Later on tonight, one of the members will be celebrating his birthday there."

"What club?"

"The only one that matters, baby. My motorcycle club, the Ace Imperials."

"What time?"

"Things will probably get started around nine or ten."

"That sounds okay. It will give me the whole day to relax and do the mundane chores I've been avoiding like, for starters, washing the mound of clothes piled on my closet floor."

"All right, then. Call me later. And make sure

and wear something tight and sexy to the party. I'll be showing you off and want all of my boys' mouths to water."

"Doug, that sounds sexist."

"Maybe, but I still want to see you in some pants squeezing the life out of that plump rump."

"Somebody's beeping in. I have to go."

"Call me later."

Jan clicked over and put the phone on speaker as she climbed out of bed. "Hello?"

"Hello, Jan?"

She stopped, looked at the phone as if it would help her ascertain the identity of the accented voice coming out of it. "Yes?"

"My name is Peter. I'm Chandler Thomas's brother."

"Oh, hi!"

"Hello. I'd like to chat with you for a bit. Do you have a moment?"

"Sure. Are you calling me from London?"

"New York, actually. I'm over here on a short promo tour with one of my groups."

"Oh, okay."

"You have a new fan in my brother Chandler. He said glowing things about you and your performance the other night."

"It was a wonderful party."

"And he sent me the song you've written."

"Sorry about the quality of that recording. It was done on my band leader's mini-mixer, very basic."

"But good enough for me to get a feel for it and I must admit I quite like it."

"Thank you."

"It's why I'm calling, actually. I was hoping that while in New York I could get you to join me and do the recording."

"Come to New York? Really? When?"

"It would have to be next week."

"Oh, that fast?"

"I know it's short notice, but we'll be flying back to London next Saturday. A good friend of mine has a studio in Tribeca on the Lower East Side. I was hoping you could fly up on Thursday."

Jan didn't fly often but knew that fares got higher the closer the trip. That it was right after Christmas and she'd bought more gifts than she'd expected, the bank account was on the lean side.

"Um . . . I'd have to . . . check a few things. See if I can get off work, and the flight schedules . . ."

"If you could let me know as soon as possible I'll have my assistant book your flight."

"Oh, you'd book the flight?"

"Sure, that wouldn't be a problem."

Jan wanted to break out into the happy dance but forced herself to remain calm. "Then let me make a call right now and see if I can get off work."

"Thank you, Jan. I look forward to hearing back from you."

"Thank you, Peter. And give Chandler my best."

"Will do."

Jan hit the button twice to make sure the call was ended, then exploded. "Woohoo!"

"What's all that noise?" Lionel yelled from down the hall.

Jan ran in and told him what had happened. "I can't believe it! I just recently told someone about the last time I was there, which was ten years ago! About how much I enjoyed it and wanted to go back. And now this happens. I can't believe it."

"Make sure everything is wheelchair accessible because as your, um, producer, I'm going with you."

"How do you figure?"

"How do you not figure? You know that without me that song would have sounded like a nineties throwback."

"Okay, then, Mr. Producer, I'll most definitely see what I can do."

They talked a bit more and then Jan left the room to call Doug. She was totally joking when she'd promised the trip to her brother. But she'd soon find out that life had more surprises in store for her than she'd realized.

41

The following Thursday afternoon Jan and Lionel arrived at New York's JFK Airport. They deplaned and thanks to the wheelchair assistant went directly to ground transportation where Peter said a car would be waiting.

"I can't believe I'm in New York," Lionel said, his eyes shining.

"I still can't figure out how that extra ticket magically appeared."

That was Doug's story that no matter what he stuck to, but Jan believed Doug's brother Nelson, who worked at LAX, had a lot to do with the magic. She'd said as much and tried to get the cost out of him so she could repay it. No way did she believe it was free, as she'd been told. It was a blessing, as Pat had pointed out. So Jan had decided to take her wise coworker's advice and not knock it or block it but to be grateful and keep quiet about it.

That Lionel was with her made the trip that much more special, as was her witnessing his first flight. The last time they'd taken a trip together was five years ago, when they went to Vegas for Aunt Brenda's wedding. They hadn't hung out together much. She'd been part of the bridal party and spent most of her time with Crystal helping her aunt get ready. Lionel and the friends who'd met him there spent their time at the pool. During the five hours on their nonstop journey, they'd talked the whole time. His helping her out with the song and her helping to get him involved in the basketball camp had brought them closer together. She'd always loved her brother, but these days she liked him a lot, too.

Downstairs, there was a man holding a sign that said BAKER. They walked over to him.

"You're here for me, Jan Baker?"

"Yes, indeed."

"This is my brother, Lionel."

"Hello, Lionel. I'm parked right outside. Let's get going."

She'd hoped they'd stop by the hotel first, but the driver took them directly to the studio. From the airport to the studio the driver was like a personal tour guide. When he found out it was Lionel's first trip to New York he gave a running commentary of the areas they passed, the buildings they saw, and the people who lived there. Jan learned a lot that she hadn't known. The drive to Tribeca felt a lot shorter than the hour that it actually took.

The studio was in a large warehouse that had

been converted to offices, lofts, and artist work spaces. They took a large, antiquated-looking elevator to the third floor, then walked down a series of halls to the studio on the other side. Peter was there, as were five rocker-type musicians: long hair, one with dreads, tats, leather, and chains. These guys were definitely being who they were and looked to be winning in their skin. For Jan, the excitement caused her stomach to flutter. It was going to be an interesting night.

"Hello, there."

"Hey, Peter. Hey, guys." Jan introduced Lionel. Peter introduced the band and the engineers who sat behind a large mixing board on the other side of the glass, including a young guy, almost twenty-five but looking sixteen with his Buddy Holly-style glasses and shock of red hair. He looked more like a nerd who should be conducting a scientific experiment in a college, not someone producing dope beats and fusing rock with funk. But that's what Peter said he did, and that he was one of the best.

"Okay, Lionel, if you'll go in the other room with the engineers and help them out I'll get Jan set up in her booth. The band is going to be out here. This is one of the best studios in New York. Everyone will blend perfectly."

"Are we going to rehearse first?"

"Oh yes, my dear. We're going to rehearse a lot."

And they did. For hours. Over and over. Take after take. At first, Jan felt a bit dubious about the rock edge that the song had been given, but the more she let loose and went with it, as Peter suggested, the more she liked it. At around midnight, Peter told them to take five.

They did. Jan went to the restroom. Peter began talking as soon as she returned. "Okay, guys. I think we're ready to do this. Jan, just relax and keep your lips close to the shield. Remember to feel the music, perform the song. Lionel, are you guys ready in there?"

"Ready, boss."

"All right, then, guys. Let's make a hit record!"

An hour later, Jan sat on a black leather couch in the general area, sipping a bottle of water, feeling totally happy and incredibly drained. She'd given everything she had, pulled energy from her toes, and left it all in the studio. Hearing the playback was proof that it had been well worth the effort. Once it was mixed and compressed she felt "What I Am" could go toe-to-toe with any hit out there.

Peter walked into the room. "Jan, how are you feeling? Ready for a good night's sleep at the hotel?"

"I can't move. But I guess I need to because I could definitely use a hot shower and a soft bed."

"You'll find neither of those here so, come on, up with you."

With Peter giving her a helping hand, she struggled to her feet. "Thank you. I can't believe how tired I am. Singing is hard work!"

"Yes, it is. You need to work out to get in better shape, so when we get called out to go on tour, you'll have the kind of stamina you need on the road."

"Wow, a tour. Sounds like a dream."

"One that could become reality. That's what daydreamers do. We make it happen."

After gathering her things, she, Peter, and Lionel walked to their cars parked on the street just steps from the studio door. The band had left thirty minutes before. The same driver who'd driven them from the airport was standing by.

She turned and gave Peter a hug. "Thanks for everything. Believing in me, taking a chance on me, pairing me with those crazy knuckleheads you call a band. They're a great group of musicians who can play their asses off. So thank you."

"It was my pleasure. Once we get this mastered down I plan to put it on ReverbNation, get some feedback, see what happens."

"That's a great idea!"

Jan knew about this platform designed for musicians to showcase their work, network with people in the industry, and where music lovers could find amazing artists not getting radio play. She'd even surfed the site a few times but had never considered it as an avenue for her own success.

"Doesn't hurt to put it out there. Even though I have friends in the business and am a producer myself, I still use the site as a way to take the temperature of the listening audience. Sometimes it works, sometimes not. One of the bands I'm managing on this tour has done very well over there, kick-started their success, really."

"The guys I just worked with?"

"No, another band. But those guys have music over there, too."

"Could you send me a link? I'd love to hear more of their music."

"Will do. So are you staying in the city for the weekend?"

"Just until Saturday. This is Lionel's first time here, so all day tomorrow we're going sightseeing, then tomorrow night we're hoping to see a play."

"I'll tell the driver to stay with you. It will make it easier to get around."

"Oh no. I couldn't possibly ask you to do that."

"You didn't ask. I offered. Don't try and talk me out of it."

"That is so generous of you." Jan hugged him again. Lionel voiced his appreciation, too. "Thanks again for everything."

"It was my pleasure."

For the rest of the stay, Jan and Lionel had the time of their lives. With a driver, they planned the stops and attractions strategically based on location and were able to see much more than catching various taxis would have afforded. Because of Lionel's wheelchair they were also moved to the front of most lines and given the best seats just about everywhere they went. Lionel learned that everything, even his disability, had a positive side.

They arrived home Saturday night. Doug picked them up at the airport and dropped Lionel off at home. He took her to the restaurant where Nelson worked. With a movie, Jan telling Doug all about New York, and Doug showing Jan how much he'd missed her, they didn't get to sleep until almost four o'clock.

The following week, life was back to normal. The post office by day, rehearsal by night, and a show at Breeze on Friday. After the show, she saw a missed call from Peter. His message was for her to visit the ReverbNation Web site ASAP. She did. And couldn't believe it. "Who I Am" was number one on three charts: funk, rock, and pop!

42

First thing Monday morning, Jan got a call.

"Hello, is this Jan Baker?"

Jan frowned at the unfamiliar voice. "Yes, who's this?"

"Hi. My name is D'Andra. You don't know me. I work with my husband, JaJuan Simmons. We own several fitness centers in the LA area."

"And you're calling me? Are you sure you have the right number?"

D'Andra laughed. "I'm positive."

"I'm sorry to sound so skeptical, but as out of shape as I am I can't imagine why the owner of a fitness center would be calling."

"I totally understand. Believe me if I'd gotten a similar phone call, even today, that would be my reaction, too. This isn't about the fitness center. Well, it is, but not in the way you're thinking. I heard your song last night. And I love it. I absolutely love it."

"Oh."

"Girl, you did your thing on that number."

"I didn't know that so many people listened to the ReverbNation Web site."

"Actually, I don't, but someone who does told my husband about you. He went on, heard the song, and immediately called me. I listened to the song, jammed to the beat. Then I listened to it again and really heard the words. Then I listened to it again and started feeling like I wanted to strut my stuff, and by the fourth time I was singing around my house with my kids looking at mama like she'd lost her mind."

"Wow, D'Andra, that makes me so excited. How you reacted is exactly how I want people to feel!"

"Girl, that song is inspired! I could relate to every single word. Did you write it?"

"Yes."

"I knew it! And you lived it, too, huh?"

"Sure did."

"I told Night that the way you sang it you had to have written those words yourself and you had to have lived them!"

"You told who?"

"Night, that's what everyone calls JaJuan, my husband. Night Simmons."

"Ah, the trainer. I've heard that name. He has a workout video."

"Several, on DVD, MP3, and YouTube."

"And a gym over in Ladera Heights. I know who

you're talking about now. Of course I've seen him. And I've heard about you. The wife who lost weight after having the baby."

"Child, I needed to lose weight long before a baby came along. But yes, after having our son I had to do it all over again and now that our daughter has arrived, it's déjà vu. I listened to that song and thought, wow, that is so inspiring. I wanted to download it, but it isn't for sale yet. So I went digging on the Internet, found your number, and here I am because, girl, I want, no, I've got to have that song. I'd love to use it as part of our routine. We have this program especially for over-weight women, many, in fact all of them, suffering self-esteem issues and this song is badass! It's just what they need to help motivate them and at the same time let them know that they're good right now, in the shape they're in, at the weight they are. It's just, girl, you just don't know how this song will motivate women. I want your permission to use it in our exercises and make a special routine."

"Stop!"

"I'm serious, Jan. I jumped my butt off that couch and was squatting and lifting and throwing punches and the music was perfect! I know I'm going on and on and you are probably wondering who is this crazy woman, but when I heard that song, I felt like I know you. Like we haven't met but I know you, because I know we've experienced some of the same things. And I just had to find you and call you and thank you, first of all. And secondly, try and get that song!"

"I'm just speechless, really. This whole thing, writing the song, recording it, came out of nowhere. We just put it on the site a week ago, just to see what would happen and here I am getting a call from Night Simmons's wife, who was in . . . what magazine was it?"

"*Capricious.*"

"Yes, that's it. Wow. This is crazy."

"Well, all I can tell you is get ready because I have a feeling your life is getting ready to change. Big time. There's something about that song that is so powerful, and the way you sing it so irreverently just like the song says. 'I don't give a damn, I'm who I am.' That is such a universal thought even if we really do care but don't want to, you know what I'm saying?"

"I know exactly what you're saying."

"So, yes, girl, I think you've got a hit right there so . . . either change your number or get another phone because I have a feeling your line is going to be blowing up real soon."

Jan would later tell D'Andra she had no idea how right she was.

43

"I'm so nervous."

"Don't be nervous, baby girl. You've got this."

After topping several charts on ReverbNation, "Who I Am" was put into rotation at radio stations across the country. Jan's phone had been buzzing all week with interview requests. Today she sat in the waiting room for her very first one, which would be given live on LA's number one pop station. Doug had volunteered to drive her there. She'd eagerly accepted. Though still apprehensive about the process and just what to expect, she felt better with Doug there.

The door to the room opened. "Ms. Baker, they're ready for you in the studio."

"Can Doug come, too?"

"Of course. Right this way."

The room was larger than she'd imagined. The famous DJ Mark Ocean, who sounded larger than life across the airways, was smaller, but friendly.

As commercials played, he removed his headset and jumped up to greet her.

"How ya doin'? Mark Ocean."

"Jan Baker."

"Doug Carter."

They shook hands. Mark looked at Doug. "Are you her manager?"

"Yes." This was said without hesitation. Jan just smiled.

"Well, have a seat over there, guys, next to the engineer. We're on right after the break."

Jan sat and looked around. It was her first time in a radio station and the closest brush with fame she'd had since *Showtime at the Apollo* ten years ago. Hearing Mark's voice, one she'd heard over the radio on so many mornings, felt surreal. Sitting here, like an out-of-body experience, one that she was jolted out of by Mark's excited on-air delivery.

"And we're back. It's Mark in the morning putting the motion in your ocean as you go to school, work, prison detail, the kitchen to get another cup of coffee, wherever you're heading we're heading there with you and on the way . . . we're bringing the 'Who I Am' artist, Jan Baker! That's right, guys, in the studio with me right now is the singer behind the song that in less than a week has taken the country by storm. It's incredible! But understandable. Everybody wants to feel good about themselves and Jan Baker is giving all of us a reason! Jan, good morning!"

"Good morning, Mark."

"Speak right into the mike, darling, so everyone can hear you. How does it feel to be an overnight sensation?"

"Great, especially since it's an overnight that was about ten years in the making. But this is surreal, overwhelming even, but really good."

"The song is so catchy, especially the hook. And you wrote this, right?"

"Yes, along with Doug"—she looked at him—"and my brother, Lionel. My band leader, Thump, wrote the original music and then producer Peter Thomas did the rocked out remix that's just . . . exploded!"

"It's exploded all right. I haven't seen a song do this since Pharrell's 'Happy.' And not many before that. So you were singing in a band before this happened?"

"Yes, it's called the Real Deal. We have a standing engagement at a club called Breeze, in Inglewood, and we also do shows around town. Doug's sister-in-law heard me at Breeze and asked us to perform at a holiday party. After hearing about an incident that happened at the club, and how I handled it, she asked if I could put what I said in a song."

"What happened at the club?"

"Well, basically—"

"She got heckled," Doug interjected. "Because of how she looks. Because she doesn't fit society's idea of an R & B or pop singer."

"And somebody in the crowd heckled her? Seriously?"

"Yes," Jan said, having again found her voice.

"But that wasn't new to me. I've always been what we call thick in my neighborhood. A chubby kid, an overweight teen, and now an average-size adult. Most women in America wear a size twelve. I wear between that and a sixteen depending on the cut and the designer. But that's considered huge in the music industry, where size zero is common."

"I hate to agree with you but have to admit that since the music video became such a crucial component to the marketing process, looks do play a major role. So how'd you handle this heckler?"

"With honesty. I signaled for them to take the music down and spoke from my heart. Told her that I'd always been a big girl and probably always would be. That's just who I am."

"Good for you, Jan Baker. Because of your courage and talent, a lot of young girls out there are feeling a whole lot better about being who they are, or as you say, who I am."

The interview was quick, lasting less than ten minutes. They played the song and took a couple callers, thanking Jan for being a spokesperson for people considered "different."

"I'm not a spokesperson," she said, correcting the last caller. "But if this song becomes the anthem for people who are marginalized, discounted, considered weird or, like you say, different, or other, whatever . . . then I'm proud to have written it and to have shared it with you."

Jan couldn't imagine life getting any better. And

then, the next morning, she got yet another phone call, this one the most unexpected.

"Hello," she said, though she recognized the number.

"Jan, hey, it's Nick Starr."

44

Jan was shocked. What could he want? Only one way to find out. "Hello, Nick."

"You're probably surprised I'm calling."

"That's an understatement."

"How could I not? Everybody's jamming to you these days. I had to call with my congratulations."

"Thank you."

"I'm feeling a little chill in the air and it's okay. I get it. You're still mad at not being chosen for my show, but please understand, Jan, it wasn't personal."

"Wasn't it?"

"Not at all. Look, this is a conversation that should be handled in person. Let me take you to lunch. I'll explain everything."

"That's not possible. I work afternoons."

"Then breakfast, right now. Just to hear me out, okay? Once you do, if you're still upset, then I'll cut my losses and move on. But if you'll listen objectively not only to what I know about this business, but how I want to help you sustain what you've got going right now, then I think we can do some big things together."

"How can that happen? I'm still the same size, the same weight. I wasn't good enough to be on your show two months ago. What's different now?"

"I was able to get the powers that be above to finally see what I saw all along. That's what you don't understand, Jan. My name is on the show, but others have money on the table and a say in how the show looks. Where do you live? I'll come to wherever you suggest so that we can move past what happened and get to what's possible."

Jan agreed to meet him in an hour. On the way to a restaurant on Slauson Avenue, she called Doug.

"Hey, juicy."

"Who?"

"That's my new name for you, Juicy Jan. The only one who can call you that is me, your man."

"Oh Lord. Keep working at the post office, baby, because a career in music or spoken word just won't work out."

"That's okay. I know how to make it juicy, though. I know how to work that out."

"I can't argue with the truth."

"So what's up, juicy girl?"

"Nick called me."

"Huh? Nick who?"

"Nick Starr."

"And just like B.B. King," Doug mumbled, "the thrill is gone."

"Ha!"

"What did that asshole want?"

"I'm heading to a meeting to find out."

"Where?" She told him. "I don't like it, Jan. He's just trying to capitalize on your success."

"He doesn't need me, Doug. He's been a celebrity for years."

"When's the last time he had a hit record?"

"He's getting ready to have a hit reality show, so yesterday doesn't matter."

"And now he wants you on it?"

"I don't know. I just think he wants to apologize formally and have us end on a positive note. There are less than six degrees of separation in this industry. You never know when a connection might come in handy. And that goes both ways."

"Jan, be very careful with that dude. Just a few weeks ago you weren't good enough. Now you're on the radio and people's iPods and all of a sudden he's got a spot. I don't trust him for a second."

"I'm not sure I do either. But I felt it in my best interest to at least go hear what he has to say."

"I'm tempted to join you."

"Not a good idea."

"Why not?"

"Because refereeing clashing egos, which I'd surely be doing, would take the focus away from why we're meeting. Besides, I'll only have an hour or so with him before coming in to work."

"That chump. He's an opportunist. And a user."

"He's also a former platinum-selling artist with a

track record in the industry and contacts that might help me. He's not my favorite person either. I'd probably choose jerk over chump. But he is still a name in the business, with a hot show happening this summer. I've waited a long time for my chance to make this happen. So I'm keeping personal feelings out of it and focusing on business."

"Make sure your focus is razor sharp. Because with a snake like him, you're going to need it."

Jan entered the restaurant and almost didn't recognize the man sitting in a corner booth, his back to the front door. Starr wore a Yankees baseball cap and sunglasses. Guess he didn't want to draw a crowd. What hadn't changed was him on his cell phone, texting and scrolling as usual.

She sat down. "Hello, Nick."

He took off his glasses and showed off his smile. After twenty years of hard, fast living, Nicholas Starr was still a fine man. "Hello there, talented lady. You're looking good."

"Not good enough for *Starr Power,* but I'm holding my own."

He had the nerve to look contrite. "Fact of the matter is, you're better than *Starr Power.* I knew that from the minute you opened your mouth. You don't need me to coach you in how to rock a mike or handle yourself onstage."

"No, but a record deal would be nice."

He sighed, fell against the back of the booth. "I should have realized that, but I didn't. I had producers in my ear talking about ratings, and what kind of people would bring the most drama and how they needed girls who were going to turn it up. I knew that wasn't you, Jan. You're too classy for that."

Are you flirting? Seriously? He was, and in spite of his jerk status it wasn't totally ineffective.

"So why am I here?"

"Because now that you're on the charts they'll finally listen to what I told them the whole ten weeks you tried out for the show. That you should be on it."

"So let me get this straight. You wanted me on the show."

"Hell yeah."

"But your producers had other ideas."

"The ones who put skin in the game, Jan, the ones who financed the show. My name is on the marquee, but I don't have total control." He leaned forward. "I know you won't believe this, but I was always for you. Maybe I didn't fight hard enough but now that you've given me radio-play ammunition, I'm ready to go back in that boardroom and do battle. I just need to know first, though, that you still want to be on the show."

The waiter came over to take their order. Jan shook her head. "Nothing for me, thanks."

The waiter looked at Starr, her eyes widening slightly at the recognition. "I'll take a tall glass of orange juice," he told her, pulling a bill out of his wallet. "And I'd appreciate it if you let me remain anonymous."

She took the one hundred dollar bill almost reverently from his hand. "I can't believe you're in here," she said breathily. "And in my section! Is there any way I can get a picture?"

"Not right now, sweetheart. But bring back your number with my juice and I'll shoot one over to your phone."

Jan watched and marveled at a true player in action. It was easy to see how Starr attracted the women. Not just his looks. Everything about him was mesmerizing. Which for Jan was all the more reason to stay focused and alert. Now was not the time for a girl crush, but to be a grown woman handling her business like the professional she was.

"So what do you think? If I go to bat for you and can get a spot opened up, will you come on the show?"

"I don't know, Nick. A lot is coming at me right now. A lot to think about."

"I understand. But you've got to know what a national platform like reality TV can do for your career and your status. You can research any of the franchises and know why reality shows are not going away anytime soon."

"I know they're really popular."

"Baby, they can make your career. I don't have to count off the names. You know the Grammy winners, Broadway stars, and super celebs doing their thing thanks to the small box."

"I do. And I appreciate your interest." She looked at her watch and stood. "I have to head to work. Let me talk to a few people and get back with you, okay?"

"Sure, sweetheart. But don't keep the Starr waiting, make me lose my twinkle."

She laughed, genuinely amused. Three months ago and the same invitation would have sent her to the moon that Crystal had mentioned. But today there was "Who I Am" and a man who called her juicy, a man who'd quenched every bit of her thirst and dimmed Starr's shine for real.

As soon as she got into the car, she rang her cousin. "Hang on, Crystal. Let me get Doug on the line. I need both of you on this." She put Crystal on hold.

"What happened?" was Doug's greeting.

"I've got Crystal holding on the other line. Let me bring her in, okay?"

"Sure."

She conferenced the call. "So, guys, long story short. Nick wants me on the show."

"I told you that's what he wanted," Doug said.

"How do you feel about that?" Crystal asked.

Jan pondered the question as she navigated traffic. "All kinds of ways. One part of me wants to tell him to shove that reality show where the stars don't . . . twinkle, and the other part says, hey, this is a shot at continuous national exposure, a way to build on the popularity of my song. To not let ego and hurt feelings keep me from taking it. Doug, I think I know your answer, but I'll ask anyway. What do you think I should do?"

"Turn him down, straight out. You don't need him now."

"Cuz?"

"I can't believe I'm saying this, but I think it's an offer you should seriously consider."

"You're right. I don't believe you're saying that."

"It's because of what you just pointed out, a way to build upon what's happening right now. You've got a hit song. *Starr Power* is going to be a hit show. Now that your name is out there and you're headed toward fame, I think you'll have more control over your story line and not have to stoop to the level some reality stars go to get more airtime. You can command it on talent alone."

"Just when I thought this situation couldn't get more complicated . . ."

"What are you going to do?"

"That's what I'm trying to figure out."

"Are you headed to work right now?"

"Yes, Doug. Are you?"

"I am now. Sounds like you can use a little support right now."

"Whatever your decision," Crystal said, "I'll support you."

"Does that go for you, too, Doug?"

"You know I've got you, babe. Whatever happens, that won't change."

Or would it?

45

A week later it was Valentine's Day. Doug was taking Jan to dinner. He wanted everything to be perfect and had worked on the evening's details for over a month. Researched to find just the right place. Shopped for the perfect gift. Had tailored a sharp black suit for their five-star evening aboard the *Queen Mary* in Long Beach. Not trusting the pictures, he'd called the place. They assured him that the ambiance was as had been described, and with reservations they'd make sure he had the perfect table with an immaculate view of the Pacific Ocean. He'd booked a table for two that very day. That's how sure he'd been about this location and what he'd planned.

Now he was on the phone with brothers Byron and Nelson, pacing the room with the phone on speaker, not sure about anything. At all.

"She's seriously thinking about doing his show! This is the same man who told her straight out that she didn't have the looks to be a singer in today's market. Who sat there in over ten auditions, watched her sing her heart out week after week, and then chose women who couldn't carry a tune five feet in a bucket but looked the part and made the cut. Now she's getting fifteen minutes and he wants to jump in the picture. It's so obvious that he's using her. I can't understand why she can't see it."

"Maybe she does," Byron said. "And maybe she's using him, too. If it gets her to where she needs to be, does it matter?"

"I don't know, man," Nelson said. "I'm kind of with Doug on this one. After all, he's the reason she's hot right now, indirectly. He's always had her back, drove me crazy talking about her, and been supporting her through this whole thing. Then Starr swoops through like Robin Hood saving a damsel, offering something that may or may not be real, and off she goes like he's the man. That would mess with me, too."

"But this shouldn't be about you, Doug. This should be about Jan and what's best for her, and supporting her no matter what she decides. Better for her to check it out and not have regrets than for you to dissuade her, his show blows up like *The Voice* or *American Idol*, the winner get a multi-million dollar record deal, and you get blamed. The last person you want to be in a relationship with is one who is unhappy, unfulfilled, and blaming you."

"What about the fact that being in a relationship

with her while she's in one with that fool will make me unhappy?"

"Ah, Doug." Nelson's voice was gentle. "Are you in your feelings? Is that what this is about?"

"Yes, and I don't mind saying it. He's a snake, and if it was anybody else she'd have seen it a long time ago. But this is the dude she had a crush on since the running was walking."

"Man, stop sounding like your mama," Byron said with a chuckle.

"I don't trust him around her."

"Him," Nelson asked, "or her?"

"Her around him. I know the kind of player he is, man. He can get in her head. I don't want her to get caught up behind his scheming behind."

"Look, bro," Byron's voice rang with big brother authority. "Why don't you just chill out, watch the show, and see what happens?"

"I guess I could. But doing that will kind of jack up the plans I had for tonight."

"What plans were those?" Nelson asked.

"Putting a ring on it. Now . . . I don't know."

After talking to his brothers, Doug made one final call. "Pops! What's up?"

"Hey now, Douglas."

"Since you're answering the phone, Mama must not be home."

"You know it."

"Where is she?"

"Ava came over and they went somewhere. They

should be back directly, or you can probably reach her on her cell."

"I'm surprised you let her out of the house."

"Boy, talk plain."

"It's Valentine's Day, Dad."

"What's that got to do with anything?"

"I guess nothing after thirty-two years."

"Didn't mean nothing to me after two years, or two months for that matter. Son, it didn't take a man-made holiday for me to wine and dine your mama. I give her flowers and presents for no reason, cards out of season, and my heart every single day of the year, three sixty-five for the past thirty-two. Ain't no box of chocolates and a card with words somebody else wrote that can top that kind of love."

"Man, Dad, the only comeback I have to that is 'wow.' Those words just shut any other argument all the way down. Funny thing, though, I don't remember you giving Mama flowers and stuff when we were coming up. Plus, half the time you were gone off fighting for your country."

"There's a lot of stuff goes on between a husband and wife that the children don't see, or at least shouldn't. Ask your mama about the letters I wrote her, sometimes daily, when I was away. Or about anything else I said. She'll back it up, might even bring out proof."

"She still has all the presents you bought her?"

"And the letters. And the cards."

"Willie Carter! Teaching a player how to play the

game! Maybe it's good I got you instead of Mama. There's something on my mind that I need to run by you."

"I'm listening."

"It's about Jan."

"Fine young woman you got there. Talented, too. Ava downloaded that song for me and your mama. You know I'm strictly R & B old school, but I have to admit that number's hot."

"I agree with everything you said, so much so that I was thinking about asking her to marry me."

"Son, I'm afraid I can't help you do that kind of thinking. That's a decision a man needs to make on his own."

"Understood. That's not the problem."

"What is?"

"Another dude."

"She's two-timing?"

"Not exactly." Doug gave Willie a brief rundown of the history between Nick and Jan, her competing for the reality TV show, being denied and then invited once her song became a breakout hit. "I don't understand why she can't see the obvious. Starr is only after her now because it will make him look good. I don't like him using her, or them being together. Or that she seems to still have feelings for him. Carter men don't have competition. That's what you always said."

"And I meant it. So why do you feel like you have to compete?"

"That's just it. I'm not going to try and compete

with the likes of a Nick Starr. And I'm not going to stay in a place where I have to wonder if that's necessary. I told her not to do it. She should have listened."

Willie's chuckle was slow and low. "Boy, if you're waiting for a woman to listen to you, you have a lot to learn, and you might die before she admits that you were right about something. Number one, you can't make up somebody else's mind. And number two, if there's no trust in the relationship, then you can't make that work either."

"I trust Jan. I don't trust Starr."

"You're not in a relationship with him, so you don't have to. Jan is the only one you need to believe. Now, the fact that you're worried somebody might take her from you tells me that you're the one who needs to step up his game."

"Me?"

"Uh-huh. That she's even looking at another man with any interest other than business, if that is what's happening, tells me you're not putting it down right. You've got to love her hard, son, and make sure she knows it. You've got to find out what it is that drives her crazy in the bedroom, and then every time you're in there send her to the looney bin."

"Uh, Dad, this might be a little too much information. It is my mama we're talking about."

"No, we're talking about you and your woman. If I've taught you boys anything it's to always do your best and be the best. I was in the service for twenty years, and was away from you children and the wife for months at a time. But every single night that I was home, and especially on that last night before I shipped out, I'd go to work, son, making sure your mama was more than satisfied, in every way. That if there was a need, I was taking care of it. When I left, it was with absolute confidence that no other man was going to turn the head of Elizabeth Carter, I didn't care who it was. Could have been the biggest star in the world, the President of the United States, and I knew Elizabeth Carter would be right there, with you children, waiting for her man."

"And she was. I can't remember even seeing Mama talking to other men, outside of the neighbors or a repairman or something."

"Of course not. She had me. I was all she needed then, and all she needs now. And one more thing. I know it was hard on my family, but sometimes those long stints away from each other did our marriage good. It doesn't hurt for them to miss you every once in a while. Let her feel her world without you in it. Then go back and rock it again.

"Trust your woman, son, and your own abilities to be the best man for her, the only one. Then go about making sure that you're setting that bar too high for any other man to reach it, or even come close."

46

It had been a week since Valentine's Day, and the wonderful dinner and evening Doug had meticulously planned, but one observing her life may have thought the holiday was still in full force. She'd awakened to romantic, sexy, or nasty text messages every morning and twice similar cards had been slid into her locker at work. Over the weekend, Doug had taken her car to get it detailed, on Sunday he'd bypassed the Carter crowd to cook them another steak dinner at his house. And in the bedroom, Doug was handling her body like it was a job and he was getting paid to work overtime. Jan didn't know what was happening, but she was loving it so much that it scared her. She found herself thinking about him constantly, unconsciously noting his whereabouts at work, feening for him on the nights they weren't together. Heck, last night, he showed up in her dreams! She was already falling in love with Doug, but if this behavior continued, she'd become addicted, maybe even possessed! The thing about it was, if someone suggested an exorcism or that she go to rehab to get over this feeling, she'd have a ready answer for them. *No, no, no!*

As if Doug's attentiveness wasn't enough to send her over the moon, Nick had called her to a meeting to discuss her being on *Starr Power.* She was headed to a meeting about an opportunity she thought had been denied her. And it had. Until the song she wrote had gotten recorded, uploaded to the Internet, and taken viral. The song inspired by a response to actions meant to hurt her had helped her in ways she couldn't have imagined. Crazy how life happened, and how the dream she'd had since she and Crystal grabbed brooms and sang in front of the mirror was becoming reality.

Jan wasn't accustomed to being in love and having life go her way, all at the same time. It was almost too much.

Following the GPS directions, Jan entered a neighborhood that looked straight out of the movies. Houses, if you could see them, sat far back away from the curb. The landscaping was so meticulous it looked fake. Flowering bushes were plentiful and vibrant, not one dead branch appeared on the lush palm trees lining the streets, and the ocean could be seen sparkling in the distance.

"You have arrived at your destination."

Jan laughed at the double meaning of the computerized statement. She had indeed arrived at the palatial estate of Nicholas Starr and, in turn, had reached her goal of being a successful recording artist. Today's visit was one step to ensuring she didn't become a one-hit wonder.

She looked at the tall wrought-iron gates of the home that was once featured in *Ebony* magazine. Last night when with Doug, she'd pulled it up on the Internet. Remembering his comments made her smile, and relieved a tiny bit of her nervousness.

"Looks like a prison."

"If it wasn't gated," she replied, "he would probably get robbed. Or run over by groupies. Or both."

"Give me his address, in case you need rescuing. Me and the Ace Imperials will jump that ten-inch fence like child's play and help you escape."

"I'll keep my phone handy. You're already on speed dial. That means my knight in shining armor is only one click away."

After she announced herself, the gates swung open revealing a vast front yard and a circular drive. To the right was a separate building that appeared to be a multicar garage. Jan parked her car in the circular drive and, after one last calming breath, got out of the car. A housekeeper opened the door and led her to an open-air dining area that was too upscale to be called a patio. Whatever the name, it was stunning. The meticulous landscaping of bushes, flowers, and trees that was seen on the street continued in this intimate garden atmosphere. Water spewed from the mouth of an upraised black panther into a fountain that flowed into a pool. A stark white awning provided relief from the sun and complemented perfectly the black glass top and stainless steel table. Bright splashes of color came courtesy of the upholstered dining chairs. She didn't sit down, though. Rather she wandered through the garden, touching the leaves, smelling the petals, and imagining how life would be if this were her house.

"Ms. Baker!"

Turning around, she was glad she'd braced herself. In white baggy pants, a white shirt, and dark glasses, Nick looked every inch the star. Sun hitting the multicarat stud diamond in his right ear cast rainbows on the glass table. He wore black sandals and carried a drink, lemonade she expected. His stance was casual, inviting. His smile produced goose bumps and caused her to wonder how many women had been seduced in this garden with those pearly whites. The thought was like ice water waking her from his spell. She could take a picture of him with her cell phone that would be worthy of any fashion or entertainment magazine. No doubt he was gorgeous. But he wouldn't be getting in the panties. This wasn't personal. This was business.

With this in mind, Jan chose to be sparing with her compliments and focus on why she was there. "Hello, Nick."

Her outstretched hand was ignored for a hug. The designer cologne she loved so much assailed her nostrils. She broke the embrace and smiled. "You have a lovely home."

"It's all right. Not as big as the one I'm designing, but it will do for now." He placed a hand at the small of her back and turned her toward the patio table, set with linen and silver. "Please, have a seat." Instead of across from her, he sat in the seat to her left. "What are you drinking, talented lady?"

"Cranberry juice, if you have it."

A different woman from the one who'd answered the door appeared out of nowhere. "Two cranberry juices. Make mine with a little extra in it." The woman nodded and left.

"What's a little extra?" Jan asked.

"Vodka."

"It's not yet noon, a bit early for alcohol wouldn't you say?"

"Vodka and cran is a breakfast drink. Besides, it's five o'clock somewhere."

Jan smiled. "I guess you're right."

"You have a nice smile."

"Thank you."

"I don't know if I ever told you, but you're a very pretty lady. A lot of people, especially these days, might say you're overweight. But you're rocking that body, believe it!"

Jan did believe it. Before leaving home she'd dressed with care: torture chamber, aka Spanx; form-fitting black maxi with a wide animal-print belt and large gold clasp, matching gold jewelry, and black leather ankle boots with a gold clasp on the side and four-inch heels. The elastic was so tight across the waist she could barely breathe, there was a fire between her thighs, and she couldn't feel her feet. But she looked good. Sometimes a woman had to keep her priorities straight.

"Thank you, Nick. No, you never told me that, never said anything about my looks. Seeing the type of women you were attracted to, it was easy to see why. I know I'm not the industry standard of beauty, but I feel good about who I am."

"Who I am," Nick sang, adopting the raspy tone she used while singing the song, and sounding excellent while doing so. "That song is fire, and you rocked it."

"Thank you."

"I requested salmon for lunch. Is that cool with you, or would you like a different meat choice?"

"Salmon is fine."

Their drinks were delivered. Nick raised his glass. "To Jan Baker, giving my show some true star power."

She smiled again.

"Damn, girl, those dimples. I'm told that if a woman has them in her cheeks, she probably has them elsewhere. Is that true?"

"It can be."

"Is it true for you?"

"I'll never tell."

"Hmm. Guess I'll have to make it my business to find out."

Jan's expression was unreadable as she set down

her glass. "Speaking of business, I don't mean to rush you, but my time here is limited."

"You're working today?"

"I told them I'd be late, but yes, I have to go to work."

"That's not going to last too much longer, you know that, right?"

"We'll see."

"I already know. I'm going to make you the star of the show, Jan. Those other wannabes are going to bring the ratchet level that's needed for a reality show to be a success, but I see you on there as I see you here now, classy, sensible, on top of your game."

"This all sounds amazing, Nick. But I can't help but remember how just a few short weeks ago I was all but invisible to you. I watched you with the other women. I saw how you treated them, how you fawned over them and flirted and, I don't know, acted interested. You were never that way with me. Now all of a sudden I'm beautiful and wonderful and the best thing ever. Besides the fact that mine is now quickly becoming a household name . . . what changed?"

Nick placed his hand over Jan's and looked deep into her eyes. "I understand why you'd ask that question and think that it's just because you have a hit song. But let me explain something to you. Those girls I see at the club I've seen every day of my life for the last twenty years. They're inter-changeable and replaceable. Yeah, I sleep with them. Wine and dine them. I'm a single man and I live that life.

"I treated you different because you're not like them. You're on the come up, but you don't act thirsty. You're confident that you can stand on talent alone. That's sexy as hell, but can I tell you something?" Jan nodded. "It was also a little intimidating."

"Me? Intimidate the Starr? You've got to be kidding."

"Not at all. I know my way around girls. But you're all woman. And I'm not sure I could handle it all. But I'd like to try."

By the time Jan left Calabasas, she was in a fog. The meeting had gone in a direction she couldn't have imagined. Nick had done everything right: apologized for his past behavior, come clean about his superficial judgments, served some of the best food she'd ever eaten, and taken her on a tour of the house Nick said she looked to belong in. When she called him on his overt flirting, he didn't back down. He went harder, told her it was time for him to settle down and he was looking for just the right woman to do that with. When their meeting ended and he hugged her in the driveway, he gave her the feeling that it might be her.

She tapped her steering wheel to engage her phone.

"Hey, Jan! I was just thinking about you. How'd the meeting go with your teenaged crush?"

"You won't believe it, Crystal."

"Why? What happened?"

Jan shared the afternoon's events. "It all sounds too good to be true. I don't know if he's being for real or just telling me what he thinks I want to hear to make sure I'll be on the show."

"What does it matter if at the end of the day, your goal is accomplished?"

"It matters because of Doug? Or have you forgotten I'm already in a relationship?"

"I'm not talking about his wanting to get personal. You're too smart to fall for that, and lose a guy like Doug Carter."

"So you think he doesn't mean any of what he said about me? Him being interested, our possible partnership, any of that?"

"I don't know if he is or not. But what I do know is that Doug Carter loved you then, before your hit record, loves you now, and will more than likely love you when the fame is over. While just a month ago, Nick turned you down for a spot on his show. So what you'll have to decide is whether or not you want to go for what's possible or if you want to hang on to what is."

Crystal's comment put her in turmoil. Because that was a decision Jan didn't know how to make.

47

The next two weeks passed in a blur. She was well into the second week before realizing that practically the only time she saw Doug was at work. When he went MIA the entire weekend, she really took notice. Friday night she'd had rehearsal. Saturday he'd taken a road trip with his motorcycle crew. Sunday she'd called and invited him to her house for dinner, but he was in San Diego at a Chargers game. In all that time, they'd made love once. Jan was going through withdrawals and, for the first time ever, discovering the difficulty in balancing a personal life with a career that had gone from zero to sixty. Ten years of trying had led to the overnight success she'd envisioned and soon, Jan felt she could quit the post office and fully embrace the life of her dreams.

On top of their regular rehearsals, she and the band were gearing up for a special fund-raiser that Frank had asked her to do at Breeze. She was working with Lionel, Thump, and now Peter to develop

more songs. On Saturday she'd finally had the
meeting with D'Andra Simmons, who on top of
wanting to buy the rights to use her song in an upcoming workout video, wanted her to participate
in it and to join their gym as well. Jan had said
she was too busy for the latter, but knew that getting exercise was the right thing to do. Plus, she
liked D'Andra. Felt that she was a kindred spirit
who, like her, had a genuine desire to make people
feel good.

Their stories were similar. D'Andra grew up in
LA and had always been big. Her mother showed
favoritism between siblings, which greatly affected
D'Andra's self-esteem. Food was her comfort. A life-
altering incident made her want to get healthy.
That's when she met a personal trainer named
Night Simmons, who was now her husband. Together they created the program called J.E.W.E.L.S.
that had led to a meeting between them.

With everything that was whirling around her,
Jan still felt a void and knew what it was. Doug
wasn't beside her, along for the ride. While preparing for the holiday show, they had been insepara-
ble. He'd been a constant support giving advice on
everything from wardrobe to hairstyle. It was an exciting time and he'd made it more so. And once the
show was over . . . that night and those afterward
had been filled with heat.

This upcoming fund-raiser show felt vastly different. They'd bought a table, so she knew that the
Carter family would be there. They'd talked last

night, but only briefly. She was living an even greater dream than she'd imagined, a surprise hit record and being on a reality show. She'd maybe even have a chance to date Nick Starr. But was the chance of having it all, as exciting and amazing as that life looked, worth losing the man who'd help make her dreams real, the one who was in her life right now?

That weekend, she told Doug she was coming over and wouldn't take no for an answer. That she missed him, and needed his curve. He'd laughed and told her he'd be waiting. Now on her way over she was nervous and didn't know why.

He answered the door wearing baggy shorts and a ripped tee, looking good enough to eat. "Hey, babe." She stepped into his arms and held the embrace as he closed the door and blessed her with a Carter kiss—hot, wet, long.

She sighed and clung to him as they went to the couch. "That's what I've been missing from my life. Where have you been?"

"I've been right here, baby. You're the one busy, living the life of a rock star."

"Yeah, one that you're supposed to be living with me."

He laughed, reached for the remote, and began surfing the channels. "You've got somebody else to do that."

She looked at him. "Who?"

"You know who. Your boy Nick."

"You're kidding, right?"

"A little bit. A part of me is serious, though. I'm still kind of put out that you're working with him."

"Well, thanks for being honest."

"You're welcome."

"Is that why you've been so scarce and we haven't had sex? Because I'm on punishment?"

"Girl, nobody has you on punishment."

"I haven't been getting my curve on, so that's how it feels."

"I'm sorry, baby, and will do all I can to make it up to you."

She snuggled against him. "Good."

"So how's it going with the Starr?"

"I haven't seen much of him actually, been meeting with the producers and honestly, things could go better in that department."

"Why, what's happening?"

"They don't get me and are trying to make me into something I'm not, something they feel the public wants or a singer should look like. Same old stuff."

"Why are they doing that when the public already loves you? That doesn't make sense."

"That's what I told them!"

"Sounds like you need to tell Nick to put his foot down and get them to back off. Remind him that they came to you, you didn't go to them."

"That's exactly what they need to know. See, Doug, that's why I need you beside me. I need a manager."

"Oh, you want my services now?"

She wriggled her eyes. "I sure do."

"I hate to break it to you, but that isn't going to happen. I'm a real dude and Nick? I can't feel that brother at all! Him and I in a room together, debating something having to do with you and he says the wrong thing? It could get ugly. I don't want that and you don't need that.

"I'm happy for you, though, Jan. I'll always want the best for you, no matter what."

She sat up and away from him. "What's going on, Doug?"

"What do you mean?"

"Why did that sound like the beginning of a Dear Jane letter?"

"Because you're tripping. Nothing has changed. I'm still here."

"It doesn't feel like it. I feel a distance growing between us. And I don't like it."

"Sometimes life happens, baby, and it spirals in a direction outside of our control. You're doing your thing and I'm here to support you. In your being busy, though, I realized that parts of my life had kind of gone by the wayside. I wasn't spending as much time with my fam, or my boys on the bike, or with your brother, like I promised I would. Speaking of, did he tell you? I'm going to start working with my friend who coaches them, come on as the assistant."

"No, he didn't tell me! That's wonderful." She kissed his cheek. "Thanks, Doug."

"You're welcome."

"But that's spending time with my brother, not with me. We still have a problem."

"No, you have a problem. I'm good."

"You're okay with the little bit of time we've spent together?"

Doug turned off the television, reached down, and began unlacing her tennis shoes. "No, but I'm okay that you're over here now." He reached for her other shoe. "I'm okay with the fact that these clothes are about to come off you." He stood, reached for her waistband, and began pulling down her pants. "And I'm okay that we're getting ready to get our curve on, just the way you like it. Right now, that's all I want to think about."

48

Doug started with her feet, massaging them with his thick, stubby fingers, planting kisses on her ankles in between rubs. Jan watched him, noted the care and concentration he took in caressing each heel and rubbing each toe. He licked his bottom lip. Her heat became damp. She moaned, low and soft, at the back of her throat. Quiet, but he heard it and got the message. He spread her legs and kissed her calf, the side of her knee, and inside of her thigh before reaching her satiny panties and licking the fabric that covered her treasure. Once, and again, his tongue stiff, the movement slow and long. Jan was on fire, wanting nothing more than Doug's sword inside her, his hands all over her, his tongue in her mouth.

"Doug, please . . ."

"Don't worry, baby," he said, his voice raspy with desire. "I've got this." He gripped the elastic waist of her panties. She raised off the couch. He pulled them down and flung them across the room, just seconds before he seized her hips, pulled her down to a horizontal position and plunged his tongue between her folds.

"Ahhhh!"

He licked her relentlessly, his pace alternating between fast and slow. He sucked her pearl into his mouth—nipping, lapping, flicking his tongue in a way that drove her crazy. It was everything and not enough at the same time. Everything because it felt so good. Not enough because she wanted him deeper.

He must have read her mind, because with one last French-kiss on her nana lips he kissed his way from there to each nipple, up to her neck, and on to her mouth. She tasted her essence as his tongue searched out hers for a duel as delicious as what was happening below as he slid inside her and began to grind, swirling his hips so his tip would hit the spot he'd memorized, the place inside her that he'd stamped with this love. She climaxed, but it was as if he didn't notice. His hips kept moving, his dick kept grooving—in, out, up, down—and side to side. She thought to ask him to stop, to let her return the oral favor, to give to him as thoroughly as he'd given to her. Just as she opened her mouth to speak he shifted his body and increased the pace, pounding her G-spot like raindrops hit pavement. Steadily, relentlessly, over and over again.

"Oh, Douglas! Ooh! Oh my God!"

"Is this good to you?"

"Yes, it feels so good."

He grabbed her butt, squeezed her cheeks and pushed himself deeper inside her. "You like it like this, huh?"

"Oh, yes."

"Well, I'm not through. I'm just getting started. Get on your knees and grab the back of that couch."

Jan had barely complied before she was once again feeling his curved member tapping her core, her breasts bobbing up and down to the rhythm of his thrusts, her stomach muscles clenching as she matched him thrust for thrust.

"This is my juiciness, you hear me?" She nodded. "All of this." He pumped harder, deeper. "Did you hear me?"

"Yes!"

"All right, then. Act like you know."

A series of staccato thrusts and Doug let out a groan, grabbing her hips tightly as he went on an orgasmic ride, then collapsed on top of her.

"Doug?"

"I know I'm heavy, baby. Give me a minute."

"No, it's not that. It's okay that I can' breathe."

He chuckled. "Then what is it?"

"Promise me we'll never go this long again with-out . . . you know?"

"Making love?" He felt her nod against his chest. "Careful, Jan. You're almost sounding like I've turned you out."

"You can delete the almost part."

On Sunday, after enjoying a rowdy brunch with his family, Jan went home. The house was empty,

but she knew it would be. Her mom was attending
an afternoon church function and Lionel was with
some of his friends from the basketball team. She
was happy that her family was out doing fun things
and glad to have a quiet home all to herself. She
needed to think, and lately life had been moving at
a pace that sometimes made that hard to do.

She went into the kitchen and put on a teakettle.
Waiting for the water to boil, she stared out the
window and thought about all that had happened
in the past few months. More specifically, all that
had happened since a man named Doug Carter had
come into her life.

A lot. And it was all good.

The whistle blew. She poured hot water over the
spiced chai mixture and let it steep. Reaching for
the sugar and then taking a lemon from the fridge,
she thought about Nick and their last meeting, and
how the conversation had begun to go in a direction that she didn't like. As much as they voiced
words to the contrary, they still didn't get who Jan
was. Sure, they liked that her song was catchy and
that her popularity would add life to the show. But
they were still trying to change her, mold her into
their idea of beauty.

And then there was Doug, and Cynthia, and Crystal, and Peter, Thump, and the band, and D'Andra,
and the thousands of fans who'd downloaded her
song who got it. Without a doubt, they accepted
her for who she was, loved her for who she was, and
had no desire to change her.

That's my new name for you, Juicy Jan.

The thought of Doug's comment made her smile. She reached for the mug of tea but then, on second thought, went into the living room and grabbed her phone from her purse. She tapped a name in her contact list and waited for the call to be answered. When it went to voicemail she thought about hanging up. At the sound of the beep, she changed her mind.

"Nick, hi. This is Jan. I was hoping you'd pick up but since this is a time-sensitive matter and I'm wanting you to know as soon as possible, I'm leaving a message. I'm not going to do your show, Nick. I've thought about it, and decided it just isn't for me. It's not who I am. Good luck with it, though. I'll be watching!"

She went back into the kitchen, knowing that she'd done the right thing and made the right choice. Nick was just a childhood crush, his reality show a vehicle to success that she no longer needed. She had a man named Doug Carter, who said he'd manage her, too. He called her his ride or die chick. She was ready to ride with him. Wherever. Whenever. Forever.

49

Later that day, Jan called Doug. "What are you doing?"

"At the club, hanging with the fellas. What's up?"

"I made a decision earlier."

"Oh, yeah? What about?"

"About the reality show. I'm not going to do it." Silence. "Did you hear me, Doug?"

"Yes, I heard you. What made you change your mind?"

"A few things, actually. The way Nick has handled this whole situation, and only reached out to me because of the song. The fact that the production team says they support me but keep trying to change my image. And there's another reason."

"What?"

"You."

"Me? How am I a reason?"

"I want you to be my manager and you said that couldn't happen if I worked with Nick."

"Wait a minute, Jan. I don't want you giving up something you want because of me."

"I'm not giving up something because of you. I'm gaining something because of you, something that Nick or no other man could ever give me. I'm gaining the experience of being loved for me, not what I do or what I can bring to the table. But just for being Jan. I'm enjoying the experience of having someone to care about my career and want to do whatever it takes to help me reach my goals. To share that dream and have someone to help make it come true. That's you, Doug Carter. I love you."

Several moments of silence passed. Jan almost regretted her moment of truth. "Well . . . aren't you going to say anything?"

"Wow, you came in a way I wasn't even expecting. That's a lot to digest."

"You don't have to say anything. I'm just glad I told you how I really feel."

"I'm glad you did, too."

"Are you planning to spend the whole night with your boys or can we get together?"

"And do what?"

"How about us going bowling?"

"Bowling?"

"Yes, we haven't been on a real date in a while and you've not taken me bowling since the first time."

"Maybe there's a reason."

"Whatever. Just because you got lucky and hit a few strikes—"

"Luck had nothing to do with it."

"And I held back just to make you look good doesn't mean we should make that the only occurrence. Thinking back, the whole experience was actually fun."

"All right, then. Let me roll through and get you now."

"On your motorcycle?"

A pause and then, "Yes."

A longer pause. "Okay."

"Really?"

"Yes, but hurry up before I change my mind. On second thought, don't hurry. I mean it. Drive safe."

She turned to see Lionel parked in her doorway, an expression on his face that she couldn't quite read. "What?"

"Did I just hear you say that you'd ride a motorcycle?"

"Yes. Does that make you uneasy?"

"Heck no. It makes me feel good, happy that you're starting to live."

"I've been living for thirty years."

"No, you haven't. You've been existing, scared to put yourself out there."

She crossed her arms and leaned against the dresser, having no idea her brother felt this way. "Keep going. I'm listening."

"You play it safe. With boyfriends, cars, job, everything. That open mike thing is the first time I remember you putting yourself out there. Fear is like prison. It'll hold you back. I'm glad you let yourself out of the cell to be free."

When Doug arrived thirty minutes later, Lionel had gone out with Bernard and her mom, in a rare night out, to support a friend who'd recently lost her mother. Their planned night included dinner and a movie. Jan was glad to see her mom doing something besides work. Lionel's words played like a loop in her head. She loved Rochelle Baker but didn't want to imitate her. Jan didn't want work and children to become her whole life.

That's if she'd even have them. At thirty, still unmarried, and no desire to raise a child alone, her chances were slim.

"You look good, babe. Those jeans do you justice. But where's the leather?"

"Where's my helmet? Let's stay focused on the important things."

Doug reached for Jan and pulled her close. "Thank you."

"For what?"

"For trusting me. I love bikes and have wanted to share this part of my life with you for a long time."

"Well, don't get too excited. Going twenty miles an hour from here to your house might not be as exciting as you'd planned."

"If we're doing twenty, then definitely not. But I've got a plan for you and my bike."

"What?"

"Don't worry. When the time comes, you'll be the first to know."

They went outside and put on their helmets. Doug got on the bike first. "Use my shoulder for balance and swing your leg over."

It took a few tries, but Jan was finally behind him. He started the bike and turned so she could hear him. "Hang on tight!"

"Don't act crazy, Doug. You know I'm scared."

"As long as you're hanging on to me, you'll be fine."

Jan believed him but still didn't take a full breath until his complex came into view. Only when he came to a full stop did she release the hold on his waist. He helped her off the bike, took off her helmet, and kissed her. "Congratulations. You're no longer a virgin. Now, was that so bad?"

"No, it wasn't. But I still prefer more metal around me while passing automobiles that way a few tons."

"Keep rolling with me. The life will grow on you."

"If you say so."

They showered together, enjoyed a quickie beneath the spray, and, at Jan's request, headed to the bowling alley in Doug's SUV. "I did something," Doug said, once on the way. "And I hope you won't be mad."

"What?"

"I was talking to Byron earlier and invited him and Cynthia to join us."

"Why would I be angry about that? The more the merrier."

"She's never bowled either and I figured her presence might keep you from being the absolute worst bowler there."

"Thank you," she replied. This reply, even though her face and tone didn't exude the same gratitude. "We are kind of on the same page, though."

"Oh yeah?"

She nodded. "I invited Crystal and Brent."

Doug laughed. "Perfect."

The couples arrived at the bowling alley within ten minutes of each other. The guys approached the game seriously, with both Byron and Doug getting repeated strikes and spares, but with Jan's and Crystal's gutter balls and Cynthia's attempt to throw with power sending her ball into the next lane, the women spent more time laughing and enjoying the old-school R & B playing overhead.

After an abysmal hour the couples decided to scrap the bowling lanes for the pool tables.

"Anybody hungry?" Doug asked as they passed the dining area. They all were. "Then, let's eat first."

It was a crowded Saturday night. The group was lucky to arrive at a table just as a group was leaving. The waiter quickly cleaned the table and handed them menus.

Doug looked at his sister-in-law. "There's no fancy food here, Cynthia. You're going to have to eat like regular folk."

Used to his teasing about her upper-class background, she just gave him a look and went back to the menu.

"What kind of fancy food?" Jan asked.

"Organic," Byron answered. "Nonprocessed."

"That's not fancy," Crystal said. "That's healthy. Brent and I have started buying organically more often. These days there's no telling what's being put in our food."

Cynthia smiled triumphantly. "Thank you, Crystal."

"No problem. We women have to stick together," she finished with a wink to Jan. "Although, and I hope you don't take this the wrong way, but I wouldn't have put a woman like you with a guy like Byron."

Byron showed offense. "Just what are you saying?"

"No, please don't get upset. It's just that Cynthia seems more the suit-and-tie, white-collar type of woman—"

Byron interrupted. "I own a suit and tie."

"I'm sorry. That came out all wrong."

Byron smiled. "I know what you meant. And you're right. Cynthia used to go after those professional types. Until she got handled by a blue-collar brother." Byron gave Cynthia a smoldering look. "Changed her life."

Crystal looked at Cynthia, who said, "It sure did."

"How did you two meet?"

She was looking at Cynthia, but Doug spoke up.

"She got on Byron's bus and got more than a ride downtown."

Quiet, contemplative Brent spoke for the first time since they'd sat at the table. "Looks like she's still riding."

The waiter came amid the laughter. They ordered food and drink.

Afterward, Cynthia continued the conversation. "Jan, I know you and Doug work together. How does you two being in a relationship affect the office, or does it?"

"It affects me more than Doug," Jan said. "I'm a private person and the post office is like a soap opera with a lot of coworkers hooking up and going out. I didn't want any part of that drama."

"Yet here you are." Jan nodded. "So, who made the first move?"

"Jan, of course." Doug said this loudly, then dodged Jan's punch.

"That is so not true. When I started at the post office, a relationship with anybody who worked there was the last thing on my mind."

"Yeah, sort of like you, Cynthia," Doug said, then waited for the waiter to deposit their drinks. "Jan was looking for one of those suit-and-tie-type brothers. But I put a Carter cuddle on her and . . . changed her life."

"You put the Carter cuddle on her, bro?" Byron laughed, reached over, and gave his brother a fist bump. He looked at Jan. "You didn't stand a chance."

Jan took in Doug's smug expression. "Don't sit over there looking all cocky. When my multimillion-dollar deal comes through I just might have to go after my other heartthrob."

"Who's that?" Cynthia asked.

"Usher," Crystal said. "He's been her idol since she was twelve years old."

There was silence for a few seconds before Doug spoke. "I'm not worried about him, or anybody else for that matter. They'd have to come through me to get to my wife."

Jan raised a brow. "Um, excuse me, but does anybody see a ring on my finger?" She raised her left hand and showed her bare third finger.

"I don't see one," Cynthia said.

"Me neither," Crystal added.

Now Jan was the smug one. She laughed confidently, having rested her case.

"Oh, right. You don't have a ring." Doug stretched his leg to reach into his pocket. He watched Jan's expression go from satisfaction to curiosity. "You shared something with me today and asked me what I thought about it. I didn't have an answer then. I do now. From the moment we met there was something about you. I couldn't put my finger on it, really, but it was like you were a walking contradiction. You were conservative and serious, but then Joey stepped to you one day and I saw a fire. And I wondered how hot it would burn. Then I sped into the parking lot one morning on my bike. You chewed me out like my mama would and I was like, damn, she must care about me."

The men cracked up. The women smirked.

"But I think what made me want to get to know you more was when I found out about your brother and why you were working so hard and why you took life so seriously. And I thought, that's a good woman, because not everyone would do what you're doing.

"And then I heard you sing. And I said, Doug . . ." He paused for effect, eyed the sentimental looks on the women's faces. "That's your ticket out the ghetto."

The table burst out laughing. Jan went for another punch.

"Naw, on a serious tip, though." Everyone became quiet. "I love you, Jan Baker." Doug stood, knelt on one knee, and opened the black velvet box he'd been holding beneath the table. "And if you agree to be my wife, I'd be a happy and lucky man. Will you marry me?"

"Of course!" They hugged as everyone around who'd witnessed the proposal clapped and cheered.

"Obviously the mail isn't the only thing he's packing," Brent muttered to himself.

Byron overheard him. "You hear that, bro?"

"No, what?"

"Brent said mail wasn't the only thing you're packing!" Jan buried her face amid snickers and chuckles. "You got a lethal weapon, brother?"

"Indeed," Doug answered as the waiter brought over a complimentary bottle of sparkling wine. "It's not a weapon that will kill you, but you'll be in heaven anyway."

Later that night he pulled out what he was packing, and over and again to Jan's delight . . . he brought the heat.

Zuri Day turns up the heat with three sexy page-turning tales of unexpected love and introduces the Morgan men, three fine brothers who have it all—except what their mama wants most for them: wives. . . .

Meet Michael Morgan in
Love on the Run

In the world of sports management, Michael Morgan is a superstar. But his newest client, Shayna Washington, may be his most lucrative catch yet. The record-breaking sprinter with the tight chocolate body has a talent and inner light Michael knows he can get the world to sit up and notice. He's certainly paying attention—and suddenly the sworn bachelor finds his focus changing from love of the game to true love. . . .

Meet Gregory Morgan in
A Good Dose of Pleasure

When artist Anise Cartier leaves Nebraska for LA, she's finally ready to put the past and its losses behind her. She's even taken a new name to match her new future. And she soon finds a welcoming committee in the form of one very handsome doctor, Gregory Morgan. Their attraction is instant. So is their animosity . . .

Meet Troy Morgan in
Bad Boy Seduction

Gabriella is a triple threat—singing, acting, and dancing—and has always lived the life of a princess. Now, her father is determined to marry her to someone who can help expand her brand and the Stone empire, not some ordinary Joe. Of course, Troy Morgan is anything but ordinary. But can bad boy Troy take a back seat to someone with more money, more fame, and more of just about everything than him?

**Pick up these books
wherever books and ebooks are sold.**

1

On a warm, overcast day in late September, the forever-grooving-always-moving female magnet Michael Morgan found himself spending a rare day both off from work and alone. After sexing her to within an inch of her life, he'd sent his latest conquest—all long hair (still tangled), long legs (still throbbing), and . . . well . . . perpetual longing—on her melancholy yet merry way. As usual when his mind had a spare moment, his thoughts went to his business—Morgan Sports Management Corporation—and the athletes he wanted to add to this successful company's stable. At the top of the list was former USC standout and recent Olympic gold medalist Shayna Washington, a woman he'd been aware of since her college days who he'd learned had just lost the mediocre sponsor who'd approached her two years prior. When it came to business, Michael was like a bloodhound, and he smelled the piquant possibility of this client oozing across the proverbial promotional floor. Along with his other numerous talents, Michael had the ability to see in people what others couldn't, that indefinable something, that "it" factor, that star quality that took some from obscure mediocrity to worldwide fame. He sensed that in Shayna Washington, felt there was something there he could work with, and he was excited about the possibility of making things happen.

The ringing phone forced Michael to put these thoughts on pause. "Morgan."

"Hey, baby."

Michael stifled a groan, wishing he'd let the call that had come in as unknown go to voice mail. For the past two months, he'd told Cheryl that it was over. Her parting gifts had been accompanying him on a business trip to Mexico checking out a local baseball star, a luxurious four days that included a five-star hotel suite, candlelight dinners cooked by a personal chef, premium tequila, and a sparkly good-bye gift that, if needed, could be pawned to pay a mortgage on LA's tony Westside. Why all of this extravagance? Partly because this was simply Michael's style and partly because he genuinely liked Cheryl and hadn't wanted to end their on-again off-again bedtime romps. But now, several years into their intimate acquaintance, she'd become clingy, and then suspicious, and then demanding . . . and then a pain in the butt.

Michael could never be accused of being a dog; he let women know up front—as in before they made love—what time it was. Michael Morgan played for fun, not for keeps. Fortunately for him, most women didn't mind. Most were thankful just to be near him. He loved hard and fast, but rarely long, and while it hadn't been his desire to do so, he'd left a trail of broken hearts in his wake.

Broken, but not bitter. A little taste of Morgan pleasure was worth a bit of emotional pain.

But every once in a while he ran into a woman like Cheryl, a woman who didn't want to take no for an answer. So when entanglements reached this point, the solution he employed was simple and straightforward: good-bye. But sometimes the fallout was a bitch.

"Cheryl, you've got to quit calling."

"Michael, how can you just dump me like this?"

Heavy sigh. "I didn't 'just dump you,' Cheryl. I've been telling you for months to back off, that what you're wanting isn't what I'm offering. This has gotten way too complicated. You've got to let it go."

"So what did that mean when we began dating 'officially,' when I escorted you to the NFL honors?"

This is what I get for being soft and giving in. If there was one thing that Michael should have known by now, it was that mixing business with pleasure was like mixing hot sauce with baby formula. Don't do it. *Any minute she's going to start crying, and really work my nerves.* As if on cue, he heard the sniffles, her argument now delivered in part whine, part wistfulness. Michael correctly deduced that she was sad and very pissed off at his making her that way. "You've been my only one for years, Michael—"

"I told you from the beginning that that wasn't a good idea—"

"And I told you that I didn't want anyone else. There is no one for me but you. I can't forget you"—Michael heard a finger snap—"just like that." Her voice dropped to a vulnerable-sounding whisper. "Can I please come over just for a little while, bring you some of your favorite Thai food, a few sex toys, give you a nice massage . . . ?"

Michael loved to play with Cheryl and her toys. And when it came to massages, he gave as good as he got. And then there was the sincerity he heard amid her tears. He almost relented. Almost . . . but not quite.

"Cheryl, every time you've asked, I've been honest. Our relationship was never exclusive. I never thought of us as anything more than what it was—two people enjoying the moment and each other. I'll always think well of you, Cheryl. But please don't put us through this. You're a good woman, and there's a good man out there for you who wants what you want, the picket fence and all that. That man is not me. I'm sorry. I want the best for you. And I want you to move on with your life." He heard his other cell phone ringing and walked over to where it sat charging on the bar counter. *Valerie.* "Look, Cheryl, I have to go."

"But, Michael, I'm only five minutes from your house. I can—"

You can keep it moving, baby. I told you from the

beginning this was for fun, not forever. Michael tapped the screen of his iPhone as he reached for his Black-Berry. "Hey, gorgeous," he said into the other phone.

"Hey yourself," a sultry voice replied.

"Michael!" *Oh, damn!* Michael looked down at the iPhone screen to see that the call from Cheryl was still connected. "Michael, who is that bit—" Michael pressed and held the end button, silently cursing himself for not being careful.

"Michael, are you there?"

"Yes, Valerie."

"Whose was that voice I heard?"

"A friend of mine. Do you have a problem with that?" Michael had never hidden the fact that when it came to women, he was a multitasker, especially among the women he juggled. But the situation with Cheryl had him very aware of the need to make that point perfectly clear, up front, and often. If a woman couldn't understand that when it came to his love she was part of a team, then she'd have to get traded.

"Not at all," the sultry voice pouted. "Whatever she can do, I can do better."

That's how you play it, player! "No doubt," Michael replied as his iPhone rang again. *Unknown caller.* He ignored it. *Sheesh! Maybe I'm getting too old for this.* Just then, his house phone rang. "Hello?"

"Hey, sexy!"

Paia? Back from Europe already? "Hey, beautiful.

Hold on a minute." And then into the Blackberry, "Look, Valerie, I'll call you back."

"Okay, lover, but don't make me wait too long."

"Who's Valerie?"

The iPhone again. *Unknown caller.* Michael turned off the iPhone. *Cheryl, give it a rest!* "Look, Cheryl—"

"Ha! This is Paia, you adorable asshole. Get it straight!"

Michael inwardly groaned. How could he have forgotten his rule about keeping his women separate and him least confused? Rarely call them by their given name when talking on the phone. *Baby* was fine. *Darling* would do on any given day. *Honey* or *dear* based on the background. Even *pumpkin* or the generic yet acceptable *hey you* were all perfectly good substitutes. But using names, especially upon first taking a phone call, was a serious playboy no-no. *Yeah, man. You're slipping. You need to tighten up your game.* He'd just promoted this beauty to the Top Three Tier—those ladies who were in enviable possession of his home number. He and Paia were technically still in the courting stage— much too early for ruffled feathers or hurt feelings. At six feet tall in her stocking feet, Paia was a runway and high-fashion model, an irresistibly sexy mix of African and Asian features. They'd only been dating two months and he wasn't ready to let her go. He even liked the way her name rolled off his tongue. *Pie-a.* No, he didn't want to release her quite yet. "Paia, baby, you know Mr. Big gets lonely when you're gone."

"Uh-huh. Because of that snafu you're going to owe me an uninterrupted weekend with you and that baseball bat you call a penis. You'd better be ready to give me overtime, too!"

"That can be arranged," Michael drawled. "Where are you?"

"I just landed in LA. But we have to move fast. I'm only here for a week and then it's back to Milan. So whatever plans you have tonight, cancel them."

"Ah, man! I can't do that—new client. But I'll call you later." Michael looked at the caller ID as an incoming call indicator beeped in his ear. "Sweet thing," he said, proud that he was back to the terms of endearment delivered unconsciously. *That's right, Michael. Keep handling yours.* "This is my brother. I've got to go."

"Call me later, Michael."

"Hold on." Michael toggled between the two calls, firing back up his iPhone in the process. "Hey, bro. What's up?" Just four words in and said phone rang. *Jessica!* Unbidden, an image of the busty first-class flight attendant he'd met several months ago popped into his head. *Is it this weekend I am supposed to go with her to Vegas?* "Darling," he said, switching back to Paia, "we'll talk soon." He clicked over. "Gregory, two secs." He could hear his brother laughing as he fielded the other call. "Hey, baby. I'm on the other line. Let me call you back." He tossed down the cell phone. "All right, baby, I'm back."

"Baby?" Gregory queried, his voice full of humor. "I know you love me, fool, but I prefer *bro* or *Doctor* or *Your Highness!*" Michael snorted. "You need to hone your juggling skills, son. Or slow your player roll. Or both."

2

Michael smiled and nodded as he walked from his open-concept living space to the cozy theater down the hall. "What's up, Doc?"

"Man, how many times do I have to check you on that old-ass corny greeting?"

"As many times as you'd like. Doesn't mean I'm going to stop saying it, though. Plus, I know it gets on your nerves and you know how much I love that," Michael confessed.

"If all of those skirts chasing you knew just how corny you truly are."

"A long way from those grade-school days, huh?"

"For sure," Gregory agreed. "And girls like Robin . . . what was her last name?"

"Ha! Good old Robin Duncan. Broke this brother's fifth-grade heart. And that was after she took my Skittles and the Game Boy I bought her."

"Using that word *bought* rather loosely, don't you think?"

"Okay, I borrowed it from the store."

"And never took it back. Some might define that as stealing."

"Hey, I pay them back every year by donating, generously I might add, to their turkey giveaway. Not to mention my anonymous donation after that arson fire destroyed part of their storefront last year."

"Payback? That's what you call it? Ha! If Mr. Martinez was still alive I'd tell on you myself. But at least you're letting your conscience be your guide."

"No doubt. Say, how is it that you have time to bug me on a Friday night? You work the early shift?" Michael walked over to an oversized black leather theater seat, sat down, and opened up the chair arm console. A moment after he punched a series of buttons, a track meet video appeared on the screen.

Gregory, an emergency medical doctor, was rarely off on weekends, normally pulling twenty-four- to forty-eight-hour shifts between Friday and Monday and often unavailable for calls. "We're training a new intern. Believe it or not, brother, I've got the night off."

"You don't say. So who's going to enjoy the pleasure of your company?"

"I thought about calling the twins. You up for a double?"

The twins Gregory spoke of were longtime friends who'd grown up in the same Long Beach neighborhood as the Morgans. As childhood cohorts, they'd made pinky promises to marry each other.

Unfortunately for Michael, one of them was trying to hold him to that bull.

"No, man, that's a code orange. I'm going to have to pass on that."

"Code orange? Lisa still bugging you to make her an honest woman?"

"We both know what Lisa's doing . . . trying to snag a big bank account. I introduced her to Phalen Snordgrass, told her that he was going to be picked back up this year."

"Talented brother right there. I'm surprised she didn't go for it."

"Man, Lisa picks men more shrewdly than I pick clients. She's looking for someone who has more time left in the NFL than two, three years. I told her she was getting too old to go after the new drafts, that she should stop being so choosy before all of her choices were gone."

"Man, you can handle Lisa's bugging. We haven't hung together for a while. Let's go out."

"No can do, bro."

"Why? What are you doing?"

"Right now I'm watching the female version of Usain Bolt," Michael replied. "And this country's next athletic superstar." He leaned forward, resting his elbows on his knees—as if he had to change positions to view his television screen. His latest electronic purchase was so large that someone manning the Space Station could see it.

"Is that so? Is she a new client?"

"Just signed her last week. She's coming over for

an informal chitchat; we'll just kind of hang out and get a feel for each other."

"She's coming there, to your house?" Michael was sure that this tidbit got Gregory's attention. Michael was long known for not mixing business with pleasure, and bringing a potential client into his Hollywood Hills pleasure palace—revise that, a *female* client to where he lived—definitely sounded more like the latter.

"Yes." Gregory was quiet, and Michael imagined how his brother looked while digesting the story behind that one word. The two men could almost pass for twins themselves with their caramel skin, toned physiques, and megawatt smiles. But Gregory was actually eighteen months younger than Michael's thirty-one years, and two inches shorter than his sibling's six foot two. And while Michael sported a smooth, perfectly shaped bald head, Gregory's closely cropped cut gave him a distinguished look, one completely befitting a man in his profession.

"Shayna's special," Michael continued. "She has that 'it' factor, similar to a Michael Jordan, a Tiger Woods, or, in the world of track and field, a Carl Lewis. This country hasn't seen the likes of her since Flo-Jo."

Gregory knew that his brother spoke of the illustrious Florence Griffith Joyner, a world-class track star who in the late eighties was known for her bright smile, long colored nails, and flowing mane. "Since when did you start focusing on track and field?"

"Come on, now. You know I never met a sport that I didn't like."

"You never met a woman you didn't like either."

"Aw, man. You wound me. I have very discriminating taste. But Shayna Washington is the real deal; on a good day she's the fastest running female in this country."

"Sounds like a winner, my brother. But I still don't understand why she's going to your home instead of meeting you at the office."

"I thought it might help to loosen her up, have a more casual meeting. When she signed, her lawyer did most of the talking. Other times we've met, she's answered my questions, but not much more than that. If I'm going to rep her, I need to get to know her; I need us to develop a camaraderie and trust. Plus, you know how the tabloids have been on me, ever since that last situation."

"All the more reason not to have her at your house!"

"That's just it. I spot them in or near the office almost every day and that's cool, because security is so on point. But so far my residence is still off their radar."

The downtown LA skyscraper that housed the Morgan Sports Management offices boasted a very efficient and loyal security staff. And chances were that since it was Friday night, he could have suggested this penthouse spread with its 360-degree panoramic views and contemporary furnishings for their meeting. But he liked to play his cards close to his chest. The competition would know soon enough that he'd just landed the next track star sensation. This was what he told his brother.

"I guess I'll have to roll solo then," Gregory said.

"Look, if the meeting wraps up early I might join y'all for a drink. But if you have to take them both on, I'm sure that will be no problem for you."

"Ha! No, that's more Troy's style."

"Maybe," Michael retorted to the comment about their baby brother. "But it's probably been so long since you've had any that you need a double dose."

"Mind your business, brother. The freak days are long behind me, and believe it or not, I've been thinking more lately about meeting that special woman and settling down."

"Will you please tell Mama that so she'll get off *my* back?"

Gregory laughed. "Better you than me. Look, I probably should let you go. I'll take the twins to dinner, maybe even follow them to the latest Hollywood hot spot. I'll send you a text on where we're headed so you can maybe join us later. I've never known a woman who made you afraid."

"Please. You know better than that." A pause and then, "I might meet up for a drink after my meeting."

"That sounds cool. Until then, have a good time with this new honey."

"Shayna is my newest client. Period. End of story." When the screaming silence transmitted his brother's skepticism, Michael continued. "You just told me I needed to hone my juggling skills. With that being so, do you think I'd be adding yet another player to the roster? Don't get me wrong, though. She is one fine specimen of a female."

"Speaking of fine females, remind me to tell you about Troy's latest situation. That boy's a trip." The youngest Morgan was a bigger playboy than Michael and Gregory combined: a fact on which all three brothers agreed.

"You met her?" Michael's eyes never left the big screen. He smiled as Shayna crossed the finish line a full two strides ahead of the second-place winner.

"Not exactly. Stopped at The Ritz for breakfast and saw them cross the lobby. They were on their way out of the hotel."

"How did she look?"

"Very happy," was Gregory's deadpan reply.

Michael laughed. "Sounds like young bro is doing his thing. And speaking of, I need to get back to doing mine." After again promising Gregory to meet him and the twins, Michael ended the call and got back down to work. Reaching for his beer before leaning back against his plush, custom-made, tan leather couch, he forwarded the Washington DVD to an interview she'd recently done on ESPN. While a bit timid for his liking, she was poised and well-spoken. Further, a certain kind of fire burned in her bright brown eyes tinged with hazel. For a split second, Michael wondered what it would be like to stoke her flame. He discarded the idea just as quickly. He would never again date a client. *Ever.* This lesson had been learned the hard way, when a determined baller with the LA Sparks had refused to accept that their passionate yet short-lived love affair was over. *Just like Cheryl.* He'd finally had to file a restraining order and she'd tried her best to sully his name. *Dang, is Cheryl going to make me have to do that again?* Thanks to his baby brother Troy's top-rate investigative skills, the near-smear campaign barely got off the ground before it was extinguished. Instead, the security firm owner had pulled in a couple favors and the former female phenomenon had been convinced—in an intellectual rather than forceful way—that damaging the Morgan name was not in her best interests. Last he heard, she'd moved to Denver and was dating a Bronco. *Ride on, b-baller, ride on.*

Michael leaned forward once again as images from Shayna attending last year's ESPY Awards filled up the screen. She'd looked gorgeous that night: tight red dress on her stacked chocolate body, five-inch heels, and spiky short hair that highlighted her perfect facial features. Unlike many female track stars with strenuous workouts, Shayna's chest was not flat. She still had her girls and they were perched against the low-cut dress in a way that almost made Michael's mouth water. *Never again,* Michael thought, even as his mind conjured up his mouth and Shayna's breasts in an up-close and personal get-to-know. *This meeting is strictly business.* He placed his legs apart and adjusted a rapidly hardening Mr. Big, repeating the words aloud this time. "Strictly business." And then he worked very hard to believe them.

Yeah, right. Good luck with that.